D1528627

PLAGUE
of
WITCHES

PLAGUE
of
WITCHES

JOHN PATRICK
KENNEDY
EDITED BY ERIK BUCHANAN

Cover Design by Idrassi Soufiane with Damonza

Interior Design by Streetlight Graphics

CHAPTER 1

April

K ANA KLAUSEN PULLED BRYCE OUT the party house's sliding doors and onto the deck, trading the deafening music and the hot dance floor for the cool breeze coming off the Pacific. She spread her arms wide, letting the wind dry her sweat. Her long black hair stirred and floated in the wind, and the dark red, spaghetti strap mini dress she wore pushed against her, the damp cloth cold against her skin. She breathed in deep and let it out in a mostly happy sigh.

Best party ever.

Her father had pulled out all the stops for her twenty-first birthday. He'd rented a beach house and told her to invite anyone she wanted. Alcohol flowed, and the bouncers allowed everyone to enjoy themselves unless they got out of hand. The DJ was playing his third set and showed no signs of stopping.

Kana had spent the afternoon swimming in the ocean, ate barbeque on the beach for dinner, and danced for the last four hours. There was just one thing she hadn't done yet, and that's why she'd pulled Bryce outside. She and the tall, chestnut-haired boy with the cool green eyes had been dating for three months. His looks had caught her eye; his sharp, almost cruel observations, and his skill in bed, had held her interest.

Bryce wrapped his arms around her waist and nuzzled her neck. In her ear, he whispered, "Happy birthday."

"Mmmm." Kana leaned back and found his lips with hers. They kissed, tongues playing in each other's mouths. Kana turned to face him and ran her fingers up his chest. His hands drifted down to her backside and she leaned into him, enjoying his touch even as she knew what was coming next.

"Tell me," Kana asked. "Is my ass as firm as Anilise Beckworth's?"

Bryce froze, his mouth falling open. Surprise, annoyance, and fear all passed over his face before he smoothed out his expression and said, "What?"

Kana shoved his arms away, anger making the motion stronger. She would not let him see how much he had upset her; how heavy her heart had become. Instead, she showed him her fury. "Did you think I wouldn't find out? Christ, you two were together every moment you weren't with me. Frankie saw you going to her apartment. Do you think I'm stupid?"

Bryce's lips curled up into a cruel smile. His voice came out cold. "I'm surprised you noticed. You never paid attention to me unless we were having sex. Hell, even then you were only half there."

"If you hated it so much, you should have broken up with me," Kana demanded.

"Anilise told me not to break with you until after tonight. Didn't want to miss your big bash, after all."

"You asshole. You…"

"Cold-hearted, self-serving, spoiled little bitch?" Bryce suggested. "Oh wait, that's you. Too busy to think about anyone but yourself."

"I'm working my ass off," Kana protested. "I'm getting my degree a year early."

"Yeah, yeah, then your master's and then off to work in Daddy's company. Life is so hard for the rich girl."

Bryce's words stung Kana. He'd spoken the truth, but it wasn't the way Kana wanted things. Her father dominated her life and choices. Every school she attended, every class she took, her father had picked them all. She only managed to convince him to let her go to UCLA instead of Harvard by promising to intern at his company in her spare time.

"Aw, what's the matter, silver spoon choking you?"

Kana swung out to slap him. He caught her hand, his lip curling up. "Try again, bitch, and see what happens."

The alarm on Kana's smartwatch sounded.

"Oh, goddamnit." Kana turned off her watch, furious.

"What?" Bryce didn't release her. "Your daddy's calling you home? Want me to tell him how you like it so he knows you're an adult?"

"Let go before you regret it."

"What, because you're dangerous?" Bryce shoved her away. "My little sister hits harder."

The sliding doors opened, and her father's driver stepped through. He stood 6 foot 4 in his shoes, his shoulders so wide he had to turn to step through the door. His sharp eyes landed on them and his eyebrows rose toward hair as short as when he was a Green Beret.

"There you are, Ms. Klausen," he said. "The DJ has a

microphone ready for you to say goodbye to everyone before you go." He saw her expression and frowned. "Is there a problem?"

"No," Kana said, giving Bryce one more glare. "Not anymore."

Kana announced her departure with a smile and told the others to party until morning. Bryce, she noticed, made a point of putting his arm around Anilise as he watched her. Anilise glared at Kana, almost daring her to start something. Kana kept smiling as she worked through the crowd amid happy birthdays and goodbyes. She settled into the plush leather seats of her father's limo and wiped away the tears daring to slide down her face.

Kana told herself Bryce wasn't worth it, that they hadn't had a deep relationship anyway. She'd wanted some companionship, some sex, someone to talk to once in a while. She hadn't believed it was permanent, but she didn't expect him to think so little of her he'd cheat on her, or to act nasty when she confronted him. The memory brought fresh tears, and Kana let them flow until they turned off the freeway.

She wiped her eyes, making sure they were clear and fixed her makeup before the limousine slid through the gates of her father's Bel Air estate. The car pulled up, and Phil opened her door. She thanked him and stepped inside the large, empty, dark house—aside from Phil, the staff left by 6. Kana's footsteps echoed through the foyer and up the stairs. She reached the top and saw the one light she expected coming from her father's study. She walked the length of the hall and knocked on the closed door.

"Come, my little black dove."

Kana smiled at her childhood nickname and went in. Her father sat behind his large black desk, looking at his computer through the reading glasses he hated wearing. His hair was gray but still thick, his light blue eyes clear and alert. His body was not as fit as it once was, but neither fat nor soft. He was her rock; had been for a long time. The ground beneath her felt steadier when she saw him, and Kana hated admitting it. He waited until she sank down in the chair opposite him to take off his glasses and look at her.

"The dean of the economics department says you are two classes away from your degree." His deep voice sounded accusatory. "In mathematics-economics."

"Yes, Father." Kana managed to hold back her first biting response. It had taken months of arguing for him to allow her to take mathematics instead of business, and he never let her forget how much he disapproved of it. "Because that makes more sense for pursuing a double master's in economics and business administration."

Kana had wanted to pursue pure mathematics, but her father would have none of it. Business, he had declared, was all that mattered. Everything else was mere nonsense; hobbies to pursue once one had made enough money. The mathematics-economics degree was the only compromise she'd gotten out of him, and that had taken months and a continuous 4.0 grade point average.

Instead of reminding him of that, she said, "Thank you for the party."

He nodded. "It was a good time, then?"

She thought of Bryce, the sneer on his face as he held Anilise, then set it aside. She hadn't told her father she was dating at all, and she wasn't about to explain she'd caught her boyfriend screwing someone else. "Yes, Father."

"Sunburn?"

"Some."

"Anyone thrown out?"

"Michael Finn and Sharon Telis shared a 20-ounce bottle of vodka on the beach and almost drowned. The lifeguards sent them home in a cab."

Her father opened his mouth. She waited, but he didn't speak.

"Dad?"

He didn't move.

"Daddy?" Fear opened a yawning pit in Kana's stomach. Memories of his first heart attack when she was four filled her mind. The housekeeper took care of her for weeks until her father was able to work again, and for months after, Kana would peek in on him to see that he was all right.

Kana stood up to grab his arm, to shake him into motion, but her hand skidded away from him like a magnet pushing against another of the same polarity. He remained frozen, his mouth half-open, his finger extended to emphasize whatever point he was going to make.

"Dad." She raised her voice. "Dad!"

"He can't hear you."

Kana spun. A tall, older woman stood in a corner Kana knew was empty when she came in. Kana stumbled back, hitting the desk. "Who the hell are you?"

The woman walked forward, her steps easy and confident. She looked seventy at least, her thin, almost emaciated, body held stiffly erect, without the slightest hint of a stoop. Her shoes were oxblood leather, her pants black wool, and her blouse oyster silk. She dressed far better than Kana's professors at UCLA. She wore her white hair in a short, severe cut. She wore no glasses, and her amber eyes burned bright in her long face.

"My name is Professor Claire White," the woman said. "I am here to see you."

Kana glanced at her frozen father. "What did you do to him?"

"Nothing that will harm him." Professor White. said. "When he wakes, he will remember your conversation and you going to bed."

"When he *wakes?*" Kana's voice rose on the last word. "Wake him up now!"

"Sit." The word's power struck Kana like a speeding truck, though Claire had not raised her voice. Kana turned and sat in the chair facing her frozen father. Professor White's shoes clacked against the hardwood, coming closer, but Kana could not move her head to see. The professor walked around and stood in front of her.

"Your mother sent me to see you," Professor White said.

Kana's eyes went wide with shock and anger. "You don't know my mother. She vanished twenty years ago."

"You were born at 1:46 a.m.," the professor said as if Kana hadn't spoken at all. "A few months after your birth, your mother cast a spell to hide you."

It was too much. "You're insane."

The professor didn't appear at all disturbed. "You can't move from your seat. Your father is frozen in time. Pretend to take me seriously, Kana."

Kana glared. Professor White caught Kana's wrist and raised it. She pushed the button on the smartwatch to see the time. "In a minute, you turn twenty-one. When you do, you will gain the inheritance your mother hid from you all those years ago."

"Bullshit."

Professor White smiled. "Language, young lady."

"Go fuck your—"

A golden glow lit up Kana's hand.

The entity woke, rising out of a slumber that had lasted… It did not know how long. Something had changed, though it did not know what. The entity remembered very little. It could not remember why it was trapped, or where. All it knew was that it was in darkness, in a cage made of something unseen, and that it needed to escape. It had to find the Promised and join with it, or it would not survive.

The Promised.

The entity pushed and slammed against the walls of its prison. The cage didn't break, but it bent. The entity gathered itself together and smashed against the cage again, ignoring the pain it caused. The cage—made from pure energy—bent again, and this time, stayed bent. The entity gathered its strength and, once more, slammed full force against its prison.

The cage shattered, energy exploding in all directions and slamming against the matter walls that surrounded it. Matter broke and flaked and burned, but the entity did not care. Matter meant nothing to it. The entity flew up, gliding through the thick matter that surrounded it until it burst free and rose high into the gas envelope that surrounded this world.

Thousands of lights greeted it.

Above was dark. Warm gases surrounded the entity, and below it, solid matter in different shapes and sizes dotted the ground. The entity sensed the billions of creatures that walked among the matter of this world and hungered for their energy. It had spent most of its own escaping its prison and would happily have fed on anything that came close. But more than energy, the entity wanted the Promised.

The Promised was life, though the entity did not know why. The entity turned toward the Promised, knowing that it was far away but still within reach. It glided through the world's gas envelope, racing above corporeals and the glowing lights and the many solid mass shapes.

It was over liquid when it slammed into a wall of energy that tore the remaining energy from its being. The entity would have screamed if it could have made a sound. It would have splashed clumsily into the water if it had mass. Instead, it made neither noise nor ripples as it slipped beneath the surface, its consciousness fading.

A corporeal, small and silver, wriggled into the entity's path, and the entity, acting on pure instinct, attached itself to the creature's mind.

The silver corporeal died in agony, its pain nourishing the entity. Another silver corporeal wriggled through the liquid nearby. The entity dug into its brain like a hooked claw, making the silver swimmer go into spasm, agony raging through its body. Again, the entity fed on the creature's pain. Then, it drifted through the liquid, looking for more corporeals to eat.

It would regain its strength, then rise and find its Promised.

Kana's eyes grew wide with horror. She could not look away even as her hand glowed blindingly bright. Then, gold light shrank in on itself, taking the shape of a spider that pulsed with each beat of her heart. Energy flowed through Kana with a tingle like an electric current.

"Your mother's totem was a spider, too." Professor White's soft voice sounded both wistful and full of pride. "She was the strongest of my students and the greatest witch I have ever had the privilege of knowing."

"Totem?" Kana couldn't take her eyes from the glowing spider. As she watched, the glow lessened and the pulsing became less obvious. Still, it sat on her hand, its faint gold shine telling her that either her world had changed, or she had gone mad.

"The spider is the external representation of the magical spirit that exists inside you," Professor White said. "You can see it, and other witches can see it. Normal people cannot."

"External representation?" Kana stared at the spider. It looked alive, and seemed to pulse as it sat in her skin, almost as if it were breathing. "Does that mean that I have a giant spider in me?"

Professor White laughed. "No. This is a physical representation. Our totems take shapes that our minds can comprehend. The true shape of the totems has been a subject of study for hundreds of years."

"But I still have spider on my skin."

"You have the image of a spider on your skin," Professor White corrected. "Think of it as a tattoo, but one that you can control and move at will. Try making it walk up to your shoulder."

"What? How?" As soon as the words left her mouth, the spider scurried up her arm to her shoulder. Kana watched, horrified and fascinated. She did not fear spiders in the slightest, but to see one crawling on her skin sent a shiver up her spine. Kana closed her eyes and shook her head again, half expecting to end her dream and wake up. When she opened them, she was still in her father's study, stuck to a chair with a glowing spider pulsing on her shoulder.

"It will take time to get used to," Professor White said, which was one of the largest understatements Kana had heard in her life. "Tell me, do you know anything about your mother?"

Kana shook her head, unable to speak.

"Thirty years ago, she was my student at Shipton University."

"Shipton?" The name pulled Kana from her revelry. Shipton was a small, exclusive university on the East Coast, attended by those whose parents thought Harvard was beneath them. "How?"

"Shipton is a witch's university," Professor White said. "There, we study the universe in a way that normal humans cannot even conceive. Your mother was one of our finest students."

"No." Magic did not exist, and the idea that Kana's mother was a witch who practiced her craft at the most expensive university in North America was ridiculous. "This isn't possible. This is ridiculous. It's…"

"You're overwhelmed, my dear, ," Professor White patted her shoulder. "You've just learned you're a witch and you have a magic spider tattoo on your body. It is rather insane, except that it isn't. Here." The professor held out an envelope, yellowed and stiff with time. Across the front, in small, precise letters were the words, "For my Kana."

Kana stared at it.

"Your mother wrote it many years ago," Professor White said. "It came to me with a note that I should deliver it to you on your twenty-first birthday. Please, open it."

Kana's hands trembled as she took the envelope. She had nothing of her mother's. Not a photo, not a book or a scrap of clothing. She opened the envelope and found thick, cream-colored paper folded inside. Kana pulled it out, and something small and metal fell into her lap. It was a ring— slim and silver. Kana stared at it a moment before opening the letter. The first words she read stole her breath away:

My Dear Kana,

This is a very odd letter for both of us. For me, because I am writing it to someone who I am uncertain will ever have cause to read it, and for you because, if you are reading this, it means you have no idea who I am.

My name is Akemi Wakahisa, and I am your mother.

If things have gone as I feared they have, you have met Professor Claire White today. She has told you that you are a witch and that I was one as well. Professor White is my academic advisor from Shipton University. She guided my research and encouraged me to learn more than I ever thought possible about our universe and others.

Unfortunately, something has gone wrong.

I cast a spell on you before I wrote this letter, making you a normal person until your twenty-first birthday. If all has worked as I planned, you will receive this letter on the same day as your magic returns to you. I do not have time to explain why, but I need you to believe me when I say it was for the best.

The ring you see here is mine. I hope it fits you and that you will wear it and think of me.

Please, please, my little love (for though you are not little as you read this, you are always my little love in my heart), please listen to Professor White. Claire is the greatest guide you could hope for. She has the strength and skill to help you reach your full potential and complete the work that I began.

I am sorry I cannot guide you myself.

Love, Your Mother,
Akemi

Kana read the last words with her vision blurred by tears. She wiped them away and picked up the ring from her lap. Tiny, intricate strands of black and gold metal wove across its silver surface. It looked so delicate in her fingers that she feared crushing it.

"It's all right," Professor White said. "Put it on."

Kana blinked her tears away and slipped the ring onto her right hand. She looked at Professor White, her stomach knotted with grief as she asked, "You knew my mother?"

"Yes, I did." Professor White smiled, and the harshness of her features faded. "I think she would be very proud of how her daughter turned out."

"I don't understand any of this," Kana whispered. "I don't understand what she's talking about. My mother disappeared twenty years ago. My father never said—"

"Your father knows nothing. Your mother never told him the truth," Professor White said. "I understand this is all very confusing and very upsetting, but I need you to trust me. Everything I have said is true. Now, we should go to your room and cast the spell of protection."

"Protection?" Kana frowned. "Protection from what?"

"From you," Professor White smiled again, appearing almost mischievous this time. "You have a great deal of work to do to reach an acceptable level for going to Shipton this fall."

"Shipton?" Kana's head started spinning. It was all too much information. "I'm not going to Shipton. I'm getting a master's from UCLA."

"If you do that, you can't study magic." Professor White gestured, and the spell holding Kana released. "And believe me when I say you *must* study magic. Come, show me your room."

Kana rose, still suspecting she was going to wake up on the beach, sunburnt and hungover, at any moment. "My mother, what happened to her?"

The professor's smile grew sad, though her eyes stayed bright. "No one knows, Kana. That is part of the reason we want you to come to Shipton. With your help, I believe we can find out what happened to your mother."

CHAPTER 2

May

V ANESSA LAKE'S CLENCHED FIST LANDED perfectly in the middle of the police sergeant's nose, breaking it and sending blood spattering. He reeled back, slamming hard against the station's counter. Her sense of triumph lasted two seconds before three more of Trois-Rivières's finest tackled her. Her head bounced off the concrete floor and stars filled her eyes. The officers grabbed her arms, pinning them.

"Let me go, you fucking assholes!" Vanessa screamed.

Three more policemen piled on, crushing the breath from her. She kicked and struggled, but the officers pinned her down, worming and twisting until each one held each limb, one sat on her back, and another knelt with his knee pressing down on her neck. Vanessa, still dazed, could barely focus her eyes on the sergeant's shiny, clean boots in front of her face.

"Right," the sergeant said. "Suicide watch."

"Wait, what?" Vanessa struggled furiously. "No. No!"

The officer's knee pressed harder on her neck, cutting off her cries. The other five officers laughed and started pulling the clothes from her body. Her boots went first, then the socks. They pulled her shirt over her head and held it there as they undid her bra. Then, they pulled away both at once. One reached around under her body and undid her jeans. Vanessa screamed, a wordless screech of rage that echoed through the police station. The men on her legs pulled her jeans off, leaving her in her panties on the cold cement.

"Let me go, goddamnit!" Vanessa yelled. "You've made your point."

"Not even close," the sergeant said. "Get her underwear. She might strangle herself with it."

"Goddamn you!" Vanessa kicked and fought and called on her magic. The raven totem on her hand flashed bright gold with a light only she could see. She pulled in a deep breath as an officer's hand closed around the back of her panties. Under her breath, she hissed, "Freeze!"

The officer yanked down her panties and pulled them off.

Vanessa stared at her wrist. The raven still glowed gold, but none of its magic released. It should have made every guard in the room freeze long enough for Vanessa to break free. But it hadn't worked.

"Take her to the bunk," the sergeant said.

The cops grabbed her legs and arms, and one took hold of her hair. Together, they carried her face down through the station, making sure to pass the drunk tank so the inebriated men there could howl and whistle at her. Vanessa's face burned with embarrassment. She called for her magic, but could not touch it. Even a simple spell to make one of the officer's shoes come undone did nothing. They put her in the last cell, her face down on the bunk. The sergeant put a leather strap across her waist and pulled it tight. They stretched her out and wrapped leather restraints around her wrists and ankles, tying them to the bunk.

"Everyone out," the sergeant said, and the other officers filed out of the cell. The sergeant leaned close to her ear. "I'm on night duty. And if I hear a single noise out of you, I will come in here and gag you, understand? I don't need your kind of bullshit in my station."

And with that, he walked out of the cell and closed the door behind him.

"Fuck you," Vanessa growled, but there was no strength in it. She twisted her wrist, looking at the still-glowing totem. "Why didn't you work? I'm not that drunk, am I?"

"No," Councilor Ambrose Levesque said behind her. "You're not."

"What?" Shock and embarrassment made the word squawk out. She twisted her neck to look over her shoulder at the short, round, balding man standing at the cell door. His large brown eyes gleamed like wet stones behind his thick glasses. He was looking directly at her, which made Vanessa blush and try in vain to pull her legs together. "What the fuck are you doing here? Stop staring at my body!"

Ambrose was an accountant and one of the most powerful witches in the province of Quebec. He sat on the Canadian national witch council and was known as cold, implacable, and ruthless to those that broke the council rules.

He was also her guardian.

"Given the number of men who've already seen it," Ambrose said, "I'm surprised you have the capacity to be embarrassed."

Vanessa looked away, shame and anger burning her

face. She tried again to call her magic, this time to blast Ambrose's fat ass off the face of the earth and to hell with the consequences. But try as she might, she could not generate the smallest spark.

"I sometimes wonder if your mother had the gift of seeing the future," Ambrose said, "and that's why she abandoned you."

"Fuck you." Vanessa snarled. She'd been dumped with Ambrose before she was three, and he'd always made certain that she was nothing to him save a burden.

"If you hate me so much," Vanessa growled, "why don't you let me leave?"

"Because you are an undisciplined, self-serving alcoholic who endangers everyone around her with no regard for the consequences."

"I am what you made me, asshole."

Vanessa's mouth vanished, her face below her nose fusing into a mass of bone covered with a smooth layer of skin. She could make no sound at all. Panic, sudden and desperate, rose up in her.

"You do not get to blame me for your behavior." Ambrose's voice was cold and hard. "You are one of the most powerful young witches in the country, but you act like a child on a permanent tantrum. And now, the National Council of Witches has informed me that your behavior will not be tolerated any longer."

Vanessa tried to force down the panic, tried to glare at him, but her body shook. She was desperate for air, desperate to make a sound—any sound. She wanted to tear at her face until she broke through it, but she could not free her arms from the restraints.

Ambrose raised his hands from his sides. Magic, so powerful it made all the hair on Vanessa's body stand on end, filled the room. Red sparks flew back and forth between his hands.

"There is a university," Ambrose said as he advanced into the cell. "One that teaches the most powerful witches of each generation. And for reasons beyond my understanding, they have called the National Council to offer you one more chance."

He brought his hands closer to Vanessa's face, and the heat from the flying sparks burned her skin. "You will go to Shipton University in Connecticut. You will obey the faculty and their rules in all matters. You will apply yourself and you will graduate because, if you do not, then I have been given permission to strip away your magic and your memories and dump you in a hospital in Churchill, Manitoba."

Ambrose pressed his hands to her face, and pain ripped through her skull. Vanessa felt the bones of her face fracture and separate into jaws and teeth. Her skin ripped apart and reformed into lips. It hurt so much that she could not even scream.

Ambrose let her go. "I have arranged for you to spend the summer in a prison work camp without your power. You can use the next three months to reflect on just how miserable I can make your existence if you do not do as you are told."

Vanessa lay on the bunk, her body limp from pain. The thought that maybe she had gone too far this time went through her mind just before she passed out.

The messaging app on Kana's phone beeped just as the doorbell chimed. Kana, in the living room, looked at her phone and nearly dropped it in surprise.

"Hi," the message said. "My name is Jade Lee. I'm a student of Professor White. Please video conference with me before you open the packages that just arrived."

Kana stared at the phone, eyes wide. Since Professor White's visit two weeks before, Kana had become half-convinced that the whole thing had been a hallucination. Only the golden spider glowing on her hand gave any credence to her memory. She had spent days staring at it, making it run over her body. She had read everything she could find about witches, but it was all just as she remembered – Salem, fairy tales, and fantasy novels that agreed on nothing and never mentioned golden spiders.

The phone beeped a second time, and a number for the video call popped up. Then, the doorbell rang again. Kana opened it and on the other side found a deliveryman with a pair of boxes and a tablet. He held out the last and an electronic pen. "Delivery for Kana Klausen."

"Uh... yes. Of course." She tucked her phone into the waistband of her yoga pants and took the tablet. She signed it, handed it back, and took the packages. They were heavy. One had 'OPEN ME FIRST' written on it in large letters with 'after you call Jade' in smaller letters beneath it. Kana thanked the deliveryman and took the packages up to her room. In two minutes, she had her laptop open and Jade's number dialed. It rang once and the screen lit up. The woman on the other side looked thin and delicate, with light brown skin and dark, straight hair cut into a tight pixie. Her wide smile revealed small, perfect teeth.

"Kana!" Her voice was loud and sharp with the tones of New Jersey. "I'm Jade Lee. So good to meet you! Professor White has been talking about you for the last two weeks straight. You're a smart cookie."

Kana smiled back. "Thank you, I think."

"Oh, it's a compliment," Jade said. "And because you're such a smart cookie with absolutely no magical experience whatsoever, it took me a while to figure out the best way to get you up to speed."

"Up to speed?" Kana repeated. "All right, who are you exactly?"

"I'm your magic instructor." Jade laughed. "I probably should have explained that, shouldn't I? I'm a graduate student studying magical interdimensional theory under Professor White. She's told me about your background and left it to me to arrange a study program that will enable you to join us at Shipton without having to go into the remedial magic program."

Kana didn't feel any less confused. "There's a remedial program?"

"Magic is hard," Jade said. "Especially at the level we practice it. Some students need help before they tackle the difficult stuff."

"Like me?"

"Nope." Jade shook her head slowly. "You need a crash course. You have to learn twelve years of magic *and* understand the basics of magic theory in the next four months. Open the first box."

Kana, still mystified, cut the box open and found a thick black book with *Theoria Motus Magicis* written in gold letters on its glossy black cover. She paged through it, looking at the strange diagrams and equations inside. They looked like a combination of quantum physics and poetry. "This will teach me how to use magic?"

"No. This is the single best tome on magical *theory* available. It covers everything from the most basic principles to the advanced work being done here at Shipton. Professor White wrote it and updates it every year. You need to read the first three chapters by the end of the week. There will be a test. You get it right, you get to move on."

Kana stared at the book. "You do realize how hard this is for me to accept, right?"

"Oh, yeah." Jade nodded. "True witchery is the best-kept secret in the world. Even those who think they believe in it go to charlatans and mystics because they have no idea what real magic looks like."

"How do they keep it secret?"

"Mainly through the MLEA and MSA: Magical Law Enforcement Agency and Magical Secrecy Agency. They keep it out of the mainstream news and stop anyone from spilling the beans."

"How?"

Jade's expression became serious. "If you tell anyone the truth about magic, they take it away, so when you try to prove it, you can't. If you use it in public in a way that proves magic exists, you get your memory erased. There are some exceptions, like saving people's lives and stuff, but those are rare. So, don't tell anyone, all right? Professor White will be pissed if you lose your magic when you've barely started."

"I promise," Kana said, thinking the whole thing seemed rather over the top.

"Good." Jade sighed. "So, you know, I envied the normals when I was growing up. My parents were all, 'Do your spells! Learn your theory!' All I wanted to do was skateboard."

Kana thought about her own father's insistence on perfect grades and business studies and nodded. "I just wanted to surf."

Jade smiled again. "Back to the topic: magic is real, you have it, and you need to learn how to use it, which brings us to box two. Open it."

Kana did. Inside was a plastic bag of blocks, balls, beanbags, and cards. Underneath them, she found a set of slim, brightly covered books. The one on top featured a four-year-old in blue jeans and a striped T-shirt making blocks float.

"*Special Magic for Special Kids*," Kana read. "You are kidding."

"Not in the slightest." Jade leaned closer. "These are the teacher's manuals, so they explain both the magic and how to train kids with it. They even have stickers in the back. Look."

Kana looked. Lines of shiny stars gleamed up at her. Kana gazed at them in horror. "Surely there is something—"

"Not for you." Jade's tone became serious again. "You know nothing about magic, and given the amount of power you probably have, you need to get your practical up to speed fast. All witch kids use these books to learn the basics, one per year from age four to twelve, two per year from twelve to eighteen. You, on the other hand, will go through them as fast as you can convince me that you have mastered the contents of each. If you get through all eight primary books by the end of July, I will be so impressed I'll give you extra stickers. Get through all the books by the beginning of September, and I'll throw in a bottle of gin."

Kana stared at the books. "It's too much."

"It won't be good gin, if that helps."

"Not the gin." Kana put the book down. "The entire thing. I didn't know anything about my mother before last month. And now I'm supposed to believe that she was a witch, that I'm a witch, and that I might be able to help find out how she vanished?"

"Yes," Jade said quietly, and Kana heard the sympathy in her voice. "Professor White told me what happened to your mother—I mean, told me as much as anyone knows."

"Why her?" Kana asked. "And why me?"

"Power," Jade said without hesitation. "Your mother was more powerful than any other witch in her generation."

"And that's why she vanished?"

Jade sighed. "I don't know. There's no information on what Akemi was doing the night she disappeared, except the letter she left Professor White and the one she gave you."

"Oh."

"But if Professor White says you can help solve the mystery, then I believe her." Jade smiled again. "Enough depressing stuff. Time to learn some magic. Open the first book to chapter one."

Kana opened the book. "Floating blocks."

"A traditional starting point. Pick up one of the blocks and try."

Kana read the instructions in the book, then took a block from the bag and held it out on her hand. "I'm going to feel really stupid if this doesn't work."

"Oh, I don't think that will be a problem," Jade said, and the gleefulness in her tone made Kana frown. Jade gestured at the block. "Go on, give it a try."

Kana still doubted herself, doubted all of it. It felt like any moment a group of her friends would jump out laughing and screaming, "Prank!" She shook her head. It was all so ridiculous, and yet… She focused in on the block, trying to make it rise off her hand. If nothing else, she would at least prove it was all bullshit. And if it wasn't, well, that would be even better. She stared at the block, willing it to rise.

It shot up into the air and splintered into shards against the ceiling. Kana gasped and ducked, covering her head as the wooden shards rained down on her.

"And that's why Professor White put the magical protections on your room, " Jade said with satisfaction.

Kana glared at the computer screen. "What the hell just happened?"

Jade grinned back at her. "Short version: magic power grows as we do, and wanes as we age. With the little ones, it's weak. Around puberty, it really takes off, and that's when we see how strong a witch is going to become. You're already well past that and into the prime of your power. So, your biggest challenge isn't making the magic work, it's not destroying everything around you."

Kana looked at the block's shattered remains scattered all

over her floor. For the first time, the enormity of what she'd done sunk in. "I made the block fly. With magic."

"You did," Jade said. "Try again, and this time, keep it floating above your palm."

For the next hour, Jade led Kana through the exercises. The work was both exhilarating and exhausting. Kana destroyed five blocks, but by the end of the hour, made three blocks float in the air at once.

"Very nice," Jade said solemnly. "You have done in an hour what takes a four-year-old three days. Only with more destruction. Good work."

"You teach this to four-year-olds?" Kana shook her head. "How do you get them to keep quiet about it?"

"Inhibitor spell," Jade said. "Makes them unable to talk about it with anyone that's not a witch. It also keeps non-witches from understanding what they're talking about."

"That's…" Kana looked for a kinder word than 'harsh.' She settled on, "draconian."

"So is being burned at the stake," Jade said. "The witch community survived this long because we figured out ways to stay hidden. Also, we generally keep out of the normals' business, unless it directly affects us."

"Such as?" Kana asked, her curiosity piqued.

Jade smiled again, her perfect teeth gleaming. "Stopping the nuclear war six times, for a start. I'll give you a history primer once you arrive at Shipton. And speaking of that…" Jade waggled a warning finger at the camera. "You will spend the rest of the week working through *Special Magic 1*. If you can do all the tricks by Friday, we can move onto book II, but don't let it interfere with your regular studies. You still need to finish your economics degree to get into Shipton's master's program. Talk to you Friday."

Kana said goodbye and closed the computer. She stared at the books and the blocks in wonder. It was all wonderful and amazing and frightening. She wanted to tell someone – someone who'd be amazed as she was – but even if Jade hadn't warned her not to, Kana didn't know anyone who'd believe her story. And to demonstrate would make her a freak up to the moment they erased her mind. Kana shuddered as she picked up the book and looked at the next spell.

If she could figure it this out, she might be able to learn why her mother disappeared all those years ago.

August

The entity oozed up out of the water. Though it had neither form nor mass, it did not have the strength to float in the air like before. The silver corporeals and the other creatures in the liquid were not a good source of food. It took most of their pain just to keep the entity alive. But slowly, the entity had gained enough strength to escape the liquid and crawl along the solid.

It came up in darkness because the light burned it. Even through the liquid, it felt the heat of the light and had to take refuge beneath the solid constructs the corporeals had put in the liquid until the light faded from the sky.

In its time in the liquid, the entity could sense the life on the solid, though it could not reach it. It sensed the globe of energy that surrounded the area, preventing any creature of energy from escaping the area. The creature was trapped as surely as it had been in its prison, only now it had space to roam and feed. And, maybe, gain enough energy to break the barrier and find the Promised.

It pulled out of the liquid and slid onto the hard surface of the solid. Slowly, it glided along the solid, searching for something that would feed it better than the silver creatures of the water. Something moved nearby—a small corporeal that skittered in the darkness. The entity did not have the energy to chase it.

It examined its surroundings. It lay on hard matter, near another darker, wider, hard surface. Above it, the lights that the large corporeals liked so much shone down. Across the large, dark surface there were more lights. It could sense larger corporeals, though none were in sight. They were further away from the water, further than the entity could go without more food. It contemplated going back into the water, wondering if it could gain enough energy to cross the large, dark matter and find larger prey.

Then, its short, sharp vibrations trembled through the gas, coming closer. The corporeal came into view on the far side of the wide, hard surface, paused, and then walked across it, making more sharp vibrations as it struck the wider, darker matter. It stepped up onto the smaller, lighter surface and leaned against the matter that divided the solid from the liquid and made a series of sharp, short vibrations while its body shook.

The entity did not know what the vibration was, but it sensed the corporeal's pain—not physical pain, but a type of pain, nonetheless. The corporeal made more noises, louder and different from before, and leaned back, looking at the sky.

The entity glided forward. It sensed the electrical connections through the corporeal's body and how all the corporeal's energy flowed down from the creature's mind and back up again.

The entity shoved itself into the creature's body.

The creature convulsed and let out another even louder and higher-pitched noise. Pain energy flowed through the corporeal and into the entity, giving it the strength to follow the flow of energy into the creature's mind. It rose up through the corporeal's body, seized its mind, and information poured into the entity like water.

The creature was a woman. Her name was Patty. She stood on the riverside sidewalk by the road, leaning on the guardrail. Her feet hurt from standing all day waiting tables in heels. Her boyfriend had dumped her that morning by leaving a note on the table and sticking her with the rent for the apartment, which she couldn't cover, and the landlord wouldn't give her a break unless she agreed to pay in ass instead of cash. All she could do was stand on the riverside and cry and scream and swear at the sky. And now, she had a splitting headache and wanted to go home.

The town's name was Newlane. The woman had some vague idea it was founded a long time ago, but she didn't know how long. She didn't care, either. Shipton University was where the rich people sent their brats to school. No one local attended, and it was hard as hell to get a job there because the pay was so good that no one ever quit. Patty wished she worked there instead of in a stupid diner where the dirty old men got drunk and copped a feel whenever they could.

Patty rubbed her head and started walking back to her

apartment. The entity stayed in her, pulling energy from her pain. The woman was tired, which meant that she needed to lie in an unconscious state for hours. The entity rode her back to her apartment, gulping down both her physical and emotional pain. It learned of the human desire for cleanliness as she showered, and the need for sex as she lay on her stomach on the bed, grinding against a pillow and whispering her boyfriend's name.

And in the midst of it all, as its energy grew and pieces of its memory returned, the entity remembered what it was.

The world the entity came from was a place without the physical changes that these corporeals called night and day. Its world existed in gray darkness, and its kind possessed the corporeals of its world to feed off their fear and pain and the agonies of the ones they killed. The more pain one of its kind absorbed, the greater its power.

The entity remembered the moment a light appeared, blinding the corporeal it had possessed. The entity thought it had found paradise, or as close to paradise as its kind could understand. It saw this world full of corporeal life, so much more advanced than the creatures in its own world. So many types of pain to feed off, so many flavors to taste, all for the taking. So much information.

The entity had made the corporeal it wore run into the light.

It remembered agony and the body of its corporeal burning into ashes. And when the pain stopped, the entity hung in the air, trapped inside a barrier it could not break. Humans like Patty but not like Patty stood around it, staring in shock. One of them, a black-haired woman, pale and slender, stared at the shield that trapped the entity, her eyes widening with excitement.

It had been she who kept it in its cage, the entity was certain.

Fury filled the entity. It needed more information. The entity ripped through Patty's mind, tearing it open like the candy bars she liked so much. The woman fell backward, mouth open in a scream that was cut short as the entity shredded her consciousness. She died, her bowels and bladder voiding as her muscles went into spasm and relaxed.

The entity rose out of Patty's corpse and floated in the air. The entity would find the witch that betrayed it and get its revenge. Then, it would find the Promised.

CHAPTER 3

September

KANA STEPPED OFF THE LUXURIOUS Shipton University shuttle bus that had brought her from Bradley International Airport in Hartford to the green campus of Shipton University. Her luggage stayed on the bus, the staff assuring her it would be delivered to her room in the graduate scholarship student apartments. A large "Welcome Freshmen" banner hung between the tall oaks on either side of the wide stone path from the parking lot. Solid, square, stone buildings crawling with ivy stood cheek by jowl with sleek, curved steel and glass constructions.

Kana was trying hard to not think of the place as quaint.

At UCLA, 10,000 new students descended on the campus every year. Welcome Week was filled with concerts, movie nights, and tours of the city. Hundreds of school clubs and teams turned out, eager to recruit. By comparison, the club and team booths that dotted Shipton's long walkway and the few hundred fresh-faced new students perusing them seemed almost a joke.

At least, it did until one remembered that Shipton

University was one of the oldest and most prestigious schools in North America.

When she told her father she'd been given a scholarship to do her double master's degree in economics and business at Shipton, he'd nearly choked on his morning coffee. Shipton students became pioneers and leaders in finance, international relations, government, and business. A Shipton degree opened doors that few other institutions managed. Three-quarters of Shipton's 1,000 students were undergraduate, the others graduate or post-graduate, and almost all of them came from money. Her father had given her the warmest, most sincere congratulations she'd ever heard from him. He'd immediately set up an expense account for her to pay any bills, and when it was time for her to fly, arranged a private jet to take her across the country. Kana couldn't remember a time he'd been so proud.

It left a sour taste in her mouth.

If he knew why she was really going, he would have been furious. If it wasn't business, if it wasn't moneymaking, he'd never have seen the point. Unless she could prove to him the financial advantage of going to Shipton and securing a degree in magic, there wouldn't even be a point to it. She sighed and wondered what her mother, who according to Professor White had been a hugely powerful magician and an avid magical researcher, saw in the man.

According to Kana's Welcome Package, the witch school was the true heart of Shipton and where much of the school's money went. At Shipton, witches conducted research into the use and limits of magic, exploring dimensions beyond their own and stretching magic to its limits. It was also the reason that the town around Shipton boasted the most powerful magic shield on Earth.

Kana sauntered down the walkway, accepting pamphlets with the indulgent air of one who has done it all before. She chatted with the man at the graduate students' society's booth before walking to a large tent with a banner proclaiming "Admissions." A smiling student pointed her toward the graduate studies table.

"Ms. Klausen," the woman behind the table said as Kana approached. "Welcome. We've been expecting you."

She handed Kana a black metal nametag with her name and major in silver. Then, she put a dark brown leather tote bag on the table. Inside sat a computer, a smartphone, a leather-bound agenda, and three leather-covered notebooks.

"You will also receive another book at the scholarship student orientation tonight," the woman said. "If you'll go through the hall's main doors and to the right, there is a lunch buffet for the graduate students, department heads, and advisors. Then, tonight at 8 is a special meeting of the scholarship students."

Kana shouldered the tote bag. "Thank you."

"And I must remind you that we cannot discuss matters relating to the scholarship program in the presence of non-scholarship students."

"Of course."

"Enjoy your day, Ms. Klausen."

Kana went into the graduate reception and immediately met the business administration department head. He talked to her of their programs over wine and the lunch buffet, where fifty other new graduate students mingled with their department heads, professors, and advisors. She had just finished her lunch when she caught sight of Professor White, dressed in a dark blue skirt suit with a white shirt and striped college tie, talking to a tall, muscular young man with hair the color of melted butter, blue eyes and high cheekbones in his tanned face. He smiled at the professor and Kana had a sudden wish for that smile to be directed at her.

She took a breath, looked away, and looked back. Yes, the cheekbones were awesome and so was the jawline beneath them. The nose had been broken at least once, but it added character rather than making him look mean or sinister. He reminded Kana of the surf types that her father would complain about any time he saw them. He was clearly a student, but unlike the other students, he wasn't dressed in expensive clothes. He wore a school golf shirt emblazoned with the Shipton logo, but the dark gray khakis and black runners on his feet came from a mall, not a boutique, and his hair was rumpled and free of product. She wondered when it had last been cut and by whom as he raised his hand to run his fingers through it. The action made his hair worse, not better, but also showed the golden cougar gleaming on his hand. Kana took a fresh glass of wine from a server and walked over.

"And this will be a continuation of last year's experiments?" the young man was asking.

"It will," Professor White said. "With the same rules. As long as you can maintain your grades and your studies, I would be very glad to have you as part of the team."

"That's not a problem," the blond man said. "My master's

thesis is on track, and my professors are all very interested in your research."

"Good," Professor White smiled. "From what I hear, the work you're doing could revolutionize the education program, so you can't let your own studies fall behind for my research. Hello, Kana. How are you settling in?"

"Very well, so far," Kana said. "It's a nice welcome."

"We do our best," Professor White said. "And, speaking of our best, this is one of the rising stars in our education department."

"Hardly that." He held out his hand for her to shake and gave Kana the smile she'd admired. "Night Donavan."

"Kana Klausen." She took his hand, making sure the spider on her own was visible. "Night? Really?"

"I'd like to say it's because of my affinity with the forces of darkness, but I think it's because my parents hate me."

Professor White chuckled. "I'll leave you two to get acquainted. Kana, I would like to meet with you after the scholarship student orientation tonight. Would you be willing?"

"Of course, Professor."

"Then I will see you at orientation. If you will excuse me."

The professor slipped out of the room, leaving Kana and Night together, which suited Kana just fine. In the four months since she'd dumped him, she had gotten over Bryce, but the warmth in her belly as she looked at Night reminded her she'd been too busy to consider anyone else. She aimed her best smile at Night. "The professor said you were in education?"

"Yes. I'm in the second year of my master's, focusing on educational theory and design. You?"

Kana tapped her name badge. "Business administration and economics."

"Both at once?" Night's eyebrows went up. "Impressive."

"My father would disown me if I studied anything else." That got another chuckle. Kana smiled back. "Why education, if I may ask?"

"I did really badly in high school," Night looked slightly embarrassed. "I only got into college out West because I played football. And while I was there, surrounded by kids who made learning look easy, I began to wonder if there was a better way to teach idiots like me. So, I started examining educational methodologies and put together a proposal. The Shipton education department saw it and offered me a place in the..." he lowered his voice, "special studies program, with a full scholarship."

"That's amazing," Kana said and meant it.

"It helped that Professor White worked with my mother. The professor read my proposal and gave me a recommendation."

"Yours too?" It was Kana's turn to be surprised. "My mother also worked with the professor."

"Small world," Night smiled. "She must be proud—your mother, I mean, not the professor."

Kana put on a polite smile and waited for him to cringe. "She died when I was an infant, unfortunately."

Night winced, embarrassment coloring his skin. "I'm sorry. My dad died young, too. It makes things... hard."

Kana nodded her agreement, though to be fair, she had

never really known the woman, so she didn't miss her. She'd missed the idea of having a mother, but the woman herself was as big a mystery to Kana as her disappearance was to Professor White. She was about to change the subject when one of the professors called for the students to come together for the campus tour.

"I know you've already seen it," Kana said, "but I'd love to keep talking."

"Sure." Night smiled at her again and Kana resisted the urge to link arms with him. She did manage to steal another glance at his biceps, though, and he stayed beside her as they walked under the old oaks toward the graduate facilities.

On the other side of the campus, Vanessa sulked outside the university president's corner office. She had been there for five hours, watching through the window as the other students arrived in luxury shuttles or expensive cars. The welcome they received filled her with envy so bitter it made her empty stomach churn.

Jail had been bad.

Vanessa had been in six fights, three of which she lost, none of which she'd started. Every meal she ate had rot in it. Her cell was the only one with roaches, and when she complained about them, she got blamed. She was given toilet-cleaning duty every day, and the women who picked fights with her made damn sure it was as disgusting a job as possible. Then, on the day they released her, Vanessa found her clothes gone, and in their place a gray plaid skirt, white blouse, sensible shoes, and a bra and panties that were about as sexy as an old Volvo. She felt like a middle-aged church lady when she stepped out of the prison gates.

Ambrose stood, leaning against the trunk of his car, waiting for her. A gray duffle bag and matching tote sat at his feet. He sneered at her and said, "I trust you had an instructive stay."

Vanessa glared at him. "You cursed my cell."

"I did. And if you do not do exactly as you are told, I will do far worse than that." He smiled as she seethed at him and nudged the duffle with his foot. "This has your clothes. The tote has your passport, student visa, bus tickets, and admission papers, along with sufficient money to buy food on the trip if you are frugal. You will catch the bus to Montreal, change there for the bus to Albany, and again in Albany for the bus to Hartford, Connecticut. There, you will wait to be picked up and taken to the town of Newlane and Shipton University. The person collecting you will know your name and have your picture. Do you understand?"

Vanessa managed not to scream. "Yes."

"Your magic will be returned to you at Shipton and further conditions given to you there." Ambrose went around his car and opened the driver's door. "It's a forty-minute walk to the bus station. Don't dawdle."

He drove off, leaving her and the bags in the parking lot.

"Fucking asshole!" Vanessa shouted after him. Then, with nothing else to do, she picked up the bags and started walking.

It took forty-three hours for Vanessa to reach Hartford, Connecticut—Ambrose booked every single connection to include at least a six-hour wait. She'd tried to change the tickets only to discover that she needed money for that and that he had only given her $10 for food. She cursed the petty asshole, then cursed him again when she discovered he'd not packed a cell phone or book in her bag and she had nothing to do but stew in her own thoughts. When she finally reached Hartford, she was exhausted and dizzy from hunger. She stepped off the last bus dizzy from hunger and nearly ran into the oversized police officer waiting for her. He held up a cell phone with her picture on it. "Vanessa Lake?"

"Yes."

"Sergeant Mulgrave, Hartford police. I'm taking you to Shipton."

After forty minutes in the back of one of the cleaner police cars it had been Vanessa's misfortune to occupy, Sergeant Mulgrave escorted her through the back door of one of Shipton's new glass buildings. He took her up the elevator to the hallway outside the president's office and left her there with instructions to wait. And now, five hours later, Vanessa was exhausted, miserable, and more fed up than she had ever been in Trois-Rivières. She had no power, no money, and could do nothing but stand there like a naughty child waiting to be fetched.

"Vanessa Lake."

Vanessa turned to face a tall, stout woman with graying black hair, thick glasses, and a computer tablet in her hand. She was pristinely dressed in a dark blue skirt and blazer with a white blouse underneath. Her makeup was perfect. Vanessa at once became very conscious of her own travel-wrinkled clothes, messy hair, and makeup-free face.

"Come with me." The woman spoke with the full expectation she would be obeyed. "Bring your bags."

Vanessa picked up the gray luggage and followed the woman to a back hallway, concrete and plain with none of the luxuries that the rest of the campus enjoyed. The woman didn't look back once—not even when she reached a freight elevator and led Vanessa inside.

The elevator went down far deeper than it should, and when it stopped, the door opened into a high-domed concrete room with no windows. Vanessa froze in the elevator doorway, gaping in spite of herself. The dome of the roof disappeared into the darkness above and the light had been inset in the walls and covered with this glass. It was empty save for a single hard-backed wooden chair in the center of the room. Three men and two women stood around it, waiting.

"What the hell is this place?" Vanessa asked the big woman.

"The magic research experimental facility," said a tall, thin man with thick blond hair and a dark blue business suit and striped tie. The other four were dressed the same, Vanessa realized, save the women, who wore skirts. The blond man stepped forward. "One of the best in the world. We built it underground to reduce the number of accidents and UFO sightings in the area." He smiled. "I am John Waterson, president of this university. Please sit."

Vanessa walked slowly to the chair and did as she was told.

"We all know your history, Vanessa," the president said. "And we are aware that you are not here of your own free will. But, now that you *are* here, you have an opportunity few others get. A Shipton degree will open doors to opportunities that most people only dream about. And you *will* get your degree."

The confidence in the president's voice made his last

pronouncement seem a certainty, even to Vanessa. The other four nodded their agreement, and the white-haired woman even smiled, which weirded Vanessa out far more than anything else. She sat in the chair, and the president stepped close to her and wiped his thumb across her forehead, whispering, "Return."

Vanessa felt her magic rush back into her, a tingle that began at her feet and spread through her entire body. She embraced it with a rush of gratitude and a gasp of relief. The president waited until she regained her composure, then continued.

"At Shipton, we expect every student to succeed," he said, "and we provide all the resources in our power to make that possible. In return, you *will* give all your effort. We will provide you with tutoring to help you master your subjects, both academic and magical. You will study for the long hours necessary to maintain your grades. At the end of this year, you will choose a major, and at the end of four years, you will have a bachelor's degree from one of the most prestigious universities in the world."

President Waterhouse stepped back to join the circle of suited men and women. "Unfortunately, because of *how* you came to us, we cannot give you the complete freedom that the other students on the campus enjoy. Ladies and gentlemen, if you please."

The president and four other witches held out their hands, whispering a chant Vanessa could not understand. Their hands glowed gold, and as one they stepped forward and placed them on Vanessa's head. Instantly, their magic wrapped around hers like wires, strong, tight, and unbreakable. They stepped back again, leaving Vanessa with her magic intact, but so tightly bound she could not use it at all. Her heart sank.

The president held out a wide black bracelet. "Put this on, please."

Vanessa took the bracelet and slipped it on her wrist. It was metal, heavy, cold, and uncomfortable. But as soon as it touched her skin, she could once more feel her magic, ready for her to use.

"This bracelet tells the five of us what magic you are doing and when," the president said. "Our magic classes require a fair amount of practical work, so we expect to see it being used quite often, but if you use it for something inappropriate or destructive, we will know, and you will be called in to explain why. It will also tell us if you attempt to leave town, which you may not do without both permission and accompaniment. Do you understand?"

Vanessa looked at the bracelet. It would be visible to everyone, and she bet every witch on the campus would know what it meant. It would set her apart from the other students even before they met her. Not that she wasn't already older and stupider than most of them.

She realized the president was waiting for an answer. "Yes. I understand."

"Good. Then we are done here." The president stepped back and gestured to the woman who had escorted her down. "Ms. Newton will take you to the dorm and sign you up for the meal plan. You will be able to move your bags into your room and get dinner before the scholarship student orientation at 8."

And with that, the president and the other four witches

stepped into the freight elevator and left. Vanessa stared after them until Ms. Newton appeared, a dark brown leather backpack in her hand. Instead of waiting for the freight elevator, she led Vanessa out the other side of the domed room and down a long hallway with a dozen more doors to a smaller elevator with a carpeted floor and wood paneling. They rode up in silence, and when the doors opened, Vanessa found herself in the marble-floored foyer of the dormitory.

Ms. Newton led Vanessa to the dorm office to get her keys, then to her third-floor room. It was large and airy with a pair of bar-sized fridges, two oak desks and—to Vanessa's horror—two beds, one of which was stacked with red luggage covered with stickers naming dozens of bands. Ms. Newton had Vanessa put her bags on the empty bed and handed her the backpack.

"Open it," Ms. Newton said.

Vanessa looked inside and her eyes bulged. The bag held a laptop computer, a folder bursting with papers in a dozen colors, a binder, paper, notebooks, an agenda with the school logo emblazoned on the shiny paper cover, and a small, flat smartphone. She looked up in surprise.

"All first-year students receive this package," Ms. Newton explained, "except the cell phone, which only our scholarship students receive. Take it out and put your thumb on the screen."

The phone was small and black and looked unremarkable until Vanessa touched the screen with her thumb. A surge of magic swirled up her arm, and the screen burst into red and gold lights before settling down to a plain black background with the time on it.

"Your phone cannot be lost or stolen. It has your schedule on it, as well as your meal plan and a special app for communicating with other scholarship students. Come with me, please." Ms. Newton led Vanessa back down the elevator. She pointed down the main floor hallway to a pair of double doors. "The orientation meeting will be there at 8 p.m. Your phone will remind you. In the two hours between now and then I suggest you eat dinner and get to know some of the campus. And since no one has said it yet, welcome to Shipton, Vanessa."

Ms. Newton left her standing in the hallway, staring alternately at the backpack and the phone in her hand. It took a few minutes before she managed to get her thoughts together enough to go into the dining hall. It was empty, with only one woman on duty in the kitchen. But that woman smiled at Vanessa, saying, "Latecomer, are you? Like burgers?"

Fifteen minutes later—after the woman showed Vanessa how to use her phone to pay for her meals—Vanessa sat in a booth eating a delicious, perfectly cooked burger and fries.

She stared out the window, watching the other students walking through the campus, chatting and laughing. They seemed so carefree and relaxed. Even the ones who walked by themselves, who looked shy, had a sense of possibility about them, an aura of hope. All of them wore clothes Vanessa knew she could never afford. They were nothing like her and she knew it. She was a fuckup, here on sufferance, under control of the faculty, and under a microscope.

So why did she feel better than she ever had in Trois-Rivières?

The answer, of course, was *because* she was no longer in Trois-Rivières. And if she did this right, she wouldn't have to go back ever again. She could escape, which is something she thought Ambrose was never going to let her do. Maybe he was sick of her, maybe he wanted to wash his hands of the responsibility of caring about her.

Maybe he was setting her up to fail.

The last thought depressed the hell out of Vanessa. She had no concept of how a university worked. She wasn't smart enough to get a certificate of completion from a community college, let alone a place like this, and Ambrose knew it. He was probably going to laugh his ass off as she failed.

But if she didn't fail, she could do whatever she wanted.

Vanessa thought on that the entire time she ate her burger. She thought about it more when she dug into the backpack and found a campus map. It filled her mind as she wandered the campus after she ate, watching the rich kids talking and laughing and having a good time.

And because she was thinking, she didn't even hear the shout of, "Look out!" before someone smashed into her and sent her flying.

The entity floated high above the Shipton campus, rage filling it as it stared down at the humans below. The Promised had come to Shipton and the entity couldn't find it.

For the month since it killed Patty, the entity had taken refuge in one of the men who slept in the alleys. Barry, as the others called him, stank and his brain was half-gone, destroyed by the poisons he drank. But his sores, delusions, and fights with the others in the alleys left him in continual pain, feeding the entity. And when Barry touched another of the alley men, the entity learned, it could drink that one's pain as well. Better still, the entity used him to learn how to control humans.

Human flesh was very different from the small, savage creatures the entity vaguely remembered wearing. It was more complex, with more possibilities for inflicting and absorbing pain. Even this half-ruined excuse of a man had more possibilities than the largest of the corporeals back in the entity's own world. Fortunately, human muscle memory was strong enough that the entity could easily make Barry move and talk naturally.

The entity had Barry walk, then run, the length of the alley, much to the amusement of the other drunks there. He made the man turn and jump, made him grab and pick things up, made him drop things. The entity made him recite speeches it had taken from Patty's memories. And when it released control of Barry's mind, Barry remembered nothing at all of what it had done.

The entity also learned that humans *dreamed*.

Human brains had specific activities they engaged in during their nocturnal cycle. A few days after the entity took over Barry, it realized that these activities created vivid hallucinations that the humans experienced while asleep. And once the entity understood the concept of dreams, it began experimenting with the mechanisms behind them.

It discovered that the human brain was stubborn, insisting on telling its own stories as it processed whatever information it had absorbed that day into elaborate narratives. Still, the entity could make Barry dream whatever it wanted for at least part of the night, and when Barry woke up, those dreams colored his behavior. When the entity gave him dreams that his fellow addicts were hurting him, he spent the day glaring at them and muttering under his breath.

The entity also learned that human flesh could not stand its presence for long and that it could not last long without it.

Its kind existed by living inside the minds of the corporeals of its world, controlling them utterly. It only switched bodies when its corporeal grew old or weak. The entity could—and planned to—live infinitely unless one of its own kind destroyed them. By contrast, from the moment it entered Barry's brain, Barry's flesh rebelled. The blood vessels swelled in his head. The pulse inside them grew irregular and strong and threatened to tear apart the vessels' delicate walls and spill their contents into Barry's brain. But every time that the entity left Barry's mind, it could feel its energy drain away—a slow, steady trickle, but enough to kill it, if it lasted too long.

And in discovering that, the entity remembered *why* the Promised existed.

The Promised had been created just for the entity: a body that could stand its presence and allow it to thrive. The entity could not remember if the Promised had been male or female, or how old it was, but it did remember two other things: the one who had created the Promised was a witch, whatever that meant, and the witch had wanted something in return.

From Patty's memories, the entity knew that witches were once believed to be humans that had powers--the ability to manipulate energy or the human mind or even change shapes, which seemed ridiculous. Humans did not believe in witches these days. Now, they were entertainment; stories to tell at night or horrible history to be remembered with a shudder. Patty had loved going on 'witch tours' in Salem, visiting the places where witches had been caught and tortured or hanged. She had devoured webpages about the Spanish Inquisition, an organization that also tormented and killed witches. But she didn't believe that witches had any real power.

The entity thought about the invisible shield that surrounded the town and the sphere of power that had trapped it and wondered.

The entity flew around the town regularly, exploring for a weakness in the shield. Once it broke through, then it would fly out into the world, find the Promised, and take control of it. Maybe then it would remember why the witch had agreed to make the Promised in the first place.

But one month after it entered Barry, the entity sensed the Promised coming to it.

The Promised flew across the country and landed only a few hundred miles away. Then, it moved across the ground, not as fast, but still heading toward Newlane. The entity stayed in Barry's brain, watching the Promised come close and shuddering in anticipation. Its excitement made Barry's pulse race and the vessels in his brain swell almost to their breaking point. The entity didn't care. Barry could die and it would matter not at all because the entity would have the Promised to possess. Then, it could take its time remembering all it had forgotten. The Promised moved ever closer to Newlane until it was just outside the shield. The entity tore out of Barry's body, letting the man collapse as it raced air toward the shield, determined to possess the Promised the moment it came inside.

Only when the Promised reached the shield, it vanished.

The entity floated in the air, stunned. The Promised, the one meant for it, whom it had connected with the moment it came back to itself, had simply... vanished? The entity scanned as far as it could for the Promised but could find no sign of it. It flew slowly forward, its path taking it over the university. The campus was filled with young adults and their parents, milling about and exploring the space.

Scattered among them were witches.

The entity spotted them at once. They were few, maybe one in ten of the students, but they emanated energy like no other corporeal, in the entity's world or this one. It was like feeling the essence of its own being flowing in waves off the witches. A new memory sparked, of defeating and devouring one of its own kind and the deep, delicious taste of the other entity's energy as it screamed and died.

It had been a witch that had captured the entity, a witch that had held it, and a witch that helped it by creating the Promised. So, would it not make sense for the Promised to be in the places where the witches were?

The entity flew back and forth over the campus, searching. It discovered that the buildings marked Administration, Education, Arts and Sciences, Scholarship Dormitory, and Graduate Studies had magic shields around them—less powerful than the one around the city, but with the same feel. The entity stayed away from them.

The witches were everywhere, blending with the others as if they were not powerful beyond measure. The normal humans had no clue at all that witches walked among them. And as it watched the witches going about their business, the entity wondered if it could enter them the way it entered the normal humans. It couldn't remember doing so, but that didn't mean it hadn't. Then, below it, a male witch slammed into a tall, curly-haired female witch, knocking them both over.

The woman's narrow face was clenched as she tried not to cry out. She was in enough pain that one more ache would hardly be noticed. The entity flew down and slipped into the female's body, intent on accessing her brain and seeing if she knew where the Promised was hiding. If not, it would use her body to explore the campus and find the Promised.

A golden raven made of pure magic slammed into the entity so hard it flew from the woman's body and into the man. He froze halfway to his feet, wincing and clutching his head. Inside him, a golden cougar almost as powerful as the raven tore into the entity. The entity broke free and flew as hard and fast as it could, back to the alley and what was left of Barry's drunk, diseased, and defenseless mind.

It now understood why humans had once feared the witches.

CHAPTER 4

VANESSA LAY DAZED AND HURTING with someone heavy on her chest. People crowded around her, cutting off her view of the evening sky. She shook her head, trying to clear it.

"Oof," said the weight as it rolled off. It was a man, tall, blond, and overly muscled with a football tucked under his arm. "Oh, man, I am so sorry. Are you all right?"

"No," Vanessa sat up. Her head ached. "Watch where the *fuck* you're going."

"I'm sorry, I'm sorry!" Another young man, taller than the blond and even more muscular, ran up. "I overthrew it. It's my fault."

Vanessa stood, then staggered as the world spun. An Asian-looking woman caught her arm, helping her stay upright.

"We should take you to the clinic," the woman said. "Get you checked out."

"I don't need the clinic." Vanessa snapped out the words and saw the woman's expression turn cold. Vanessa pulled her arm away. "I have somewhere to be in ten minutes."

"They'll understand if you're late," the blond said.

"No. They won't." Vanessa looked down at the grass stains

on her skirt and the tear in the elbow of her blouse. It was bad enough to have to wear the clothes to begin with, but to show up to orientation like this? Everyone who wasn't looking down on her yet would start. She growled and picked up her backpack. Then, she panicked, tearing open the pack to check the laptop. It looked undamaged, but how would she know? She would have to check it later and find out, which led to yet another panicked thought. "Where did my phone go?"

The blond looked chagrined. "It hit the tree."

"Fuck."

The blond picked up the phone. His eyes widened when he picked it up. "You're a scholarship student. Me, too. I'm Night. In education."

"Night?" Vanessa doubted it. "Really?"

"We think it's because his parents hated him. I'm Kana," the Asian-looking one said. She was impeccably dressed, Vanessa noticed, like all the other rich ones, but unlike Night, whose clothes looked more city mall than swanky boutique. She held out a hand with a glowing spider on it. "I'm doing business economics."

"Wonderful," Vanessa muttered, shaking her hand. Rich *and* magical and had just seen Vanessa slammed into the ground like a rag doll. It wasn't the worst first impression Vanessa had ever made—that honor belonged to a hungover morning when she was fifteen and vomited on her new English teacher—but it was close.

Night held out her the phone. "Here. It's not broken. They can't break, in fact."

She pulled it out of his hand, looked at the screen and the

time, and found he was right. She shoved it in her backpack. "Good."

"We've got to go to orientation, too," Kana said. "We'll walk you."

"Do what you want." Vanessa hobbled away, leaving Night and Kana to fall in behind her.

The Scholarship Student Orientation was held in an old-style lecture theater, with rows of seats arranged in descending semi-circles to a small platform with a lectern. Behind it, sitting in a line of chairs, were the president, the four professors Vanessa had met before, and three others. Vanessa stepped left into the second row and sat. Kana and Night went down to the front.

"Kana!" a short, thin Chinese woman ran up to Kana and hugged her. "So good to meet you in person! Here!"

She handed over a bag. Kana pulled out a bottle of gin covered in shiny star stickers and burst out laughing. The Chinese woman grinned. Vanessa sighed and sank down into her seat. All around her, students spoke to one another like they were already friends. They all wore clothes that Vanessa could never afford and jewelry to match. Up close, even their hair looked rich—shiny and conditioned and perfectly in place. Vanessa slouched lower in her seat.

The students buzzed and chatted until the university president stood and walked to the podium. He smiled at them and launched into a smooth, well-prepared welcome speech that Vanessa didn't follow at all. She tried, but her head pounded and she was feeling wretched. Given a chance, she would have happily lain on the floor until everyone left, but she'd be damned if she would show any weakness in front of the rich kids. So, she sat, letting the president's pompous speech about new beginnings wash over her. In the midst of it, his tone became stern. She looked up and saw him watching her, fire in his eyes.

"In the three hundred fifty years our institution has taught the most powerful witches in North America, we have had accidents." The president's eyes swept away from Vanessa and onto the other students. "Some were merely destructive. Some were fatal. Some were so terrible that they almost destroyed the town. As a result, we have developed methods to safeguard our students, our facilities, and the town around them."

The president reached into the podium and pulled out a large book. "Each new student will receive one of these books. Once you touch it, it will only open to your hands, and will always find its way back to you. Inside it are the rules for using magic on university grounds and the town beyond. Before you use *any* magic outside of the classroom, you must read the rules and take the quiz inside the book. Once you have, you will become part of the Shipton coven."

He raised his hand, and the school's crest—a ship with sails in full rigging—floated on his palm, the sails billowing in a wind that only the ship could feel.

"And then, ladies and gentlemen, your true studies will begin."

He stepped down from the podium to polite applause from the senior students, joined in a moment later by the first years. A white-haired older woman took his place at the podium.

"I am Professor White," she said. "At this time, we'll ask all new students to come forward and receive their books. Once you have, you are encouraged to go to the Scholarship Bar for the orientation party, or to whatever other entertainment you have planned tonight. Night Donavan, Jade Lee, Vanessa Lake, and Kana Klausen, I need to speak to you each before you are released for the night."

Vanessa and the other new students lined up to get their books. Vanessa took hers and went back to her seat, examining the blank black cover. Inside it, on the first page, was written, "Rules and Regulations of Magic Use at Shipton University." She closed the book, sighed, and sat back until the rest of the crowd dispersed. Once the last of the others had left, Professor White said, "Vanessa Lake, Night Donavan, can you both come here, please?"

Vanessa stuffed her book into her backpack and came down the steps. Night joined her a moment later. Professor White smiled fondly at Night before turning to Vanessa. "Vanessa, Night is doing his master's degree in education and has been working with me on several experiments. He is an intelligent young man and an excellent teacher."

"We've met," Vanessa said, and her tone made Professor White's eyebrows rise. Night had the good grace to look chagrined.

Professor White's head tilted, and Vanessa could see her suppressing her curiosity. The professor turned to Night and said, "Ms. Lake has come to Shipton under special academic circumstances, and the faculty has made a commitment to help her pass all her classes. With that in mind, I would like to ask you to take on the role of tutor for Ms. Lake. The university will pay you for your work. Are you able to do that?"

"Uh…" Night looked rather stupid when surprised, Vanessa discovered. She enjoyed the moment it lasted because when he closed his mouth any sense of him being less than smart went away. He looked at Vanessa and nodded, "Certainly, I can manage it. If Vanessa wishes."

"Ms. Lake?" The professor turned to her. "Would Night be acceptable?"

The words, "It's not like I have a choice" were on Vanessa's lips, but she quashed them and settled for, "If he can avoid running me over again, sure."

Night's expression held both chagrin and irritation this time, which Vanessa enjoyed more than she should.

"Then I'll leave it to you two to settle the time," Professor White said. "Classes don't start for four more days, but I suggest meeting tomorrow to get organized."

"We can figure it out later," Night said. "You'll want to ditch your stuff before tonight's party, right?"

Vanessa, who hadn't known there was a party, nodded and followed Night out. The elevator was already closing before she reached it, which perfectly suited the way her day had been going so far. She hit the button and waited. Night stepped up beside her.

"Tomorrow is another orientation day," Night said. "Campus rules and stuff, plus a barbeque lunch. Nothing starts before 11, so do you want to meet at 10?"

"Sure," Vanessa said without enthusiasm.

"So, you know, my grades sucked in high school," Night said, which surprised Vanessa enough to make her look at him. He smiled. "Football was all I was good at and that's how

I got into university. But I figured it out, and I can help you do it, too."

"Night, I'm tired, I'm *sore*," Vanessa gave him a look on that one, "and I'm too broke to get a drink. So, skip the pep talk, all right? I'll see you tomorrow."

The elevator doors opened and a stream of students flowed out. Several gave her a look, most wincing when they saw the state of her skirt and her blouse. Vanessa watched them go, laughing and talking. Her anger, burning like embers since her collision with Night, surged into full flame. She was a shadow compared to them; a poor loser among so many rich kids. Vanessa stepped into the elevator, pushed the button for her floor, and leaned against the wall, arms crossed.

"Tomorrow," Night said as the elevator door closed. "Bring your schedule."

Kana watched Night trailing after Vanessa to the elevators with a certain pang of—irritation, maybe? It was far too early for jealousy, Kana was sure, but she did want to spend more time with him. She sighed internally and turned back to Professor White.

"I am sorry to delay you," the professor was saying. "And I promise I won't keep you too long tonight. But I did want to take some time to go over your magical study program, Kana, since it will not be the usual one."

That caught Kana's full attention. "It won't?"

"Usually, students begin with a four-year program to teach them the core of advanced magical studies before going into the magical research program," Jade explained. "Of course, they also take twelve years to learn the same material that you did in a single summer."

"It wasn't that hard," Kana said. "Except for the magical theory."

"The magical theory is not grade-school material," Professor White said. "It's not even introduced until first-year university. You did well to understand it."

"A lot of it is close to mathematics," Kana said. "And math I understand."

"Good." The professor smiled. "In order for you to begin work on your mother's research as soon as possible, I have arranged a specific study program for you. It will take your magic from high school level to bachelor's degree level within a single semester if you are willing to dedicate all your time to it."

"All my time?" Kana asked. "I'm supposed to be working on an MBA as well."

"And you will begin working on it next semester," Professor White said. "As well as beginning graduate studies in magic, while you continue your mother's research and hopefully, find out what happened to her."

"I see." Kana frowned. "Professor, what was my mother researching?"

"I can't tell you yet," the professor said. "Your mother's research was so important that the university council declared it secret. Only those who sign the university's non-disclosure agreements can see her work."

"Why?" Kana asked. "Was she doing something dangerous?"

"Revolutionary," Jade said, her eyes sparkling. "If her research was to come to fruition it could change the nature of existence itself."

Kana's skepticism must have shown on her face.

"You think I'm exaggerating," Jade said. "I'm not. I've seen it."

Kana frowned. "You've seen her work?"

"Much of Professor White's recent experiments are based on your mother's. I work with the professor, so I signed the papers to gain access to it."

"It is a standard Shipton University magical and legal non-disclosure agreement," the professor added. "Once you sign it, you won't be able to talk about your mother's projects with anyone who is not directly involved with them."

"You can try," Jade added, "but people either won't listen or will not understand what you're saying."

"So, in order to study magic, I need to sign a secrecy agreement?" It felt wrong to Kana and her tone and expression said so.

"No," Professor White said. "You need to sign the secrecy agreement to access your mother's research. Without it, you can still study here and get your undergraduate magic degree, as well as your MBA and M.Ec."

"But without the secrecy agreement, I don't get to find out what happened to my mother."

"Without you signing the secrecy agreement, *I* don't get to find out what happened to your mother." Professor White sighed. "You need to understand, Kana. I have been searching for twenty years. And for the first time, I think we might have a chance to understand."

"I don't get it," Kana said. "Why do you need me? You've been doing witchcraft forever. I barely know any."

"It's not about skill," Professor White said. "It's about power. Your mother could generate power that I can barely imagine, and I know you can do the same."

"She's right," Jade said. "Some of the magic your mother was doing requires more power than the professor and I could generate together."

"And you think I could do that?" Kana's skepticism was clear in her voice.

"I'm overwhelming you," the professor declared, shaking her head. "Too much at once. I'm sorry."

"It's not that—"

"Meet me here tomorrow morning at 9:30," Professor White said, the faintest hint of pleading in her voice. "I will show you what I mean and then you can choose if you want to study with me or not. If not, I'll help you set up your other classes. Will you do that?"

Kana hesitated, unsure.

"Trust me," Jade said. "It's worth it."

The eagerness in Jade's voice and expression was infectious, and not just because of Jade's smile. The woman was actually eager to do research, something that Kana had not seen her entire time studying business and economics at UCLA. Kana felt the eagerness rising in her, too, and she nodded. "All right. I'll see you tomorrow morning."

"Thank you." Professor White's smile returned. "Enjoy your evening."

"Come on," Jade said. "I'll show you your room. Have you been yet?"

Kana shook her head. "They said they'd take my luggage for me. I haven't seen it."

"Your keys are in your welcome package," Jade said. "Master's students get private suites. Follow me."

Vanessa stepped out of the elevator and into chaos. Students milled in the hallway, trying to talk over one another. It seemed like everyone knew everyone else already and each person was busy trying to communicate with three other people at the same time. Several eyes went toward her and eyebrows rose in surprise. Before anyone could ask her who she was, Vanessa pushed through the crowd, gripping her backpack's straps. The younger students gave way and she reached her room without talking to any of them. She opened the door, stepped inside, and froze.

Her suitcases were exactly where she left them, but the other side of the room looked like a whirlwind hit it. Clothes and books lay scattered on the desk and bed, and a solid, compact woman with bright, red-dyed hair lay in the midst of them. She wore tight black jeans, a red and black plaid jacket, and a black T-shirt with a picture of two cherries hanging off the barrel of a pistol and the words "Renegade Virgins" on it. Her black combat boots hung off the end of the bed and a cigarette burned in her hand. The woman blew out a cloud of smoke that, instead of floating to the ceiling, hung in the air a moment, then whisked out the open window.

"Close the door, for fuck's sake," she said urgently. "Before one of the Glindas sees me smoking and reports it."

Vanessa stepped in and let the door close. "Glindas?"

"Goody-goodies. From Wizard of Oz?"

Vanessa, still bemused, nodded.

The girl looked her up and down, eyes narrowing. "Christ. You're not one of them, are you?"

"What?" Vanessa put her backpack on her bed. "No."

"Cause you sure dress like them." She lay back and took another drag. "You want one?"

"God, yes." They didn't allow smoking in the prison, and Vanessa hadn't had time or money to buy any in the two days since she'd gotten out. The other girl pulled a pack of cigarettes out of her shirt pocket and tossed it. Vanessa caught it with one hand.

"Holy shit." The girl rolled up to sitting. "You, too?"

"What?" Vanessa looked down at her arm and the bracelet there.

"Looks like they're sticking the felons together." The other woman rolled up the sleeve on her jacket, revealing another black bracelet. "At least they aren't as ugly as the one I wore in jail. That fucking thing was day-glow orange. I'm Cassandra."

"Vanessa. What did you do?"

"Burnt down a drug store trying to create a distraction so I could steal some condoms." Cassandra grinned. "At least I got to use them before they caught me. I had the orange bracelet for three years. They sent me here last year, switched it for black, and told me if I got a degree they'd let me take it off. You?"

"Got shitfaced and lost a fight with six cops. Got a light?"

"We're witches," the other woman snapped her fingers and

the tip of Vanessa's cigarette glowed red. Vanessa took a deep puff.

"You know how to get rid of it?" Cassandra raised her hand and made a circle in the air. The smoke from Vanessa's cigarette immediately whisked out the window. "Most useful spell I've learned. Keeps the smoke stink out of the dorm room."

"Can't they track you doing that?" Vanessa nodded at Cassandra's bracelet.

"They can tell I'm doing magic in the dorm, which is allowed," Cassandra said. "They can't tell what sort of magic without looking closely, and unless something goes really wrong, they're not going to look. How old are you?"

"Twenty-two. Why?"

"Because I'm twenty and I want booze." Cassandra leaned forward. "Want to get shitfaced?"

"No money."

Cassandra frowned. "They didn't give you your stipend?"

"My what?"

"Stipend. Every student who doesn't come from money—and that's not many of us, let me tell you—gets a stipend. Check your phone."

Vanessa took the phone out of her bag, stared at it, and blushed. "I've never actually owned a smartphone before."

"What?" Cassandra sounded shocked. "Where were you? 1990?"

"Trois-Rivières."

"I have no idea where that is."

"Be thankful."

"Right." Cassandra pulled out a phone similar to Vanessa's,

but with a sticker on the back showing a guitar with blood dripping off the headstock and "Ripped Holes" in gothic lettering. "I'll show you."

She took Vanessa through the steps to find her account balance. Vanessa stared at it, stunned. "This is monthly?"

"Yep. And they pay for your books, tuition, and room, so you can just use it for coffee, booze, smokes, and clothes."

Vanessa stared at the amount, trying to take it in. With her food, housing, and books covered, the monthly stipend was more than enough for Vanessa. She could buy new clothes with it and have money left over—lots of clothes if she went secondhand.

"You can get cash out of the campus bank machines with this phone," Cassandra said. "So, get changed and we'll go downstairs and mock the rich shits unless you want to stay here all night doing nothing." Cassandra's head tilted to the side. "Got anything decent to wear?"

"Probably not." Vanessa unzipped the duffle bag. "They gave me these clothes when I left jail."

"Ugh." Cassandra stood up. "You're too tall, so I can't lend you a skirt. But my tits are bigger, so my jean jacket should fit you if you roll up the sleeves. Can you find something to wear under it?"

An hour later, Vanessa sat on a couch near the bar in the scholarship dorm lounge room, drinking vodka and Coke from a large red cup. She had exchanged her ripped blouse and stained gray skirt for Cassandra's denim jacket over a tight white camisole and a navy blue maxi skirt she'd found in the bottom of her bag. It was the only skirt that had enough fabric to make it easy to walk in and didn't look like part of a business suit.

Magic decorations glowed on the walls, warping in shape and style as different witches touched them. In a corner, a group of grad students was engaged in a drinking game that involved floating beer cans. In another, the younger, sober students were laughing and trying to play Jenga with their magic. So far, they were being stunningly unsuccessful. The room had more witches than Vanessa had seen together in her life, and she felt incredibly out of place.

"Feeling old?" Cassandra asked, grinning.

"I am old," Vanessa grumped. She shoved her chin at the young ones playing Jenga. "What are they, seventeen?"

"Probably." Cassandra took a drink from her own red cup and made a face. The bartender had refused to serve her any alcohol and mixed her a Shirley Temple. She pointed a thumb at the graduate students. "So, hang out with the other oldies."

"Shut up, punk," Vanessa growled. She had less in common with the graduate students, she suspected, than she did with the kids.

"Getting grumpy in your dotage?" Cassandra grinned and dodged her swipe. "Got to piss. Right back."

Cassandra headed across the bar to the crowd by the bathroom door. Vanessa took another sip and reveled in the smooth taste of the rum and Coke. Whatever else could be said of Shipton, and Vanessa really hadn't figured out anything about the place, they at least stocked excellent booze.

"You're the happiest person sitting alone I have ever seen," a new voice said. Vanessa looked up. The man was thin but had muscles on his arms and chest under his tight AC/DC

T-shirt. His gut was flat, his jeans were ripped at the knees, and his sneakers were scuffed. He had black hair and sharp brown eyes that watched her looking at him.

"Ian," he said by way of introduction. He sat in a chair beside the couch. "You're new here?"

"Yes. You?"

"Not even a student. Townie all the way."

Vanessa snorted. "Then what the hell are you doing here?"

"Hanging with my kind." Ian gestured around the room. "There are precious few other witches in Newlane outside the university, so I like to visit the campus parties. Can't even light a cigarette with magic around normals. I don't recognize your accent. Where are you from?"

"Trois-Rivières. Quebec."

He frowned. "Is that near Toronto?"

"No."

"Just my luck. Now I sound like an idiot."

"Yep." Vanessa took another sip. "Are you?"

This time Ian smiled, one side of his mouth pulling up higher than the other. "Sometimes."

Vanessa didn't smile back at him. Ian was cute, in a scrawny kind of way, and had an edge to him that the little rich boys lacked. Also, looking at him made her remember it had been months since she'd gotten laid. Not that he was making her panties damp, but it was nice to know someone found her attractive. "Vanessa. Is crashing parties the only fun you have, Ian?"

"In this town, yes." Ian took a drink. "I'd rather be at work."

"Which is my cue to ask what you do so I can be impressed?" Vanessa kept her tone light.

"Figured me out already. I work on bikes."

"Motor or pedal?"

"Motor. Got my own parked out in the lot, if you want to see it."

"Wow." Vanessa made her eyes wide as her tone turned mocking. "Your pickup skills are terrible."

"True." His lopsided smile grew larger. "But I do have a bike."

Ian reminded Vanessa of a certain type in Trois-Rivières—full of themselves and out for a good time. The smart ones knew they were ridiculous and played on it, which was exactly what Ian was doing. Vanessa shook her head. "Does that ever work?"

Ian grinned. "Not on anyone sober. Speaking of which, buy you another drink?"

Vanessa laughed in spite of herself and held out her glass. "Rum and Coke."

"Back in a moment." Vanessa watched him head for the bar and decided the back view wasn't too bad either. She smiled to herself. She knew his type. He'd buy her a couple of drinks, try to make her laugh, and try to get in her pants. If he was a decent guy, he'd accept her refusal with good grace and get her phone number. And she might even give it.

Which made her realize that she didn't know what her phone number was.

She pulled out the cell phone and opened it. She had just found the settings screen and was scrolling down looking for the number when someone landed on the couch beside her.

"Vanessa!" Night wore the happy expression of the pleasantly drunk and sounded positively delighted to see her. "I was worried you weren't going to come."

"Worried?" Vanessa repeated, skepticism filling her voice. "Really?"

"Really." Night put on a serious expression that, thanks to the alcohol in him, looked funny more than anything else. "Meeting your peers is important here. Especially when you may be depending on them for group projects in magic."

"My peers?" Vanessa put the phone away as she looked over at the freshmen, five years younger than she, rich and prosperous, looking at each other and trying to find conversation. "Those aren't my peers."

"Classmates, then," Night said. "You should go introduce yourself since you missed Welcome Day."

"No thanks."

"I can introduce you if you want."

The man was like one of those oversized dogs that doesn't realize you're not a pet person and keeps rubbing against you anyway in the hopes you'll pet them. "Yeah, because that will go over so well. No."

Night leaned back, looking embarrassed. "I'm just trying to help."

"Well, I don't need help."

"Look, I know we got off to a bad start, but—"

"Bad start?" Ian said. "Oh, what did he do?"

"Ian." Night's voice turned as cold as the Quebec winters. "Don't you get tired of coming here every year and trolling the new girls?"

"See any other witches in the town?" Ian turned to Vanessa. "You didn't tell me you knew this one."

"I don't." Vanessa wondered why Night sounded so scornful and decided she didn't care. Besides, it was another chance to embarrass him about it. "Night slammed into me and knocked me on my ass this afternoon."

"Wow, bad luck." Ian sat back in the chair he'd vacated, took a drink, and smiled at Night. "You must be embarrassed as hell."

Night didn't rise to the bait. "Accidents happen."

"That's what my mother said." Ian smiled at Vanessa, that half-smile that was part sneer and so familiar from the boys back in Trois-Rivières.

"It would still be good for you to meet the other first-years," Night insisted. "You need to take this opportunity to make connections."

Vanessa felt her irritation at Night blooming all over again. At least oversized, drooling dogs didn't talk. "And yet, I don't want to."

"First-year?" Ian's eyebrows rose. "I figured you for a graduate student. You're not like, seventeen, are you?""

"I'm twenty-two."

"Thank God. I'm twenty-three. I don't rob cradles, Night's insinuations aside."

"You don't stay with anyone, either," Night said. "What was the longest? Two months?"

"Six, and we parted by mutual agreement."

"I'm sure. This is a student party, Ian," Night's voice didn't warm up at all. "You shouldn't really be here."

"And yet, I don't want to leave," Ian said, his eyes still on Vanessa.

"I do," Vanessa stood up. She didn't want to ditch Cassandra, but she couldn't deal with Night anymore. "Ian, still want to show me your bike?"

"You should stay on campus the first night," Night protested. "It's a bad idea."

"And yet, I am doing it. Ian?" Vanessa walked past Night and out the door. She glanced back and saw Ian behind her, his lopsided smile back on his face, heat in his eyes. She smiled back, turned, and nearly ran into Kana.

"Careful," Kana said with a smile. "I'd hate to be your second collision of the day."

"Second?" Jade said behind her.

"Sorry." Vanessa squeezed out the door, Ian right behind her. "Night's in there. Have fun."

Kana stopped in the door, curious. Vanessa led Ian to the parking lot and pointed to a beat-up motorbike. "Yours?"

"Right first guess," Ian said back. "You really want to get out of here?"

"Fuck, yes." Vanessa squared off with him. "Two things, though."

"Yeah?" Ian sounded both wary and curious at once.

"First, I'm not some easy rich kid," Vanessa said. "If you do anything I don't like, I'll end you. Got it?"

"Loud and clear."

"Second, I need to text my roommate."

"Before or after we leave?"

"After."

Ian smiled, got on the bike, and stomped the starter. It roared to life. "Then hop on. I'll show you the town."

"Got to be better than here," Vanessa muttered as the bike roared into life. But even as she clung to his back, she wondered what Cassandra would think and if the woman would forgive her. Part of her even wondered if Night had been right and she should have introduced herself to the nice, smart, rich kids, all still there making connections.

CHAPTER 5

Jade led Kana out of the elevator and down the long underground hallway to the magical training and research rooms. Kana peered through the open doors along the sides. A few rooms had desks, but most were empty concrete shells with high ceilings and plain walls.

"Bleak, isn't it?" Jade called over her shoulder. "Like one of those underground bunkers survivalists build but without snacks. You'll get the whole tour this afternoon, but Professor White wants to do one experiment with you this morning."

"Is that what this is for?" Kana asked. "Magical experiments?"

"Yes," Jade said. "Except for those spells specific to the outdoors, all undergraduate magic and most magical experiments happen here. It minimizes the messes when mistakes are made."

"How bad were the mistakes?" Kana asked.

"Remember the admin building? It was a lovely eighteenth-century revival up until the mid-'80s when an experiment went wrong and it blew up."

Kana shuddered. "And you want me doing this, do you?"

"Not her," Professor White said from the door of a room

up ahead. Today she wore purple slacks and a grey blouse, both expensive. "Me. Come in, Kana."

Kana stepped inside a large concrete room as bare as the others, save for a large double circle painted on the floor. The space between the circles was filled with patterns. Kana recognized some from the *Theoria Motus Magicis,* but most were unfamiliar. The professor let her look at it for a time, then walked around the circle until she faced Kana.

"Most witches have done some minor group magic at this point," Professor White said. "We don't teach the more powerful spells to those under eighteen, so the things they do are simple—friendship spells, future reading, minor weather spells to keep the rain off their picnic. Mostly we teach them the rules and ethics of witches in human society—not to cheat on their homework, put bugs in normals' clothing, change traffic lights. You have to drill it in before they even know how to do those things. Then we start them on group magic because it's the ability to work in groups that produces the most powerful magic, including magic which protects our society."

"And what do you do with it?" Kana asked. "I mean, how does the community use its magic?"

"Discreetly, mostly," Professor White said. "Magic in human society is difficult because it cannot be obvious."

"So, no getting rich and powerful?" Kana asked it as a joke, but Professor White took it seriously.

"Oh, there is a fair amount of that, but nothing obvious. No manipulating the stock market or people's minds to make deals. It's unethical, and if anyone figures it out it puts us all in danger. No interfering with politics except in case of emergency."

"Like stopping a nuclear war?"

"Yes, that certainly was one of them. But there simply aren't enough of us to make a difference on a major level. Less than one in five thousand people are witches, and most of those don't have great power. We are a small minority, and even with all our abilities, having normals know about us, fear us, envy us, would be dangerous in the extreme. So, we limit ourselves."

"I'll get you a copy of *Witch Ethics*," Jade said from the other side of the room. "It's required reading from all undergraduates. That will explain most of it."

"Excellent idea, Jade," Professor White said. "What I want to talk to you about, Kana—what I want you to do if you study with me—requires a sharing of power at a much higher level than most witches are capable. Could you stand at the edge of the circle and focus your magic, please?"

Kana did, and the near-unnoticed background buzzing of the magic filled her being. The spider on her hand glowed bright gold. Jade and the professor moved to points equidistant from her and each other and summoned their own magic. A cat glowed gold on Jade's hand and an octopus on Professor White's.

"Very good," Professor White said. "Now, you two are going to direct your magic into the circle, and I am going to control it. Kana, watch Jade."

Jade knelt at the circle's edge and put her hands on the floor. Light, yellow as summer buttercups, spread through the lines of the chalk circle, making it glow. Professor White knelt next, more stiffly, and a dull orange glow spread from her side. The two colors mixed and spread through the lines. In the center of the circle, a large ball of glowing energy began to form.

"This is the first group magic spell that university students do," Professor White said. "It is an exercise to teach the students to control magic in a group situation. The ball of energy is volatile and unstable, so if someone loses their focus, it melts. Each person in the group takes turns controlling the energy in the middle of the circle, making it change shape. For example,"

The ball of light shifted, changed color to dark red, and took the shape of a Mobius strip with pulses of energy running around the single surface, unstopping.

"And now Jade," Professor White said.

Jade closed her eyes, and the shape coalesced into a spinning cube with each side a different color. It picked up speed as Kana watched, the flashing colors blending together to white.

"Now you, Kana," Professor White said. "Put your hands on the lines and direct your magic into it."

Kana put her hands down and willed her magic to flow into it. Energy, shining a brilliant electric blue, flowed out of her body and into the chalk. Jade's eyes went wide, and she muttered something under her breath that Kana didn't hear. On the other side of the circle, Professor White smiled, her amber eyes exuding satisfaction. Kana turned her attention to the circle, felt her magic mixing with the others. The touch of magic to magic was at once as intense as electricity buzzing through her brain and as intimate as a lover's touch on her flesh. She could sense the other two and feel their magic's power.

"Now, look at the shape," Professor White said. "Feel the shape of the energy. Let me know when you think you have it."

Kana turned her eyes to the shape. As she watched it, her sense of the magic extended, spreading out from her body to the lines on the floor, then upward to the magic floating above the circle. "I think I have it."

"Can you turn it back into a ball?" the professor asked.

It was easy—stunningly easy, in fact. No sooner had she thought it than the shape morphed into a perfect sphere. Kana held the sphere in her mind like electric cotton candy, tingling and pulsing and ready to be shaped to her whims.

"Can you make a new shape?"

Kana barely heard her, so intensely was she absorbed with the shape of the magic. She breathed deep, feeling the magic entering her lungs. She closed her eyes, and with the sure knowledge that the magic was hers to command, imagined the shape she wanted.

"Holy shit," Jade said.

Kana opened her eyes. A giant Japanese-style dragon flew in the middle of the circle, riding up and down on invisible air currents, scales shimmering through a rainbow of colors.

"That's wonderful." Professor White sounded exhilarated and immensely pleased. "I'm not surprised, knowing your lineage, but still it's quite remarkable. Please return it to a ball, then focus on pulling your magic out of the circle without taking any other magic with you."

Kana turned the dragon back to a ball with ease. The

next part was harder. She opened her eyes and looked at the swirling magic on the floor. Strand by strand, she pulled her magic away from Jade's, then from Professor White's, until she had gathered back all her own magic to herself. The power faded, slipping out of Kana like breath and leaving a void inside her.

"How the hell did you manage a dragon first out?" Jade demanded as she stood up from the circle. "It took me weeks to do more than the circle."

"Power and affinity," Professor White's voice trembled, with exhaustion or excitement, Kana wasn't sure.

Kana breathed deep, feeling the void that the magic left behind slowly fill. She could still feel the power flowing through her fingertips. She stared at her hands. "My mother, she was this powerful?"

"She was." Professor White sounded proud of her. "And it was that power that enabled her to do the research she did. Without it, she could not have done her work."

Kana stared at the void where the ball of energy had been. "And she wouldn't have disappeared."

"That is true." The professor sighed. "Great talent is always demanding, Kana. She knew there were risks to her work, I believe, but it was worth it to her. She was driven."

"And if I look at her work, you think you could find her?"

"I think if someone recreated her work, then we could figure out what happened to her."

"And that someone has to be me?"

"That someone needs to be a person with power and an affinity for magic as strong as your mother's," Professor White said. "With the experiments she was doing, the person who is guiding and controlling the magic needs to be incredibly powerful, and you are the only one I've found with that kind of power. I teach witches every year, the best of the best, and none can do this. I wasn't certain you could, of course, but I hoped."

"I see." Kana looked at the circles painted on the ground. "What my mother was working on… Was it really so important?"

"Yes," Professor White said without hesitating.

"So where can I sign the agreement?"

"Follow me."

Vanessa arrived at the cafeteria in her clothes from the night before and nursing a tremendous hangover. She'd woken in Ian's bed to the shrill alarm on her phone at 9:30. She wanted nothing more than to shut it off and sleep all morning, but she would be damned if she would give Night the satisfaction of seeing her arrive late. Ian cursed the noise of the phone but still pulled on his clothes and gave her a ride back to Shipton. Vanessa went to her room, ignored the snoring Cassandra, grabbed her backpack and walked into the cafeteria with five minutes to spare.

There was no sign of Night.

Vanessa thought some rather uncharitable things and went to the counter. The breakfast menu was extensive; she ignored it all in favor of a large cup loaded with nearly equal parts of coffee, cream, and sugar. Vanessa took a sip at the counter and sighed with relief. With luck, Night wouldn't show up at all and she'd be able to sleep until lunch.

"Vanessa!" Night's voice rang across the cafeteria and into her head. She sighed, turned, and saw Night sliding into a booth beside the window in what was no doubt the sunniest part of the cafeteria. Vanessa cursed Ambrose, this time for not putting sunglasses in her suitcase. She took another sip and walked across the cafeteria. Night watched her come, a frown on his face. He didn't look at all hungover, the bastard.

"Glad you made it," Night said.

"Aw, were you worried?" Vanessa asked, her voice saccharine sweet.

"Uncertain," Night said evenly.

"Just because you were being a jerk last night? Give me some credit."

"I wasn't being a jerk; I was trying to help."

"Well, you weren't succeeding."

"And did going off with Ian help you get to know your peers any better?"

"No," Vanessa spoke slowly as if explaining to a child. "It helped me get laid. Which makes everything better except dealing with you."

Night's eyes narrowed. "You know, I'm not actually a jerk."

"You're not my older brother, either, so quit acting like it."

"I'm also not the one who agreed to have a tutor, so stop being a jerk," Night snapped.

"You think I had a choice?" Vanessa demanded. "They want me to have a tutor, and they picked you."

"You could have said no."

"No, I couldn't."

"This is a university, not a jail."

Vanessa held up her arm, letting her jacket sleeve slip back to show her bracelet. "Trust me, I know the difference."

Night's eyes narrowed. "Just tell me what classes you have."

"Fucked if I know."

Night 's eyes rolled so hard his whole head moved. "How can you not know your classes?"

"Because no one told me what they are." Vanessa opened her bag, dug through it, and came up with a welcome folder. She paged through it and found her schedule. Her first semester classes were English, French, Statistics, Formal Logic, and Art History. She also had Remedial Magic Studies, which pissed her off, but didn't surprise her at all. Leave it to Ambrose to make sure she couldn't even practice the one thing she was good at. She slid the schedule to Night. He just stared at her.

"What?" Vanessa demanded.

"Everyone has to pick their own classes," Night said.

"Well, I didn't. They got picked for me."

"Fine," Night tapped the sheet. "Which course do you think you'll need help in? French?"

"*Je suis née au Trois-Rivières.* I think I'll manage."

Night grimaced and looked away. Vanessa smiled at his embarrassment but felt a prick of guilt. He was trying to help her after all, but he was such a jackass. When he looked back, his expression was harder but determined.

"There're three days of orientation left," he said. "Today is all about campus rules and regulations, both mundane and magical, and a tour of the magical facilities. Go to them. Tomorrow there is a crash course in note-taking. Be there."

"I thought you were my tutor." It was a tease more than anything else. "Why am I going to that?"

Night leaned his elbows on the table. "Because I'm the one teaching it."

It was enough to give Vanessa pause. Night took advantage of it.

"I'm doing a master's degree in educational theory. I'm developing practical applications that will allow bad students like me and *you* to get through without struggling nearly as much. So, unless you're a secret genius, show up. We'll meet on Thursday morning and I'll go over your textbooks. I'm assuming that you went to the bookstore like everyone else yesterday morning?"

The condescension in his tone raised her hackles. "No, I didn't."

"Why not?"

"Because I was still on the bus from jail." Night's eyes narrowed, and she could tell he didn't believe her. "I spent the summer in the Correctional Camp outside of Trois-Rivières, and was told that when I got out, I had to come here and pass or get my memories erased, so forgive me if I'm a bit behind on everything."

Vanessa hadn't meant to let that much out, but it was worth it for the shock on his face. She could almost *see* his brain rewiring itself to deal with the new information. At last, he said, "That's horrible."

"Yeah."

Night frowned, his lips pressing together. When he spoke, he sounded more puzzled than anything else. "Why here?"

"How would I know? Because they can keep an eye on me, maybe? "

"No, that's not it. They could do that anywhere." Night shook his head, still frowning. When he looked at Vanessa, his eyes were narrowed again and his brow down, as if examining another species. "Do you know how much it costs to come here?"

"No idea."

"Sixty-thousand a year for undergraduate tuition. One hundred-thousand for graduate."

Vanessa's mouth fell open.

"Books, living expenses, dorm rooms, the meal plan are all separate," Night continued. "This is the most exclusive, expensive university in North America. Most witches only dream of coming here. Hell, the only reason I'm here is that they liked my work on educational theory and practice enough to offer me a scholarship. So why did they send *you* here?"

"I…" Vanessa shook her head. "I don't know."

"Me either." Night looked down at her schedule then gave it back to her. "Put that away and come with me."

"Where?"

"We're getting your books, then I'm taking you on a campus tour. After, you will attend every orientation event for the next three days, and we'll meet every morning to go over study concepts and answer any questions you have. Because no matter what else, you need to pass."

For the first time since she'd met him, Vanessa had no desire to argue.

Professor White led Kana up to her large modern office on the third floor of the administration building. The room had a desk with a computer and a lovely view of the campus, and the wall was covered with whiteboards with what looked at first glance like advanced mathematics. Only when Kana looked closer did she realize half the symbols were magical.

The professor opened a folder on her desk revealing a single sheet of paper and an old-fashioned fountain pen. She held the pen out to Kana. "Press the tip of this against your left thumb."

Kana took the pen, but instead of pressing it to her skin, she turned the sheet of paper around and read it top to bottom. The writing was in legalese, but the gist was clear enough: by signing the paper, Kana was restricted to speaking about her mother's work only to those directly involved with it. Kana looked up. "Just you two?"

"Yes," Professor White said. "Until you design your own research project. Then whoever is involved will also need to sign an agreement to research your projects."

Kana stared at the pen in her hand. She understood the principle of a non-disclosure agreement. Her father used them all the time for business deals. It was just that she didn't like the idea when it came to learning about her mother. She wanted to be able to tell her father what happened to the woman he said he'd loved, but what if the agreement prevented her from doing so? Of course, if she didn't sign it, she would never know either, and having come this far, she didn't think she could tolerate that at all.

Kana touched the pen's nib to her thumb tip. She felt a prick of pain, and her blood flowed up the nib. The professor pointed to the signature line on the bottom of the paper. Kana signed, her blood flowing from the nib to the page.

"And now you are bound," Professor White said. "Thank you, Kana, because I do believe that you are the only one capable of carrying out your mother's research. Here."

The professor opened a drawer and took out a thick stack of papers bound with plastic coils. The front page said simply, "Experimental Series 1278: Proposal by Akemi Wakahisa."

Kana took it, opened it, and after a quick glance at the table of contents, turned to the experiment abstract. She read through it, frowned, then read it again. She looked up at the professor, whose eyes now sparkled with anticipation.

Kana cleared her throat and read aloud, "'The use of interD theory and the extrapolation of D through means of a Mu access and Declenzian neo-mathematics could result in intra rather than interdimensional travel, both on the spatial and temporal dimensions.'" She looked at the Professor. "Does that mean what I think it means?"

"Akemi Wakahisa thought so," Professor White said. "Enough that she made that experimental series the basis of her doctoral thesis. But in order to grasp exactly what she means, you're going to need to read far more than just her proposal."

"I want all of it," Kana said. "Everything you have. Every single scrap."

"There are boxes of papers," the professor warned. "Most of them at a level you can't comprehend."

"I'll learn," Kana said, her tone leaving no room for argument. She looked down at the abstract again. It was almost too much to believe, and yet, if it were true the implications were staggering.

"Time travel," Kana whispered. "My mother was studying time travel."

When darkness fell, the entity hunted.

It took three days and all of Barry's strength for the entity to recover after the golden raven and the golden cougar's attacks. The entity left his corpse lying in the alley, its fury driving it forward in search of prey and a new host.

The witches had *hurt* it. The entity wanted revenge, but to attack a witch directly was too dangerous. The golden creatures living inside them could destroy the entity. It needed to find a different way to attack. Something they wouldn't expect.

It glided toward the university, watching all the activity in the bars around it. The young humans were out enjoying the night, and the witches were no exception. The entity followed them through the night, feeling their emotions as they laughed and danced and worked up the nerve to speak to one another.

One particular witch caught the entity's attention. The young man was much like the others, bursting with energy and sexual frustration and nervousness. The one difference was that his eyes kept straying to the waitress, who was young and pretty with dark brown skin and a low-cut shirt showing ample cleavage. Even while talking to the others at his table, the young witch's eyes kept following the waitress, focusing on her short skirt every time she leaned over a table.

The waitress was not a witch.

It was easy to enter the woman's body and mind. Pain flared in her head, but she gritted her teeth and kept going. Her name was Janice and she was going to a community college for a certificate in restaurant management. She couldn't afford to lose money by stopping for a headache. The entity rode her mind as she smiled and laughed with the customers and served their drinks and avoided getting groped with practiced ease.

On her break, the entity took over Janice's body, wrote a note, and slipped it into the pocket of her apron. When she returned, the entity took over just long enough to leave the note with the young witch. And when the waitress's phone binged a few minutes later, the entity made her not look at it. And that was all it did until the end of her shift.

Only when Janice's shift ended did the entity take total control, making her slip into the kitchen to steal a paring knife before following the other waitresses out the door and saying goodnight to the bouncer. It texted the witch—Billy Sanderson was his name—and offered to meet him in the park by the university.

During the twenty-minute walk to get there, the entity plundered Janice's mind for every single sexual thought, act, and moment. It learned of her first boyfriend, first kiss, first blowjob, and everything she had done since. By the time the university came into sight, the entity had everything it needed to seduce a stupid young man. Humans were far more complicated than the corporeals of its home world, but the desires were the same: food, sex, strength, and power.

When the entity reached the park, Billy was there, pacing back and forth and looking cold and nervous. The entity put a soft, sultry smile on Janice's face and stepped forward. "Hi there."

Billy smiled back, saying, "I'm glad you texted."

The entity kept Janice's voice low. "I saw you watching me."

Billy's fair skin made his blush glow even in the darkness. The entity made Janice laugh, which made Billy blush more and say, "I was obvious, wasn't I?"

"You were, but I liked it." The entity stepped forward and took Billy's hand. "I like honesty. It's refreshing."

The entity led him into the park. It had flown over the place during the day, spotting the quiet places where lovers stole kisses and caresses. It led Billy to the fountain, now turned off for the night, its water reflecting the lights above. The entity sat Janice on the edge, pulling Billy down beside her. He looked confused.

"Moving a bit quick for you?" the entity asked.

"No. I just..." Billy swallowed and shifted nervously. "I just didn't expect you to like me, is all."

"But I do. At least as much as I can like anyone from only seeing them." The entity put Janice's hand on his knee. "So, I thought I'd start by seeing how well you kiss and go from there. Okay?"

"Uhh..."

Billy's stunned expression amused the entity as it leaned Janice in close and pressed her lips to his. His mouth was slack, but only for a moment. He opened it, and the entity slid Janice's tongue into his mouth, licked the roof of Billy's mouth, and pulled back. With a low, breathy voice, it said, "We are way too exposed here. And I want more."

It stood up, held out a hand to Billy. "Do you?"

"Yes." Billy took her hand, and the entity led off the paths to a large copse of trees where no one could see them from the outside. The entity pushed Billy's back against the thick trunk of an oak and raised his hand to her breast, whispering, "Kiss me hard."

Billy did, his hand cupping the soft flesh of Janice's breast. The entity lowered Janice's hand to cup his crotch and stroked. Billy moaned, and his other hand came up to caress her breasts.

The entity made Janice moan as it tugged the zipper down on Billy's jeans and slipped Janice's hand inside. He stiffened in surprise and started trembling as the entity put Janice on her knees and took Billy into her mouth. Billy, so caught up in sensation, didn't notice her take the short, sharp knife from her purse. The entity stood up, grabbed his hair, and pulled his head back. It kissed Billy's neck, making him moan even louder.

Then it drove the knife into the side of his throat.

He jolted with the shock of it, his mouth opening into a scream. The entity pulled the knife sideways, hacking Billy's windpipe open below his vocal cords. The scream that should have come out became a hiss. Billy tried to run away, but the entity held tight, allowing his agony to flow into its body. The entity felt the magical golden creature that lived inside Billy raging. It could do nothing without Billy's direction, and Billy didn't have enough life in him. His legs buckled and he slipped out to the ground, his wide eyes losing their focus.

The entity kept its grip on Billy's hair, feeding on his agony. The golden animal inside him lost cohesion, melting as Billy's body failed. The entity reached for it, and as the last of the life faded from Billy's body, drained the magic from his flesh.

A rush of power far greater than any it had felt in this world filled the entity, and with it, the sure knowledge that the entity could use the magic it absorbed.

With a thought, the entity made the blood covering Janice flow off and into the ground. More magic remained inside her flesh, making the entity shiver with the pleasure of it, the heat like molten metal, hot and dangerous and so full of power.

And with that power came memory and the sure knowledge that the Promised was a witch.

CHAPTER 6

October

VANESSA WASN'T USUALLY A FAN of early morning sex, because, early morning. Ian liked it, though, and since she'd used him last night to celebrate the "A" she'd scored on her Formal Logic quiz, she wasn't going to begrudge him a quick fuck before she headed back to campus. The only problem was, she couldn't stop thinking about Night.

It wasn't even sexy thoughts, which would have been annoying but understandable in the circumstance. No, she was thinking that she owed the man an apology. Night had been obnoxiously useful—obnoxious because damn near everything he said felt condescending, useful because without him she'd probably flunk. They met twice a week for Night to review her work and her study habits. He sounded disappointed when she didn't get things done, which was far more irritating than if he'd been angry. It made her work harder every time, and now she was passing.

The alarm on her phone went off, filling the room with a loud pulse of retro dance music. Ian groaned and shifted his hands, pressing down hard on her shoulder blades.

"Hurry," Vanessa gasped as the bed shook. "I've got class."

Ian's thrusts grew harder. "Why… are you in such… a hurry?"

"Magic class. We get our test back today." Remedial magic class was so easy, Vanessa slept through it half the time. "Professor told me that if I wasn't early and awake for this one, things would go badly for me."

"God!"

Vanessa wasn't sure if the word was a condemnation of her professor or an exclamation of surprise as Ian finally went over the edge and groaned to a finish. After a moment of his weight pressing down on her back, he slipped out and rolled off her. "Thought all your marks were great, thanks to that asshole."

"Night's not an asshole," Vanessa said, unsure why she was defending him.

"The way you talk about him he is. Don't know why you see him."

"He's helping me pass English and Statistics." Vanessa heard the tinge of jealousy in Ian's words and added, "Other than that, I don't see him."

"Good. He's a douchebag."

"Whatever." Vanessa stood up to find her clothes. She felt more drained than usual from a late night of sex and booze. But then, she always did after a night with Ian. She suspected it was because she was getting old and immediately shoved the thought away.

"Do you like being a student?" Ian asked as he watched her shimmy into her tight jeans. There was a strange tone in his voice—the jealousy was gone, and in its place were both curiosity and disdain.

Vanessa shrugged. "Better than jail."

"Yeah, that's about it." Ian lit a cigarette. "It's like work. Wouldn't do it if I didn't have to. And one day, I won't."

"Yeah?" Vanessa pulled her hair back into a ponytail. "Got a plan?"

"Oh yeah."

The relish with which he said the words sent a twinge through Vanessa's stomach. "Is this something I shouldn't know about?"

"Depends." Ian grinned again. "You want to get rich with me?"

Vanessa shook her head. She'd heard that exact tone before, in the voices of Trois-Rivières's drug dealers. "Ian, I'm on all sorts of probation, so whatever you're planning, I don't want to know."

"You think it's illegal?" Ian tried to sound offended but didn't succeed.

"Is it?"

"You said you didn't want to know." He slapped her ass. "Let's get you to school."

Vanessa tried not to think about it as they rode to the university. Her relationship with Ian was based on a mutual love for smokes, booze, and sex. She was fond of him in a general way, but no more than that, as she sure as hell wasn't going to risk getting her memory erased for whatever plan he thought he could pull off. The last thing she could afford was trouble. Her magic was her life, and she wasn't going to lose it again. She said goodbye in the parking lot, and after a shower and change of clothes, went to the magic studies laboratories.

To her surprise, the professor was the only one in the room. The small, neat, fiftyish woman with cornflower blue eyes and raven black bobbed hair didn't look up from the book she was reading when Vanessa came in. Vanessa checked her phone, saw she was early, and pulled out her notebook. The professor had assured them that the next classes would further expand on the previous materials, which meant, according to Night, that reviewing them was in order.

Vanessa remembered Ian's tone as he mentioned the man. She wondered at it and what had happened between them. Sure, Night was a pain in the ass, but he was a smart pain in the ass, and with his help, Vanessa was doing well in her classes.

"Vanessa." The professor put a plant on her desk. "Make it bloom."

"Uh… All right." Vanessa raised her hand and muttered the spell. The plant shuddered, twisted, and the small buds on the sides of it blossomed out into large red flowers.

"Very good." The professor nodded and put the plant aside. She stood up, raised her hand, and a cylinder of magic webs surrounded Vanessa. "Break the spell."

"Where's the rest of the class?" Vanessa asked.

The professor's head tilted, and a spark of electricity zapped Vanessa, making her yelp. The professor repeated, "Break the spell."

Vanessa gritted her teeth, forced down her anger, and used her magic to feel the shape of the cage. It had been pre-cast from a hidden pentacle on the floor. Vanessa directed her energy to the floor, made the pentacle visible, and dragged the sole of her used Doc Marten over one of the lines, breaking it.

The room erupted in flames.

Vanessa yelped in surprise and jumped to her feet. Every chair and desk had become a bonfire. The professor became a screaming column of flame. The air stank of burning wood and overheated metal and cooking flesh. Vanessa's throat seared with the heat of the air. She could smell her hair smoking. Her eyes went up to the sprinklers, expecting them to go off any second.

They didn't, which wasn't possible.

Which meant that the fire was also impossible.

Vanessa slammed her hand to the floor, shouting "Dispel!"

There were other ways to dispel magic, but this spell tore the illusion apart and sent a shock through the caster. Ambrose used to use it on her when she hid from his rages.

A bright white magical burst filled the room. The professor yelped in pain and stumbled back. Vanessa rose to her feet, gathering her magic as her hands clenched into fists. "What the fuck are you doing?"

The professor, still gasping, opened the door, stepped out, and turned off the room's light. For a moment she stood, silhouetted by the hall light. "Escape."

Then the professor closed the door and everything went black.

Kana leaned back and stretched. She sat at her desk, wearing her pajama bottoms and T-shirt. She had no classes today, which was good because she'd been up all night looking at Akemi's files. She folded her hands together and put her elbows on the desk to prop up her chin. Beyond her laptop, her window gave her a lovely view of the campus and the memorial to the murdered young witch. It looked ragged now, after days of rain and fall winds.

The young man's murder had shocked the campus to its core, even more the witches, who all knew one another by sight, if not by name. They'd had two memorial services—one for the campus, and one for the tight-knit witch community. Students were warned to go out in groups or stay on campus. The administration announced they'd move the memorial inside for the winter at the end of the month.

Kana listened to the warnings and felt sorry for the student, though she did not know him. Aside from Jade and Professor White, her interaction with the other witches was limited to the cafeteria and the bar. The rest of the time, she was up to her neck in intensive magical studies and her mother's research. She hadn't even gotten to know Night very well, though she'd intended to. Even when she was taking extra classes to finish her undergrad degree she hadn't worked as hard. For the first time in her life, Kana was able to do pure research. Every aspect of magic fascinated her, and her mother's work fascinated her most of all.

Boxes of Akemi's research sat in stacks around her desk, narrow paths between them to allow access to the bed, closet, and door. The professor had been as good as her word, but the sheer volume of her mother's research was daunting. The problem with magic, the professor explained as she watched the custodians haul in the boxes, is that it did not digitize easily or well. Magicians mostly used notebooks and chalkboards for their research, and Akemi had been no exception. Each box contained dozens of giant paper sheets, covered with complex calculations and scribbled notes.

Fortunately, Akemi had also been meticulous in her tracking. Each box contained an itemized list of its contents and a report summarizing the experiments contained within. Those had filled every waking moment Kana wasn't working with Jade and Professor White. Since she'd received them, Kana had managed to read through the abstracts of every experiment Akemi had run.

Time travel required far more power than any single witch possessed, even a witch as strong as Akemi. It was different than the shields around the city and the university buildings. Those were passive, relying on small amounts of magic drained from each witch who lived inside the shield. When they were hit, the shields converted magic into heat and sent it blasting up into the atmosphere. It was huge, powerful, automated magic, needing almost no energy to *control* once the shield was set in place.

Time travel was the opposite.

Akemi's theory revolved around using magic portals to transfer matter both physically and temporally. The problem was that no one had ever done it successfully. To open a portal between locations was easy enough (it was part of second-year undergraduate magic studies). But such portal was a construct of pure magical energy, capable of transferring magical energy. They were volatile, short-lived, and nearly impossible to control. But in a paper she wrote during her second year of experimentation, Akemi claimed to have found a solution:

> *While there have been many discussions in recent years of the best way to combine powers and multiply their effect, the most efficacious answers come from the medieval writings of Monsieur De Vangelous, who worked with a coven of twelve to create some of the most powerful magic known at the time...*

Kana made a note to look up the works of Monsieur De Vangelous.

> *De Vangelous used three key methods to maximize the power of his spells:*
>
> *He brought the witches together as a coven, binding their powers to one another.*
>
> *He had the witches dwell under one roof and cast spells that increased their ability to share their power and his access to it.*
>
> *He "mined" the daily magical energy given off by the witches in a manner similar to that used by the Shipton University magical shields and power sinks, and stored that magic for later use.*
>
> *I therefore propose to follow in Monsieur Vangelous's footsteps and ask the university to allow the experimental group to occupy Coven House Three and begin the process as detailed in the following proposal...*

It took two hours of working in darkness for Vanessa to break through the six layers of the professor's trap. The last was the most irritating of all: the professor had simply locked the door. By the time Vanessa broke the lock and stepped out into the hallway she was tired, angry, and ready to beat her professor into a bloody pulp and fuck the consequences.

All she saw was a paper taped to the wall across from the door. It read: "Vanessa Lake, please report to the president's office."

Vanessa tore it down, crumpled it into a ball, and stomped through the underground hallways to the freight elevator. She boiled with anger all the way up and was ready to explode when she stepped inside the president's waiting room. It had a pair of leather couches, a glass and metal coffee table, and a desk with Ms. Newton standing in front of it. Before Vanessa could speak, Ms. Newton thrust a water bottle at her.

"Have a seat and drink this. Please." Despite the courtesy, Ms. Newton's tone brooked no argument. Vanessa took the bottle and dropped onto the closest couch. Ms. Newton put a plate of chocolate chip cookies on the coffee table "Have some cookies, too."

Vanessa was in no mood to be delayed, but the look in Ms. Newton's eyes made it quite clear she was going nowhere until she did what she was told. So, Vanessa opened the water—too cold to drink fast so she was forced to sip—and took a cookie.

A minute later Vanessa took a second cookie. Then a third. They were *really* tasty. She saw Ms. Newton watching her and flushed. Vanessa mumbled around a mouthful, "Thank you for the cookies."

"You are welcome," Ms. Newton sounded quite pleased. "Are you cooled down yet?"

Vanessa shook her head.

"Take your time, dear. Professor Grindal's actions were rather unconscionable. She and the president are having a discussion about it right now."

"Oh." Vanessa wondered what, exactly, that discussion might sound like and how much trouble she was going to be in when it ended. The thought kept her angry while she munched another cookie. She'd just finished her water when the inner office door opened.

"Vanessa, could you join us, please?" the president said. "And bring the cookies, if you would."

Vanessa went in. The office was large, with a corner view of the campus. The desk and small conference table looked sleek and modern—black, white, and dark gray—as did the comfortable, ergonomic chairs. Vanessa didn't care. Her eyes locked on the smug-looking professor at the table.

"Please sit," President Waterson said, indicating the chair opposite the professor. "Are the cookies good?"

"Yes, sir." Vanessa sat, her eyes still on Professor Grindal. She put the cookies down, out of the professor's reach.

"Ms. Newton's own recipe." The president helped himself to a cookie and slid the plate over to the professor. He took the chair between Vanessa and Professor Grindal. "Whenever she bakes for her grandchildren, she brings some in."

"Why did you sign up for remedial magic?" Professor

Grindal demanded. "Did you expect to use it as an easy credit?"

Vanessa's anger flared up anew. "I didn't sign up for your course."

"Yet, you are in it," the professor sounded no less angry, "despite being far more advanced than most of the undergraduate witches. How dare you waste your time and—"

"Professor, enough." The president's voice, calm and smooth, stopped the professor mid-rant. The president turned to Vanessa. "Please, Vanessa, tell us how you picked your classes."

Vanessa put her hands in her lap to keep from reaching across the table and punching the professor in the face. Between gritted teeth, she said, "I didn't pick my courses. They were picked for me."

"That is odd." The president frowned. "Normally, we send a counselor to work with students who… arrive in the way you did."

"From jail?" Vanessa snapped. "Well, I didn't get one. I didn't get anything but twenty bucks and a bus ticket."

"That is ridiculous," Professor Grindal said. "No matter what sort of trouble she got in, she should have been tested the minute she walked through the door. She's Rachel Meadows's daughter, after all."

Vanessa stared at the woman. Her voice shook as she asked, "Who?"

"Rachel Meadows. Your mother."

Kana walked through the near-empty cafeteria, a bowl of chowder and a large cup of coffee on her tray. When she'd grown too hungry to think she'd exchanged her pajamas for jeans and a sweater and comfortable shoes, more out of a sense of decorum than any need. A large number of students—all undergraduate, of course—ate in their pajamas, no matter what time of day. For Kana, getting dressed before searching for food was the least she could do to respect her graduate status. She spotted Night sitting in one of the booths by the windows. And was especially glad of that decision. Books lay all over his table, and a half-empty plate of fries and a half-finished milkshake bracketed the notebook in front of him. Kana wove through the tables and stopped in front of his.

"Got room for another?"

Night raised his head from his notebook, saw her, and smiled. He had a very nice smile; open and friendly but not too big. It warmed her belly and made her smile back without thinking. She noticed that his soft, yellow hair was still too long. She resisted the desire to reach out and stroke it. Night looked at the table and the smile turned embarrassed. "I think I have room. Just let me…"

He cleared the books from the other of the table and piled them into a slightly precarious stack. Kana put her bowl down and Night's nostrils flared.

"That smells amazing," Night looked at the remains of his fries and sighed. "Now I'm thinking I should have had the chowder."

"If you like, you can savor the smell while I eat it in front of you." Kana slid into the booth across from him. She picked up her spoon and stirred it, sending up a waft of steam and the thick, rich smell of seafood and cream. Kana smiled. "Mmm. So good."

Night breathed deep. "You are evil."

"I know." Kana spooned up a mouthful, blew on it, and slipped the spoon between her lips. She made an exaggerated expression of joy, and Night rolled his eyes and turned to stare out at the trees instead. Kana followed his gaze and saw the last of the leaves still clinging, their bright fall colors turned dull brown as they fought the fall winds that would soon turn to winter.

"Getting cold out there," Kana said. "I think I need a bigger jacket."

Now it was Night's turn to smile. "This is sweater weather. The real cold isn't coming for a while yet."

"California girl." Kana tapped her chest. "If it isn't bikini weather, it's too cold."

"How did you survive this long?" Night asked. "I've heard it gets below 60 in LA in the winter."

"Going to Hawaii at Christmas helped." Kana ate more of the chowder. "Not going to do that this year, though. Too much to do."

"How goes the work?"

"It's been incredible." She wanted to tell him about Akemi's research, but even the thought of doing so tied up her tongue. Instead, she said, "Working with Professor White and Jade has expanded my magic so much. We've done things I didn't even think possible."

"Sounds fun." Night smiled. "I think I'm jealous."

"Don't be," Kana protested. "It's exhausting. I'm so far behind I think I'm first."

Night chuckled, which made him look even cuter. She'd liked the look of him from the beginning, but for most of the last month, he'd been busy with classes, assignments, tutoring Vanessa, and working with Professor White's experiments. They'd barely had time for more than passing conversations in the bar. Of course, since she had him here in front of her...

"Any chance you're going out tonight?" Kana asked.

Night gestured at the pile of books before him. "Paper to write."

"Too bad. I could use the company. Another night? You choose."

"Well, I'm done with this by—" Night stopped, his brows coming down. Kana followed his gaze out the window to the common. Vanessa was staggering across the grass, her face paper-white against the golden-brown of her tousled hair. She stumbled a few steps further, leaned back against a tree, and slumped to the ground.

"What the hell?" Night muttered.

"What's the matter with her?" Kana was far less than pleased that his attention was being taken away so easily. It came out in her suggestion, "Is she drunk?"

"I don't think so." Night slid out of the booth. "I think something's wrong."

He left his books and food and headed for the door, moving at a jog. Kana considered leaving him and eating her chowder. If he was more interested in Vanessa than her, there was no point in pursuing. On the other hand, if Vanessa were in trouble and she didn't help, what would Night think of her?

Kana sighed, took another spoon of the chowder, slid

out of the booth, and followed. The cold wind blew through her sweater and chilled her almost instantly. She hastened to where Vanessa sat under the tree, her head in her slender hands. Even sitting, Vanessa looked tall and gawky, but in a way that would be catnip to some men. Kana wondered if Night was one of them and then tried to shove the thought aside as Night knelt near Vanessa, but not close enough to touch.

"Vanessa," Night said gently, and when she didn't look up, raised his voice. "Vanessa!"

Vanessa raised her head. Her green eyes shone with tears, and she was shaking, though not with the cold. She blinked like she couldn't focus her eyes well enough to see him. Then her brows came down. "Night?"

"Yes. What happened?" He frowned. "Did Ian do something?"

Vanessa's head titled, her brow coming down. "No, Ian didn't fucking do something, you idiot. I…" She looked down and Kana saw a picture clutched in her hand.

"What's that?" Kana asked.

Vanessa heaved in a shuddering breath. "This… Professor Grindal says this is a picture of my mother when she used to come here. She says I look and sound just like her."

Kana leaned closer and looked at the picture. Save for her rather conservative haircut, the woman could have been Vanessa's double. "She looks like you."

"Vanessa?" All three of them turned to see Cassandra, backpack over her shoulder and eyes narrowing, running toward them. Cassandra's face was red with exertion, and her chest heaved as she skidded to a stop. "I got your message. What's wrong?"

Vanessa held out the picture, her hand shaking. Cassandra frowned at it. "Who is this?"

"Rachel Meadows," Vanessa whispered. "Professor Grindal said she's my mother."

"I don't understand," Kana said. "Why are you so upset?"

Vanessa's hands shook, making the picture wave back and forth. "I don't know who my mother is. I've never known. And I've never seen that woman before in my life."

It took an hour for Cassandra and Night to convince Vanessa to go inside. Kana left them in the lobby and bought another cup of coffee before going back to her room. She sipped at it, warmth spreading slowly through her body as the elevator rose. For the first time, she felt something like sympathy for Vanessa. She wasn't clear about the story of Vanessa's upbringing, but it didn't sound pleasant. At least Kana had always known her mother's name, even if she didn't have the slightest clue what happened to her.

When she reached her room, Kana put the coffee down beside the pile of experimental reports on her desk and dug into them again. There were so many, and she had been so busy that she'd barely had time to scratch the surface. She dug in and started reading the next paper.

Her phone chimed.

Kana pulled it out of her pocket, frowning. She didn't remember giving the number to anyone but Jade. She opened

it and saw one new message from the Scholarship Network—
the social media site reserved for Shipton's witch students.
Curious, she opened it.

> **Night:** Sorry we didn't get to finish our
> conversation. I am free Friday if that works for you.

Kana felt a smile pulling up her lips and a warmth inside
that had nothing to do with the coffee. She tapped "reply"
and wrote:

> **Kana:** Friday is fine. 8 p.m. in the student pub? We
> can go out from there.

She did not expect the wait for Night's reply to be nerve-
wracking. She tried to focus on the papers in front of her but
couldn't until the phone chimed again.

> **Night:** See you then!

The exclamation mark made her feel even warmer, and
not just because it was a yes. The quickness of the reply told
her that Night was no longer with Vanessa, and that gave her
immense satisfaction. Kana sighed happily and then stopped.

She realized that, just like Vanessa, she wanted answers.
The only difference was, Kana was certain that the answers
could be found somewhere in Akemi's experiments.

Which meant the easiest thing would be to run them
again.

Kana sat and stared at the boxes, her mind whirling, for

the better part of an hour. It was a ridiculous plan, given how little she knew about magic, but Kana's desire to know the truth had gotten the better of her. She opened the word processor on her laptop, put fingers to keyboard, and typed:

Proposal for the Continuation of the Studies of Akemi Wakahisa on the Mechanism of Temporal Travel through the Application of Magical Mechanics

CHAPTER 7

THREE HOURS, ONE LARGE PEPPERONI, hot pepper, and mushroom pizza and a half-bottle of vodka later, Vanessa watched Cassandra stare at the picture of Rachel Meadows. In the interim, Vanessa had spilled everything she knew about her childhood. As far as Vanessa was concerned, she was an orphan, raised by Ambrose Levesque as an annoyance to be tolerated. Now, with Cassandra staring at the picture and shooting glances from it to her, Vanessa felt her stomach churning.

"Professor Grindal was sure?" Cassandra asked.

"Sure enough that she gave me this picture." Vanessa took another sip from the vodka bottle. "Rachel was one of her favorite students. She'd wondered what happened to her. I had to tell her that I didn't know, that I didn't know my mother. She looked so disappointed and muttered about maybe making a mistake, but look at her!"

The young woman with the curly, golden-brown hair smiled out of the picture. The eyes were shaped a little differently, the face slightly wider, but there was no mistaking the resemblance. Vanessa took another drink. "If she's not my mother, who the hell is she? And if she is, why didn't Ambrose tell me?"

"Did you ask him?"

"I…" Vanessa stopped. She frowned. "I must have asked him at some point. But I can't remember."

Cassandra handed back the picture. "If you asked about your parents, you'd remember the answer."

"Yeah." Vanessa ransacked her memories. "I always knew he wasn't my father. But I can't remember asking him who my parents are."

"That is… weird." Cassandra frowned at the picture some more and chewed on her bottom lip, then she pulled off her flannel shirt and tossed it aside. Underneath, she wore a black camisole tucked into her jeans. She scooted to the head of Vanessa's bed. "All right, I want to try something."

Vanessa's eyebrows rose. "I didn't think you swung that way."

"Ha ha." Cassandra's expression told Vanessa exactly how lame her attempt at humor was. "No, I want to read your memory."

"What?"

"Family skill," Cassandra smiled. "My mother used it on me when I stayed out late to see what I'd been doing. The night my high school boyfriend and I went all the way, I made sure to stay out late. Should have seen the look on Mom's face."

Vanessa, remembering her own high school boyfriend, and the dozen others since then, felt the blood rising to her face. "Why do you want to read my memory?"

"Because you don't recognize the woman who is supposed

to be your mother and you have no memory of ever asking after her. That's not right. So, I'm thinking someone messed with your head and I want to see."

Vanessa didn't like the idea at all. "How much will you learn about me?"

Cassandra raised her hand, three fingers pointing at the sky. "I hereby promise to stay away from your sex life, your drug use, and your juvenile delinquency, Girl Guide's honor."

Vanessa managed a smile. "You were a Girl Guide?"

"We were all sweet and innocent once," Cassandra said. "And for what it's worth, I can't do anything except read. To mess with someone's mind requires a major ritual, and I'm far too lazy to set it up. So, will you try?"

Vanessa suspected this was not a decision to make inebriated. She didn't like the idea of anyone seeing into her mind, but even worse was the thought that someone had already gone in and messed with her memories. "What do I do?"

"Lie down and put your head in my lap."

Vanessa lay down, putting her head on Cassandra's crossed legs. It was unexpectedly comforting. Cassandra rested her fingers against Vanessa's forehead. Her touch was gentle and soothing.

"Now, close your eyes and take slow, easy breaths," Cassandra said. "Start thinking about being a kid. Don't focus on one moment or another, just drift through your memories."

Vanessa did her best. Memories bubbled slowly to the surface. High school was a blur of drugs, sex, and skipping class. Before grade three she'd been homeschooled by Ambrose. She remembered hours of sitting at the dining table, working through magical problems as well as English, French, math, and science. She didn't remember any trips, any days at the beach or summer vacations, not even when she was little. In fact, before her time sitting at the table there was…

A blank.

Vanessa opened her eyes. Cassandra sat back against the wall, frowning again.

"He fucked with my memories." Vanessa sat up. Fury burned bright inside her. "Ambrose fucked with my memories."

"We don't know it was him," Cassandra said.

"Who the fuck else could it be?" Vanessa grabbed her phone and called Ambrose's number. It rang through to the answering service. Vanessa swore and hung up. "Fucker. I'm going to go back there, and I'm going to kill him."

"He'll have the whole Quebec Council of Witches on his side by the time you get there." Cassandra held out her hand for the bottle. "Plus, you leave, they erase all your memories."

"That fucking asshole." Vanessa wanted to throw the phone across the room, to go out and get in a bar fight, anything to shake her feelings of helplessness. Instead, she handed the bottle to Cassandra. "What am I supposed to do now?"

Cassandra took a long swig. When she put the bottle down, she was frowning again. For a time, she sat silent, until at last Cassandra said, "The first thing we need to do is find out how you ended up with Ambrose."

"How are we supposed to do that?" Vanessa asked. "You going to go to Quebec and beat it out of him for me?"

"Tempting," Cassandra said. "But no. I have a friend on the MLEA."

"What?" The Magic Laws Enforcement Agency was the magic community's equivalent of the FBI. "How?"

"When you get arrested enough, you get to know people." Cassandra smiled, though it was a tight smile. "He's a sergeant. Every time the local cops arrested me when I was a kid, he'd show up, claiming to be my parole officer, and take control of the case. Man, he dished out nasty punishment. One time he made me blind and deaf for a week."

"And that didn't stop you?"

"I was a willful child." Cassandra shook her head. "And stupid. Anyway, he's been like a mentor since I straightened up. Helped me get through my house arrest, recommended me for Shipton. If it weren't for him, I'd probably still be in jail."

"Nice, I guess." Vanessa doubted it. Police, in her experience, were rarely helpful.

"No, he isn't," Cassandra said. "He's a ball buster. But said if I needed anything, I could call him. And if someone fucked with your memory, that's something worth calling about."

Vanessa desperately wanted to know what happened, but at the same time, she really didn't want any more police in her life, especially from the Magic Laws Enforcement Agency. She'd faced them a few times when she'd been a teenager, and they scared the hell out of her. "I don't know."

Cassandra handed her the bottle back. "How's this: we don't tell him about your memory. I'll say you have some questions about your adoption. If Ambrose took you from your family legally, there will be a record of it. If not, then we might get an idea of what really happened. We might even find out whether or not Rachel Meadows is your mother."

Vanessa thought about it, took another long swig of the bottle, and said, "Ask him. I don't know if he'll find out anything, but if he does…"

"It's better than not knowing?" Cassandra ventured.

"Yeah. That."

Janice sat in the third row of a storefront church in a rundown mini-mall on the outskirts of Newlane listening to the Reverend Marcus McCrae preaching as if to a full cathedral. And in her mind, the entity plotted how to get more magic.

From the moment the entity absorbed Billy's magic, it drained away like water from a bucket with a slow leak. The entity tried to keep it, but just like water, the magic slipped through its grip. It tried leaving Janice's body and taking the magic with it, but the magic was anchored to the flesh that held it. Before the sun had set on the first day, it was almost gone. By the next morning, the last of it had vanished.

The entity needed the Promised.

If the Promised was a witch, as the entity remembered, it could host the entity and hold magic at the same time. And with magic, the entity could subjugate its brethren and bring them through to this world with its plentiful corporeals to live off. It could become the greatest of its kind.

But until it found the Promised, it needed a different kind of power.

Janice's body was strong and young, which meant it could host the entity for much longer before it broke down entirely, but it also meant she had less pain for the entity to feed off.

And while it gained some from her coworkers' aching legs and emotional misadventures, it wasn't enough to keep it strong. That was where the reverend came in.

Janice walked past the reverend on the way to work. The man stood on a small stepstool, preaching on the streets. The ones surrounding him were a mixture of street people looking for entertainment and a few true believers whose lives, from what the entity could sense, were miserable indeed.

Since then, the entity made Janice sit in Reverend Marcus McCrae's church twice a week. The man had a good voice and a good message for those looking to be castigated for their sins. They were all sinners, he assured them, and certainly worthy of damnation in the deepest burning pits of Hell. Even so, there was hope for those who obeyed Christ's commandments and did as Reverend McCrae told them.

The more the entity heard the reverend preach, the more it suspected that the man could be of use on many more levels than as just a conduit to absorb pain from others. Reverend McCrae had the charisma that made humans pay attention, believe, and follow. It was a characteristic the entity could exploit.

But first, Janice would give it one more feast.

Professor Grindal's office hours were 10 to 12 on Tuesdays, which meant Vanessa had to wait most of the week to see her. She tried to bury herself in her studies, but her mind kept straying to the possibility that Rachel Meadows was her mother. What the hell happened to the woman? Why had she abandoned her daughter? Had she died suddenly and left Vanessa with Ambrose? And why Ambrose? No one in their right mind would leave a child with that man. Did that mean that Rachel wasn't in her right mind when she died? Was she even dead?

Night tried to be helpful, which for Night meant making suggestions that were no help whatsoever and getting offended when Vanessa told him to fuck off. Cassandra had talked to her friend in the MLEA, but she hadn't heard anything back yet. So, all Vanessa could do was study and work and drink and fuck herself stupid when that didn't help.

She didn't tell Ian what was wrong. She just gave him sex in exchange for allowing her to get shitfaced at his house and be driven to school in the morning. It was a hollow arrangement, but it gave her an outlet; a way to fuck out her anger, and if Ian didn't like it, he didn't complain. Nor did he say anything when she got shitfaced after they finished.

Which is why, when Tuesday came, Vanessa felt about as awful as it was possible to feel without actually being sick. Twenty minutes in the shower didn't help, and the two cups of coffee she poured down her throat roiled around in her stomach like they were racing to see who would get thrown up first. Even so, she managed to dress decently—blue skirt, black leggings beneath because it was chilly, tank top under an oversized sweater she'd found at a secondhand store— and brushed her hair and teeth so she could pretend to be an upstanding student. And if she had Doc Martens on her feet, well, the better to kick ass, and she really wanted to kick someone's ass.

Cassandra came with her. Unlike Vanessa, who was

hoping to make a good impression, Cassandra had opted for her usual tight jeans, Doc Martens, and a band T-shirt from Blanket Hornpipe's "Three to One and Bound to Lose" tour under a thick red and black plaid wool shirt. Vanessa was torn between worrying about the impression they would make and wondering where Cassandra got her shirts.

Vanessa knocked at the office door—open—and Professor Grindal actually smiled at her.

"Vanessa, good to see you." Professor Grindal frowned at Cassandra as she tried to place her. "And... Cassandra, is it?"

"Yes, Professor," Cassandra said. "I took your basic magic course last year."

"Yes. And did quite well, as I recall. How are your studies this year?"

"So far, so good."

"Excellent." The professor sat back in her chair. "So, what brings you two here today?"

"My mother," Vanessa said. "I mean, the woman you think is my mother. I mean..."

Cassandra smoothly took up where Vanessa stopped. "Vanessa thinks that Rachel Meadows might be her mother, but she doesn't know anything about her. So, we thought we'd start by asking you what you remember and what might have happened. Is that all right?"

The smooth confidence in Cassandra's tone caught Vanessa off guard. The two didn't have any classes together, and despite being Vanessa's best friend on campus, they rarely saw each other outside the dorm or the various bars that Cassandra dragged Vanessa along to on weekends.

"That's fine," Professor Grindal said, "though I'm afraid I

don't know much after her time here. She finished her master's degree in interdimensional magic theory and practice, then got married and had a child whom I thought was you, Vanessa."

"She really looks like Rachel?" Cassandra asked.

"Right down to the attitude problem." Professor Grindal smiled. Her big blue eyes lost their focus on Cassandra as she peered into the past. "She was full of fire, our Rachel was. Had a mind of her own, knew exactly what she wanted to study, and wasn't going to take no for an answer. I was her thesis advisor for her master's degree. We fought like cats and dogs about it but in a good way. The way you were ready to fight me, Vanessa, after I ran you through the magic traps."

"She knocked you on your ass and beat you so your own family couldn't recognize you?" Vanessa asked, frowning.

Professor Grindal's mouth went wide. She stared at Vanessa and then, to Vanessa's utter surprise, began laughing. Vanessa shut her mouth and waited.

The professor wiped a laugh-tear from her eye. "Oh, my, I haven't heard that sort of talk since my high school days. Do you still want to do that, Vanessa?"

"Uhhh…." It had not been the reply Vanessa had been expecting. "Not right now, no."

"Good." Professor Grindal leaned her elbows on her desk, her small face turning serious. "You can't get into fights, Vanessa, not with that bracelet on. They'll throw you out of here, and honestly, given what I've seen, you're too good to let your life go to waste like that."

"Oh." It was not the response she'd expected, but then, she wasn't sure what she had expected. The professor *cared,* which of course made her think of Night's clumsy attempts to be helpful and made Vanessa wonder if she was being an asshole to all these people.

"As for Rachel, I'm sorry. I haven't heard from her in twenty years. Not since she got married. Rachel didn't even give me a forwarding address. Have you tried the office?"

"Yes," Cassandra said. "They don't have her current address or anything else since twenty years ago. Neither does the alumni office."

Vanessa switched her gaze to Cassandra. "I didn't know you'd done that."

"I had some time yesterday," Cassandra answered. "Was going to tell you last night, but you didn't come home."

"Oh."

Cassandra turned back to the professor. "So, you didn't see her after she got married?"

"Once," Professor Grindal said. "She came back to help… what was her name… one of Professor White's students…. Rachel brought her infant daughter with her, whom I thought was you, Vanessa. Then after that, she went off and I didn't hear from her again."

The entity walked Janice toward the campus late on Wednesday evening. Janice would miss her shift at the bar, but then, if the entity's plans went well, she wouldn't ever go back. The night was quiet, with few people around. Newlane was a working town and rolled up its streets during the week, but the entity now knew enough about university students to expect to see a few out late. It had been on the Shipton campus a dozen times, but always in its energy form. It did not venture on campus in human form but stayed in the park and the shops nearby. One coffee shop in particular was a student favorite. It stayed open all night, had free internet and large, comfortable booths for students desperate to study and write.

One witch went there every Wednesday night. He bought a large cup of coffee and pored over his notes as though his knowledge of history and biology actually meant something.

The entity walked Janice's body past the coffee shop to the darkness of the alley between it and the campus. Its target had not arrived yet, which was exactly as the entity planned. Janice grew cold as the entity watched the university campus, but the entity didn't care. In fact, the more miserable Janice looked, the easier it would be to lure him in.

At last, the witch came out of the campus gates. He was tall, lean, and walked with the slow, stumbling walk of the exhausted. He had a backpack on, and his eyes locked on the coffee house like it was his salvation. The entity watched him until he was only a block away.

Then it turned and slammed Janice's face against the wall.

The woman's nose cracked with the first blow, blood spurting from both nostrils and the split flesh on her bridge. Janice wanted to scream, but the entity locked down on her vocal cords. It adjusted the angle, and this time Janice's eyebrow split. Blood poured down the side of her face and into her eye. The entity tore off her coat and threw it to the ground. It used the knife—the same one that killed Billy—to hack through her purse, spreading the contents over the alley pavement. Then, the entity sank down against the wall and waited.

The witch stepped into sight.

"Help me," the entity made Janice's words come out in a pained croak. "Please. Help me."

The witch turned, saw her, and his eyes went wide.

"Holy shit!" He knelt beside her. "What happened?"

"There were three of them," the entity said. "They grabbed me on the way to the coffee shop. I just wanted to get a coffee, but they shoved me against the wall and threatened me with a knife. Please, I need to go home."

"You need an ambulance." The witch reached for his phone.

"No, please," the entity said. "If my mother finds out, she'll make me leave Shipton. Please, I just need to get back to my apartment. I just... "

The entity made Janice look down at her destroyed purse. It allowed her body to start crying, then looked up at the witch. "I can't stand up by myself right now."

The witch hesitated, his expression clearly saying that it was a bad idea. But he held out his hand and said, "All right. Let's get you up."

The entity grabbed his hand, pulled on it, and released it with a small cry of pain. "Sorry, I think I hurt my wrist, too. I'm sorry I'm such a mess."

"It's all right. Can I put my arm around your back?"

"Please."

"I know you don't want to go to the police," he said, as he crouched beside her and wrapped his arm under her shoulders, "but if there're people out here mugging other people, they should really know, so it doesn't hap—"

His words ended with a startled gurgle as the knife

slammed, hilt deep, into his throat. The entity felt it bounce
off the witch's vertebrae and exit the back. The witch wrenched
backward, tearing the knife out of his neck. The entity leaped
at him. It hadn't hit anything vital with the first stab, just
silenced him. It slashed at the witch's neck, but the man got
his hands up. The blade bit into his fingers, hacking one off
and leaving a second hanging by a flap of skin. The witch
tried to scream, but the hole in his throat sent half the air out
in a squeaking rasp. The entity charged forward, slamming
into him and driving the knife in and out of his belly like
the needle on a sewing machine. He fought, but the entity
ignored his blows. It didn't care how much damage Janice
suffered. All it wanted was a dead witch.

"Hey!" someone shouted across the street. "What the
fuck?"

The entity pulled the knife out of the witch's guts and
once more slashed deep into his throat. This time it hit the
jugular and blood rained out of the gash. The entity held
tight to him, savoring his pain. The witch's heart stuttered,
and his magic drained into Janice. The entity savored it and
wished it could use the magic to burn away all the university's
buildings and reveal the Promised. But even as it reveled in
the sensation, it knew that the young witch's power would
barely dent the shields around the campus buildings.

So instead, the entity released control of Janice's body and
retreated into her brain.

Janice stumbled back, releasing the witch and staring at his
bloody, slashed form. Her eyes went down to the bloody knife
in her hand, and she started screaming. The entity fed on her
terror until the police put her in the back of the car. Then,

it flew across the city to where the Reverend Marcus McCrae lay back smiling as he watched one of his followers getting dressed. The entity floated in the room until the woman left and slipped into the reverend's mind. The reverend winced and rubbed his head, but that was all. The entity waited until the reverend was asleep before it started shifting through the man's memory.

That night, the Reverend Marcus McCrae dreamed of witches.

CHAPTER 8

November

K ANA STEPPED OUT OF THE dormitory elevator, walked
past the cafeteria, and paused by the pictures of the
two young men murdered by the waitress. The words "In
our memories" hung above them, and in front stood a small
table with a candle that never stopped burning. Kana's breath
caught in her throat, not for the young men personally, but
for the horrid, useless way they had died. It seemed so unreal.
From the gossip Kana had heard, half the campus knew Janice.
She'd been working at the Harrison Pub and Grill for three
years and didn't know either of the men personally, though
the police said that she'd texted with her first victim before
she killed him. The waitress claimed she didn't do either of
the crimes, even as she stood over the body of the second
witch, holding the knife she'd used to cut his throat.

It didn't make any sense.

Kana sighed and walked outside to let the cold air clear her
head. The last of the leaves were gone from the trees and had
been raked away from the yellowing lawns. The air smelled of
water, and the breeze that blew through the campus carried

the wet promise of rains to come. It wasn't snow weather—
yet. The temperature hovered around freezing, just above or
just below, but never dipping long enough to bring down
snow. Kana wrapped her leather coat tight around her and
wished heartily it would hurry up already. Snow was nice.
Kana enjoyed snow every time she went skiing. But this gray,
cloudy misery she could certainly do without. She'd much
rather be sitting in the pub with Night, talking about magic,
than standing out in the cold.

She smiled, remembering that she had done exactly that
the last two Friday nights. Night had been delightful company,
his work with education, fascinating, and his muscles excellent
eye candy. Thinking about it warmed her up and kept her
mind off the coming meeting for another thirty seconds.

Then she thought about the meeting.

Kana pretended it was the cold making her hands tremble
and shoved them deeper into her pockets. It had taken her
two weeks to write the proposal in consultation with Jade,
who thought it was an amazing idea, and three hours to nerve
herself up to send it. She had not expected an answer for at
least a month. Instead, Professor White had sent her an email
the next morning, giving her the time for her appointment. It
happened so fast, Kana was worried the professor was going
to give her a long lecture about working beyond her ability
and send her away.

Kana spotted Jade outside the administration building,
smiling and breathing deeply of the cold air. She looked like
she was enjoying the weather, which was enough to make
Kana dislike her intensely. How could the woman be happy
when Kana was cold, miserable, and nervous? Kana chuckled

at the stupidity of her reaction, so she, too, was smiling when she reached the administration building.

"All ready?" Jade asked as she opened the door.

"As I'll ever be." Kana opened the inner door. "So, no."

"Don't worry," Jade said. "Professor White approved your mother's research. I can't see her denying you."

"I'm not my mother," Kana pushed the elevator button. "I don't know nearly as much magic as my mother did. Even with all the extra work we've been doing to get me up to speed."

"She had the advantage of a lot more time," Jade said. "But you understood her research well enough to put together the proposal. And the way you picked to tackle it is brilliant."

"Let's hope the professor thinks so." The elevator opened and they stepped in. Kana spent the ride up staring at the wall. Jade left her alone and stayed quiet as they waited in the hallway outside Professor White's office. Kana appreciated it. She needed the silence to gather her nerves. It was one thing to examine her mother's disappearance, it was the height of hubris for someone with so little experience to try and complete Akemi's experiments.

Professor White opened her office door and smiled. "Kana, Jade, come in."

The professor sat behind her desk and gestured to the two chairs before it. Kana sat, hoping her nerves weren't showing. What she wanted to do was high-level magic, something she was stunningly unqualified to do. It was tantalizing to read her mother's theories on imaginary numbers and unseen dimensions turned real by the application of magical force, to be on the very edge of understanding it. Kana felt like she stood on the bank of a raging river, unsure if her swimming skills were enough to take her through to the other side or if she would be snatched by the current and dashed apart on the rocks that surely lay beneath the surface.

"Your proposal was most interesting," Professor White said

"I know it's presumptuous," Kana began, but Professor White held up her hand.

"It is not that," the professor said. "It is ambitious, certainly, and took a certain amount of nerve to send in such a proposal given that you've been studying magic for less than six months, but there's nothing in it that is unreasonable, given the proper guidance."

"Which is why I specifically asked for Jade to be the lead on the project until my own magic skills are enough to take on that role," Kana said. "And for you to be the supervisor since at this point you are the only other one I can talk to about my mother's work."

"It looks like you're asking for a fair amount more than that," Professor White said. "You want to create a coven and have them live together?"

"The university has been using covens for experimental groups for a long time," Kana said. "Akemi's notes indicated that she got permission to do just that as part of her experiments."

"Akemi was doing her doctoral thesis," Professor White said. "You are not."

"Which is why I need you and Jade to guide me, going forward."

The professor's eyes narrowed. "I think we should all take a walk."

Twenty minutes later, they stood outside Coven House Three. The building was square, concrete, and stood three stories with a flat roof. The front lawn was short and immaculately kept, and the doors and windows clean. Kana, who'd been imagining something more gothic, possibly with a tower festooned with gargoyles and ravens nesting under the eaves of a dark shingled roof, felt vaguely disappointed.

Professor White opened the door and ushered them into a large foyer with a dining room on one side and a lounge on the other. White sheets covered the furniture in both rooms. The wall in front of them was blank, save for a single door in the center with the words "Lab One" written on it.

"Go on," Professor White said, pointing at the door.

Kana kicked off her boots, left them on the mat, and went to the door. It was big and metal and solid and resisted moving at first. Kana pulled hard to get it open and stepped inside.

"Oh." Kana's voice came out small. "Wow."

The room's white concrete walls rose the height of the building to the ceiling skylight. It had no other windows at all save a narrow band of thick glass inset in one wall. Kana stepped up and peered through. On the other side, she could dimly make out a control room.

"It's like the university labs, only above ground." Kana turned a slow circle. "It's impressive."

"It most certainly is," Professor White said from the doorway. "The coven houses were built in the 1990s for experimental groups studying magic requiring long-term use of space. It has this lab, plus three more underground. It also has residence space for up to twenty witches. Have you got parameters for the witches you recruit?"

"Yes," Kana said. "Akemi used a specific experimental protocol to determine the power and control of potential research assistants. We'll use the same one. Then, we'll run a group spell to determine compatibility among the assistants."

"And will you be limiting it to witches in the university?"

That question gave Kana pause. "I was planning to, yes."

"Don't," Professor White said. "If you do, you'll be limiting the available pool of powerful witches. Open it up, and I'll ensure that those in the town and nearby get the information as well."

Kana frowned, unsure.

"The outside witches will sign a secrecy agreement just like the students," Jade said. "The secrecy of the information will be preserved, and you may get some powerful help."

"Also, do the initial testing on campus," the professor added. "You can do the group experiment here, afterward."

Kana's eyebrows went up. "Does this mean we can use it?"

"That depends." The professor leaned back against the wall and crossed her arms. "Where will you get the funding, Kana?"

Now it was Kana's turn to smile. "I'm a Klausen, Professor White. I can fully fund the entire research project out of my trust fund without going broke. Of course, if I do it that way, the university gets no access to the results, so it would probably be better if the university funded it instead."

"Now that's your mother's confidence." Professor White's smile grew wider. "I'm sure Shipton could come up with matching funds."

"I'm sure Shipton could pay for it all."

Half an hour of haggling later, Kana and Jade stepped out of Coven House Three into the cold fall air. Kana breathed in a deep breath, let it out, and turned to Jade, her lips pulling up into a huge grin. "Two weeks to get funding approval, then it's a go. We did it."

The women stared at each other, grins growing wider by the second. Almost as one they threw their hands in the air and shouted, "YES!" Their arms came down and wrapped around each other, squeezing hard. Both laughed for sheer joy and danced together, shaking up and down.

"Tonight, we celebrate," Kana declared, pulling back enough to see Jade's face. "Tomorrow, the real work begins."

"Like recruiting the other suckers for *your* magical research project?"

"Like that, yes." Kana put her arm through Jade's and pulled her toward the graduate students' pub. With her other hand, she pulled out her phone and sent Night the words, "We got it!" She hadn't been able to tell him what the proposal was, but he knew she was working on something. Before they were halfway to the pub, Night replied.

Night: Excellent! Meet you at the pub tonight!

Kana grinned and began planning. If there was ever a night where she would love to go home with someone, it was tonight, and so far, her chances were looking very good indeed.

"Murder!" Reverend Marcus McCrae shouted into the three-quarters full storefront church, making the congregation jump. It was a good turnout for a weeknight; better than most weekend turnouts before the entity had come. It had scoured the lower-class neighborhood that Reverend Marcus called home, searching for the destitute and the mentally unstable. Night after night it filled their minds with evil dreams and the promise of soothing help if only they visited Reverend Marcus's church. And thanks to the entity's urgings, the reverend gave them tales of hellfire and damnation and the comfort that it wasn't their fault.

"Murder," Reverend Marcus rolled the word on his tongue, his nostrils flaring. "That's what it is, but not murder like Cain and Abel. Not with a rock to the head or the jawbone of an ass or a knife to the guts. No. The death of a person's body is a tragedy for those left behind, even if that person is bound for Heaven, but I speak of something more insidious. I speak of the murder of a person's soul and a person's dreams. That, my friends, is as evil as the murder of the body."

The congregation, primed in their dreams to believe him, nodded their agreement.

"Do you not look around you and wonder why others have more than you?" he continued. "That others are healthier and wealthier and live easier lives than you, though you work as hard as they?"

The crowd nodded and muttered their agreement.

"It is not an accident," Reverend McCrea said. "It is not a mistake of destiny. Nor is it God's will, because God loves all his creations equally and does not want to see misery for any of them. No, it is something far worse. Far fouler. It is EVIL!"

This time the congregation's agreement was louder, the mutters turning to calls of "yes" and "praise God."

The entity sat in the back of the reverend's mind and listened, content. The congregation wasn't ready to be whipped into a frenzy yet, but they were getting closer. Every night the entity gave more dreams to the destitute and the mentally unstable. Each day more found their way to Reverend Marcus McCrae, whose fire and brimstone sermons told them what they dreamed was real and gave them a reason to believe. Soon, they would be ready to move. They just needed the right spark to turn the kindling of hatred the entity had planted in their minds into a burning flame.

Then, the entity would hunt, and it already had its next target picked out.

Kana practically floated out of the scholarship student bar. She was drunk, but not terribly so. She'd kept her intake slow and steady, letting the euphoria of the project and all that it might mean give most of her buzz that evening. Jade had drunk six or seven beers—Kana lost count—then begged off, pleading exhaustion and papers due. Night stayed with Kana, watching with amusement as she attempted to give details of the project without giving any details of the project.

"It's so frustrating," Kana said as they stepped outside into the cold air. "I want to tell you everything."

"Magical NDA's are a massive pain in the neck," Night agreed. "Though given how hard you're trying, it must be desperately exciting."

"You have no idea," Kana spun on the spot. "It's…

incredible. It's amazing. It's… a riddle, wrapped in a mystery, inside an enigma."

"It's Russia's response to Germany during World War Two?"

Kana stopped, amazed. "Holy crap, someone else who actually knows the source of the quote."

"Winston Churchill, radio address, 1939." Night smiled at her. "I'm in education after all, I should know some stuff by now."

"True." A cold breeze hit Kana, making her shiver. "Do you know how to keep a lady warmed up?"

"Take her inside?" Kana's head tilted and she sighed with exasperation. "Oh please, you're not that dense."

"I'm not, " Night agreed, walking closer. "But I wanted to give you an out in case you weren't saying what I was thinking."

"Very sweet." Kana met him halfway and leaned into his body. "Now be my windbreak."

Night wrapped his arm around her, hugging her close. The warmth of his body seeped through his sweater and into Kana's coat. Her shivering stopped, and he wrapped her own arms around him. She tilted her head up and saw him looking down at her, a smile on his face different than the one she'd worn in the bar.

"Well," Kana said, "kiss me already."

"You sure?"

"I'm sure," Kana leaned back a bit. "Are you? Is there a reason you're hesitating? Is there someone else you like?"

"No, no, and no, in that order," Night said. "I've just seen a few too many cases that started with the guy forcing a kiss on the girl when she didn't like it. It didn't end well for either of them."

"Well, I'm asking. You're not forcing a kiss on me." Kana frowned. "When you say ended badly, ended badly how?"

"She left school." Night flushed. "And I may have punched him a few times."

"Impressive," Kana said. She stopped, frowning. "Wait, did this happen here?"

Night looked away. "Maybe…"

Kana's mind, drunk though it was, managed to put the pieces together. "Holy crap, it was Ian. Vanessa's boyfriend. What did he do?"

"Drove a friend of mine away from the school." Night sighed. "She was a good student, finishing a degree in education. She started dating Ian and… I don't know. She was tired all the time, unfocused, sick. I thought he was feeding her drugs, so I confronted him. He shoved me, and, well, I'm a lot bigger than he is."

Kana winced. "How bad did you hurt him?"

"I only hit him a few times," Night said. "And I told him to stay away from my friend, but by then… Well, the damage was done. She broke up with him and left school."

"That is… bad." Kana snuggled back in close. "Glad you didn't get kicked out."

"He didn't tell anyone," Night said. "Too embarrassed at getting his ass kicked, I guess."

"Well, I'm not going to kick anybody's ass." Kana leaned her head back. "As long as I get kissed, that is."

Night grinned, "Well, I would hate to make you do that."

As far as first kisses went, it was pretty good. Night had

soft lips and a strong mouth, and he didn't shove his face against hers. He kept his tongue back until hers ventured out, then responded in kind. After a few long breaths, he pulled his face away.

"That better?" he asked.

"Oh, much better," Kana said.

"Then I'll walk you back to the dorm," Night said.

"Just to the dorm?" Kana asked, keeping her voice teasing.

"I thought that would be enough for a start."

"You thought wrong." Kana caught his lapel and pulled him close again. "Can I be honest?"

Night's eyebrows rose. "Haven't you been?"

"Not honest enough, apparently," Kana said. "I know we don't talk much during the week because we're both up to our asses in work, but I really, really want to celebrate this with someone. You're beautiful, you're strong, you like me, I hope, and I like you."

"That's good to know."

Kana pushed her body harder against his. "I'm not asking for a big relationship commitment. If that happens later, good. But tonight, I want company."

"I understand, but…"

"But nothing," Kana said, exasperated. "I am lonely, Night. I haven't had sex in months, I want to have it with you, and from what I'm feeling, you're not opposed to the idea."

"I'm not," Night's voice came out lower than before. "But I don't want having sex with you to wreck the chances of having a relationship."

Kana grinned. "Then you'd better be good at it, hadn't you?"

CHAPTER 9

A PILLOW HIT VANESSA'S HEAD WITH far more force than necessary. The blow jolted her awake and made her realize that her skull was pounding, her stomach turning and that she wasn't in her dorm room. She opened her eyes and glared at Ian, who raised his pillow high.

"Fucker," Vanessa muttered. "Hit me again and I'll turn you into a toad."

"Man, I wish that worked." Ian lowered the pillow, a dreamy look on his face. "Imagine if we could turn the rich into toads and take all their money. Anyway, get up."

"Fuck off or I'll turn you into a corpse and *feed* you to the toads."

Ian pulled the covers away and smacked the pillow down on her bare ass. "You told me that, no matter what, I wasn't allowed to let you miss the experimental testing today. So, get up before I decide on a better use for that lovely ass than sitting at a desk."

"How can you be so energetic?" Vanessa grumbled as she sat up. She felt absolutely awful and exhausted to boot. It hadn't been that late an evening, she was sure of it. "Why aren't you hungover?"

"Genetic luck," Ian declared. "I may not have been blessed with money, but at least I'm pretty and have a good constitution for drinking. Now up and at 'em. Don't want to miss the big experiment, after all."

"This isn't the big experiment," Vanessa grumbled as she sat up. Ian tossed her panties and jeans at her in quick succession. Vanessa caught them both. "This is the application process. First, we get through this, then we do the big experiment, whatever the fuck it is."

"And you're going to do it?" Ian's asked.

"No choice. I missed a month of advanced magic. The prof. said if I joined the experiment, he'd count it in place of my missed assignments."

"Sucks to be you." Ian finished dressing. "Is Night going to be part of the group?"

"Damned if I know," Vanessa said. "He needs money, so probably. Why?"

"No reason," Ian said, though his tone suggested otherwise.

"Whatever," Vanessa grumbled. "Just get me there, will you?"

Ian's bike was loud, the sound driving like a spike into Vanessa's aching head as they zipped through the streets to the campus. At least it dulled the permanent spin cycle that her mind had been in since she'd learned about Rachel Meadows. The little information Professor Grindal had shared hadn't helped, and Cassandra's friend in the police hadn't gotten back to her yet. Nor had Ambrose answered a single one of Vanessa's phone calls. And so, she kept drinking at Ian's place, knowing he'd wake her up in the morning.

She wasn't sure the mornings after were worth it. She felt awful every time.

They pulled up in front of the dormitory. Vanessa got off the bike. "I'll see you later."

"Yeah," Ian said. "Later."

He was still there, sitting on his bike watching her when Vanessa glanced back from the dormitory door.

"Candidate four in place," Kana said. "Recording on?"

"One moment." Jade leaned over and hit buttons on the recording stack on the wall. "Sound on and... Video on."

"Thank you." Kana activated the microphone. "Is the candidate ready?"

"He is," Ian said on the other side of the glass. He was in one of the smaller experiment rooms under the university. He gestured at the 3-inch block of aluminum on the concrete stand in front of him. "I just need to bore a hole through this?"

"That's right," Kana said. "We'll time it."

"No worries," Ian said. "Metal is one thing I know."

"Begin when you are ready," Kana said. "Timer starts now."

Ian lowered the welding mask over his face. For a moment, he clasped his hands in front of him. Then he pointed at the block of metal.

"Heat in the room rising," Jade said. "Here we go."

The experiment was simple: to convert focused magical force into heat and burn a hole through the center of the aluminum block without cracking it or destroying it. High school-level witches had to do a similar one using a block of potassium whose melting point was 64 degrees Celsius. The aluminum block Ian was facing had a melting point of 660 degrees Celsius. To melt a hole through the aluminum required much stronger magic, focused and sustained for a long period of time. Akemi had only considered witches who could melt through the aluminum in two minutes or less for her research team.

"Thirty seconds," Jade said.

In the center of the aluminum block a red spot appeared. Ian's posture didn't change. If he was at all worried, it didn't show. The red spot expanded to exactly an inch in width and glowed yellow. The rest of the block didn't change color.

"Excellent control," Jade said.

"Hm." Kana had been skeptical when Professor White suggested she throw the applications open to any witch that could generate the necessary power, and given what she knew about Ian now, she was pretty sure she didn't want him unless absolutely necessary. Unfortunately, even with the open call, she got only eleven applicants. They were seeing eight today, and so far, the first four had not passed the Akemi standard. If she couldn't get at least five other passes, Ian was going to have to be on the team.

She hoped Night was all right with that.

Their first night had been fun and slightly awkward, as good first nights usually are. The three times since had been more fun and much, much less awkward. Neither had pressed on with the idea of developing a deeper relationship, but both knew the possibility was there. Both also knew exams were coming, papers were due, and the winter holiday was coming up fast. With all that, they agreed not to delve into the relationship part of what they were doing until January.

But my, it was nice.

"Hole is forming. One minute. Impressive."

Kana pulled her attention back to what they were supposed to be doing. She had run the experiment herself and broken through the block in forty-three seconds. Jade had taken seventy-five. "If he gets through at all I'll be impressed. Who's after him?"

"Night," Jade said. "The back of the block is glowing yellow. Ninety seconds."

"Better than anyone else has done so far," Kana sighed. Having him and Night on the same team would be awkward, but if there were not enough candidates, he would be on the team. Kana watched the back of the aluminum block melting, leaving a perfectly round hole. Ian stayed in place a pair of seconds longer, then dropped his hands and raised his mask. "And done."

"Ninety-seven seconds," Jade said. "Very nice. Thank you."

"My pleasure."

"I'll escort you to the waiting area," Kana said. "If you could remain, that would be appreciated. The test shouldn't take too long."

"Sure, I have nothing else to do today," Ian said. He picked up the welder's tongs from the side of the room, removed the aluminum block with practiced ease, and put a new one on the stand.

Kana left the control room and escorted him back through

the halls and up to the cafeteria. Eight students sat waiting there, drinking coffee. Vanessa, Kana noticed, was not yet among them. She got a coffee for Ian and turned to where Night waited. "You're up next."

"Right."

Night rose and Ian took his chair, smiling. "Good to see you, too."

"I'm amazed you made time to come here," Night said. "What with your busy schedule."

"It's winter," Ian said. "You'd be amazed how much work drops off for a motorcycle mechanic in winter."

Night didn't say anything else as Kana led him to the elevator. Only when they were inside did he say, "Him? Really?"

"Beggars can't be choosers," Kana said. "He's not in yet, but if he is it's because there's no one else, and that means you two have to get along. Right?"

"Don't worry," Night said. "I won't be the one to start anything."

"Not reassuring," Kana muttered as the elevator door opened. To her surprise, Vanessa stood beside the lab door. Kana's felt her eyebrows rise. "You're early?"

"I didn't feel like waiting in the cafeteria," Vanessa said. "Too many people. I go after Night, right?"

Kana checked her clipboard as an excuse to hide her face. "You do."

"I'll wait."

A part of Kana wanted to leave Vanessa waiting in the hallway until Night was finished. Kana recognized the thought as petty and instead said, "Come into the control room, if you like."

"All right."

Vanessa took a spot near the wall, and Jade sat down by Vanessa. In the other room, Night had already picked up the welding mask and was settling it on his face. Vanessa nodded to Jade. "Recording on."

"Sound on," Jade said as she hit the switches. "Video on."

"Thank you." Kana leaned to the microphone. "Is the candidate ready?"

"I am," Night said.

"Excellent. Timing begins from the moment you put down the mask. When you're ready, go."

Night pulled down the mask and pointed his fingers at the metal block.

"Room temperature climbing," Jade leaned forward. "That's the fastest so far."

The metal began glowing red, then yellow.

"Thirty seconds," Jade said. "Very impressive."

A moment later it began to flow, sliding down the front of the block and slipping to the side as if being shunted. Kana suspected Night was doing exactly that, clearing the way so his magic had nothing between it and its target. It was a minor piece of magic, but one that Ian hadn't used. Even so, Night was going faster.

"One minute," Jade peered at the block. "And... through. Sixty-three seconds. Nice."

"Much better." Kana activated the microphone. "Good work, Night. Can you remove the block and set up the next one? Then you can come into the control room if you want."

"Will do." Night pushed up his mask. He raised his hand and muttered under his breath. The block rose into the air. He lowered it gently to the side, then walked to the wall and picked up another one, setting it on the clear spot on the stand.

"All right, Vanessa," Kana said. "You can get ready."

Vanessa left, passing Night in the hallway. Kana heard Night wish her "Good luck," and then Night was in the control room, closing the door behind him.

"Nice time," Kana said. "Best so far, in fact."

"Aside from Kana," Jade added. "She beat you by twenty seconds."

"Good to know," Night said, smiling at Kana. "Always nice when the boss is the best in the group."

Kana smiled back at him. "Glad you appreciate it."

"In place," Vanessa's voice came through the speaker. "Ready when you are."

Kana turned back to the window and saw Vanessa with the helmet on, the front tilted up. Kana leaned to the microphone. "One moment. Recording?"

"Sound on. Video on."

"Test begins when you put down the helmet," Kana said. "When you're ready."

"Right." Vanessa pulled down the helmet and pointed at the block.

Immediately the center glowed cherry red.

"Wow," Night said.

Kana said nothing, her eyes on the block. The red changed to yellow, then to white. Aluminum began flowing. Soon, the back of the block began glowing red.

"Thirty seconds," Jade said.

The back of the block glowed yellow, then white. Aluminum spilled down the back of the block as the hole broke through and widened. A moment later, it was perfectly round.

"Done!" Jade clicked the stopwatch. "Wow, indeed."

"How fast?" Kana asked.

"Forty-five seconds." Jade held up the watch for Kana to see. "Two seconds slower than you."

Kana felt absurdly smug that Vanessa hadn't beat her time. She shoved the thought aside. Given all that was riding on these tests, she shouldn't be petty about being victorious. Vanessa lifted up the mask. "Is that good?"

"It's awesome," Jade said into the microphone. "You're all done. Kana, did you want to take them up, or should I?"

"Uh... I will. See you in the hallway, Vanessa." She turned to Night. "You'll be contacted for the main experiment on Monday, then after we review the results, we'll put it all together."

Night smiled at her. "Does this mean I'm in?"

Kana sidled close and whispered, "Later tonight if you've got the time."

Night tended to blush when surprised, which amused Kana to no end.

"Unless we can find five more like Vanessa," Jade said without looking up. "So yeah, you're in."

"Thank *you*, Jade." Night said, giving Kana a look that was supposed to be annoyed but was completely ruined by the smile under it. Night stepped out into the hall and raised his hand for a high-five for Vanessa. "Well done! That was amazing."

Vanessa gave him a long, steady look until he dropped his hand. She shrugged. "It was all right. I've done it before at home."

"At home?" Night shook his head. "I didn't do anything that hard until I finished my first year of university."

"Yeah, well." Vanessa looked at the floor, a sour look on her face. "Ambrose liked to push me."

"Are you coming to the cafeteria?" Kana asked, moving closer to Night. Again, petty, but she wanted Vanessa to see their relationship. Why she was insecure about the woman was beyond her, since Night clearly only liked her as a student. She felt like she was trying to stake her claim, which was ridiculous given the boundaries they'd put on their relationship.

If Vanessa noticed anything, she didn't show it. "No. Email me the results. I've got to study."

The entity floated high above the street, watching the witch saunter out of the bar. She was a red-haired thing with a plaid flannel jacket and tight jeans tucked into high black combat boots. Her backpack hung off one shoulder, and she moved with the happy ease of the slightly drunk.

The entity had tracked her for two weeks since it had moved into the mind of Reverend Marcus. The witch liked to go to bars and watch bands. Three nights a week she went out alone and rocked along with whatever band was playing in the local bars. That night, she'd been at a country bar, listening to a band play a rather uninspired set of cover songs.

The entity knew the routes the witch took back to campus. This night, it would take her past the alleys where men slept rough. The entity had spent the previous three days forcing an alley man to make a knife from a sharp piece of metal and some cloth. When the witch got close to the alley, the entity would take over his body and stab the witch to death.

The witch's phone belted out the lyrics to AC/DC's *Highway to Hell*. She pulled it out of her pack, looked at it, and her face lit up. She put the phone to her ear. "Sarge! About damn time. Where have you been?"

She stopped walking, her brow furrowing. "Are you sure?"

Her brow furrowed more at his answer, her lips pushing hard together. Anger filled her face and she sighed, the air escaping her in a long, controlled breath that released her displeasure.

"That's fucked up," the witch said. "Way too fucked up. All right. I'll stick closer to her. But someone will have to take over the Janice case."

The entity froze in midair.

"… No, we've had no luck tonight, either," the witch said. "I'm sure there's something going on, though. It doesn't make any sense otherwise. Talk to you soon, Sarge."

The witch put her phone away and started walking again. The entity stayed high above her, its plans forgotten. Something was wrong, though the entity wasn't certain what. But as a creature accustomed to ambushing and being ambushed, it had senses finely tuned for a trap, and suddenly, this witch felt like one. It searched; reaching out its awareness to see who else was in the area. It sensed no one, could see no one.

And yet, the witch had said 'we.'

The entity reached out again, this time searching for magic.

Four bright glowing spots of magic surrounded the witch. One walked half a block ahead, another half a block behind. A third was across the street, and a fourth was right beside her. All four kept pace with the witch, moving as she did. A shiver went through the entity as it realized what it had nearly done.

It followed the witch all the way back to the campus. The four magical spots followed as well but never closed the distance with her. It wasn't until the witch disappeared into the shielded dormitory that the four turned away, going off in four separate directions into the night.

The entity pondered what it meant all the way back to the storefront chapel. It slipped into the Reverend Marcus's sleeping mind and crafted a vision of an angel to speak to him.

"I am Raguel, listen unto me," the entity said in his mind. "The enemy is crafty and strong. It knows that we hunt it. But soon, so very soon, we shall strike the enemy, and they shall know fear."

The entity just had to figure out how.

CHAPTER 10

KANA STOOD IN THE LARGE experiment room in Coven House Three, studying the floor. The candidates would come in a moment, and Kana wanted to be sure the designs that she, Jade, and Professor White had spent all weekend drawing were correct. They were based on Akemi's work but were augmented with advancements that Professor White had added over the last twenty years. Kana was inordinately proud of the work they'd done over the weekend. It was not just the double circle of the shield, but also a third, smaller circle in the center, with a concrete post and a single, metal lattice hexagon prism resting on it.

Jade walked the other side of the circle, double-checking the lines. She looked up and spotted Kana watching her. "Nervous?"

"Very." Kana swept her eyes around the circle again. It looked right, but given what she was going to do with it, she couldn't risk any mistakes.

"I won't waste your time telling you not to be," Jade said. "I always end up a bundle of nerves when I'm doing this sort of work."

"Good to know." Kana managed a smile. "I think."

"But *you're* totally going to be fine," Jade grinned at her.

"Is it safe to come in?" Night called from the door.

"Yes. Just don't touch the circles," Kana said.

"I promise."

Night came in and immediately went over to examine the circle. Jade joined him, and they talked to each other in low voices as Jade pointed out the details of the circle.

Vanessa came in soon after, wearing clothes that looked slept in and dark circles under her eyes that made her face look haunted and ten years older. She also looked pissed, which led Kana to suspect that Ian, who came in behind her and looked enormously smug, hadn't told her he was part of the group until just that morning.

Ian's smug look vanished as he looked at the pattern on the floor. From his expression, he had no idea what he was seeing. Ian cast glances toward Night and Jade and tried to listen in but made no moves to join them. Vanessa didn't bother coming over to look. She leaned against the wall, eyes half-closed as if opening them all the way hurt. Kana half-hoped Vanessa wouldn't be able to do the work, so they wouldn't have to deal with her hangovers and binge-drinking.

Cassandra arrived last—still two minutes early—and whistled when she saw the pattern. "How long did that take to draw?"

"Cassandra?" Vanessa's eye went wide open. She pushed off the wall, looking ready to both punch and hug Cassandra. "Where have you been?"

"I'll tell you after," Cassandra said. "I promise."

"You'd better." Anger and relief filled Vanessa's voice.

Kana stepped forward. "It took all weekend. Professor White, Jade and I did it together."

"Nice work." Cassandra shook her head. "Damned if I know what it does, though."

"You and me both," Ian muttered.

"Good morning, everyone," Professor White's voice came in over the speakers. "I will be your observer and recorder for this experiment. Can everyone take their positions, please? You will find your initials marked on the floor outside of the circle where you need to stand. And of course, do not cross over the patterns, please."

Kana went to the top of the circle, Jade to the spot on her right, Night on her left. The others circled until they found their places. No one was foolish enough to step onto the patterns on the floor. Kana watched Vanessa take a place between Night and Jade and saw Ian move to a spot on the other side of Cassandra. Six places, equidistant from each other.

"Everyone, please listen," Kana said. "This is a test of our compatibility as a team. We are going to create an energy shield based on the research of Professor White, using the pattern in the circle. We will record the results of the experiment, and all those who are found compatible will be invited to join the research group. Understood?"

Nods around the circle.

"Rehearsal run, please," Professor White said over the speakers. "No power, just focus."

"Right." Kana rubbed her hands together once and then clapped them. "Keep your eyes on me and follow my movements at all times. Breath synchronization first, please."

"Inhale." She breathed deep, pulling air through her nose to her diaphragm. Around the circle, the others did the same. "Exhale."

Five times they did it until all six breathed in unison.

"Raise hands, please," Kana said, raising her hands high, envisioning her magic. The other six followed the motion perfectly.

"And down." As one, the six squatted and held their hands above the circle. "At this point, we release our magic into the circle. According to Professor White's calculations, we need to stay in this position for thirty seconds."

Kana counted off the seconds in her head. "And up."

They rose, and their hands pointed toward the center of the circle.

"Good," Kana said. "Just like that. If something goes wrong, I will shout 'break.' If I do, break the circle by dragging a foot over the marks and then get back as quick as possible. Everyone understand?"

Again, heads nodded around the circle. Kana turned to the window. "Professor, we are ready."

"Excellent," Professor White said. "Sound and video recording on. Seismic activity, air pressure, magic variability, and structural integrity monitors are all recording."

"Thank you, Professor." Kana tried telling herself this was no different than leading a group project at UCLA. She gave it up a moment later. This was nothing like those projects. This was magic; fantastically powerful forces that she didn't even know existed six months before. If she did it wrong, it could hurt the other five people in the room, all of whom, she realized, were waiting for her to start.

"Right, synchronize breath please," Kana said. "And this time, summon your magic."

Kana focused on her magic until it became a pulse throbbing through her body. Her hands glowed, red first, then yellow, white, and finally, electric blue. Yellow magic glowed from the hands of Night, Jade, Ian, and Cassandra. Vanessa's hands shone white, almost as brilliant as Kana's own blue.

"Hands up," Kana said. As one, the six raised their hands, the other five all watching her. "And down."

Kana exhaled and squatted, the others following, and six sets of hands touched the circles together.

Their magic filled the outer circle, and suddenly, Kana could feel them all.

It was different than before when she and Jade and Professor White had worked together. This time, she could feel everyone's magic, waiting for her command. She felt the separate threads of power, identifying each person by their magic as easily as staring at their faces. She sensed Night as a cable of kindness and strength, laced with intelligence. Vanessa was a fire of passion, anger, and hope. Jade was a knife's edge of intelligence and desire for knowledge. Ian's magic was slippery, like a serpent, but strong. Cassandra's was a rock of self-confidence, control, and skill.

Gently, as Jade had taught her, Kana braided the magic together, no longer six separate strands of magic, but a single woven power far stronger than before. The outer circle glowed white, and the magic spread inward, filling in the equations and symbols before spreading to the inner circle. As expected, the equations had done their work. The magic, powerful before, had grown tenfold. The electrical tingle became a crackle that sent her hair standing on end and her heart racing. She wanted to seize it directly, to feel the true power of the spell between her fingers but knew doing so would likely kill her. She fought back the temptation and instead concentrated on the inner circle. That was the final control point, and it was from there that Kana needed to direct the magic.

The power rose, a brilliant white, cobra-deadly energy that resisted the confines of the spell. It snapped and hissed like a sparking wire. Kana and the others rose to their feet, arms raised into the air, their combined power both feeding the spell and controlling the raging magic.

A single muttered command from Kana and the magic expanded, growing into a mesh net of energy, its brilliant light filling the room. Kana watched it a moment longer, then called, "Release."

As one, the others released their magic. The power in the circle faded, and above them hung a mesh of magic far more powerful than anything Kana had seen before.

"Stage one complete," Professor White said over the speaker. She sounded satisfied, but not surprised.

"Thank you, Professor," Kana said. "Everyone, please go to the control room."

"Stage one?" Night looked up the magic shield. "What's stage two?"

"You'll find out in a minute."

She watched the other five leave and waited. Professor White's voice came over the speaker. "They are all here, Kana."

"Thank you, Professor." Kana turned her attention to the post in the center of the circle and the hexagonal prism sitting on it. She closed her eyes and focused her magic on the part of the experiment that Kana hadn't told them about. Because the other thing Akemi used this experiment for was learning how much she could trust her associates.

If the shield was cast correctly, it would contain far more magic than any single witch could throw. If it didn't, that meant someone wasn't doing their part fully. Analyzing the failure point would show exactly which member of the team was the problem and allow Kana to eliminate them before they affected any other experiments. But first, she had to try to make the shield fail.

Kana sent her magic to fill the small circle, felt the equations that filled it and the lines that connected it to the hexagonal prism on top of the small concrete stand. She poured energy into the shape until she felt her breath grow fast and her knees weaken. Kana stumbled a few steps backward. She took one more breath, closed her eyes and said, "Release."

The hexagonal prism shot up into the shield like a rocket and exploded in a roar of magic energy and a blast so bright it turned the darkness behind Kana's closed eyes white.

Kana opened her eyes. The shield crackled with the energy of the blast, but none had escaped it. The hexagonal prism had vanished, swallowed up by the force of its own energy release. Kana let out her held breath and stumbled to the wall. Five seconds later, Night burst into the room, the other four hard on his heels. He ran to Kana and caught her arms tight enough to hurt.

"Are you all right?" he demanded. "What did you do?"

"Tested the shield," Kana said. Despite the volume and brightness of the explosion, neither her ears nor eyes hurt. She smiled at Night, enjoying his nearness, then at the others who stood, mouths open, looking at the glowing mesh above their heads. "Congratulations. It works."

The entity, deep inside Reverend Marcus's mind, felt something calling it—a faint, pulsing beat thrumming below human hearing. The entity was at once intrigued and suspicious. It left the reverend and rose in the air, seeking the source. The calling came from the university, which was not at all surprising. What did surprise the entity was that, in the magic that made up the calling, it felt something far more important.

It felt the Promised in the shape of the magic.

The entity floated toward the calling, concentrating harder, trying to understand how the calling was being directed, and if it could find the identity of the Promised by following the magic. It was almost too late when it realized it was falling into a trap.

The calling became an irresistible pull. The entity tried to resist, but the force dragged the entity across the sky. In desperation, the entity flew down, allowing the calling to drag it forward as it moved closer and closer to the ground. The entity sent its awareness ahead, spotting a young human girl leaning on the wall of a store, her phone in her hands. The entity used all the strength it possessed to alter its direction the few inches necessary to enter the human's body.

It slammed into her with the force of a truck hitting a wall.

The girl screamed and fell, her phone hitting the ground. The entity dug hard into the girl's brain and lodged there as her hands clutched her head. The pull on the entity faded, though the siren call of the magic of the Promised still tempted it.

Kana had paid for the dining room to be cleared and catering to be brought in, including champagne mimosas for everyone. Now she stood back, a mimosa in her hand, watching the others babble to one another about the experiment. She even pretended not to notice that Cassandra had grabbed a mimosa, despite still being underage. Kana waited until everyone had their champagne in hand, then raised her glass.

"Attention, please," she said. "I want to tell you that each one of you did your part amazingly. No one messed up, no one failed to give their all, and together we created a self-sustaining shield that will last approximately three days. Congratulations."

The other six—Professor White had joined them—raised their glasses and drank.

"Now," Kana continued, "before anyone gets seconds on the mimosas, do you all understand the terms of being part of the experimental group?"

"I don't get why we have to live here," Ian said. "Why can't I stay at the shop?"

"I need your energy," Kana explained. "The experiments we'll be running this year will require higher levels of magic than we can produce consciously, so we'll also be channeling your daily unconscious magical energy output to the power sink."

"Power sink?" Ian frowned. "Where?"

"There are crystals embedded into the structure of the building," Professor White said. "With them, we can store a large amount of magical energy before experimenting."

"Also, the proximity will enable us to better sync our energy," Kana added. "And we'll pay an additional stipend for any inconvenience this might cause. Any other questions?"

"What are your experiments?" Cassandra asked. "I mean, the shield is one of Professor White's experiments. I saw the report on it last year. What are you working on?"

"She can't tell you yet," Professor White said, stepping forward. "The work is secret, and only those in the experimental group and the university's magic faculty will know what work is being done."

"The experiments are in line with the university's ethical guidelines," Jade added. She grinned. "In case anyone thinks we were planning something evil."

"We should be so lucky," Cassandra said. "Still, I'm not sure I want to go in not knowing what I'm doing."

"You don't have to," Kana said. "I will tell you everything about the experiments after you sign a non-disclosure agreement. If you don't want to be involved, you'll still not be able to discuss it. If you do, you can sign the contract and join the experimental group."

"How long do you expect the project to take?" Night asked. "I mean, the whole series."

"Ten years." Kana grinned at the expressions around the table. "At least, that's how long it took the first time. But don't worry, your contracts will only cover from now and to the end of the academic year. I'll spend the summer going over results and prepping the next set of experiments. Then I'll call for a new team. This year's team will have first refusal rights."

"Come this way, please, " Professor White said as she led them to a small table by the front window. Eight papers and eight old-fashioned pens lay waiting for them. "Please make sure you have the paper and pen with your name on it. This is very important."

The group picked up the papers and read through them. Kana watched Cassandra and Vanessa frown and saw Ian's eyes open wide.

"And with this, my blood," Ian read, "I do affirm that I will be true to the bindings that are held within this paper until Experimental Group 2739 is disbanded, or until the experiments for which the group was formed are complete and made public." He looked at Professor White, his eyes wide. His head tilted to the side and his voice came out disbelieving. "My blood?"

"It's standard," Night said. "I've signed three of these so far, all related to magical projects. This one is no different."

"At Shipton, we take privacy very seriously," Professor White said. "This is a magical document as well as a legal one. If you sign it, you will not be able to talk about Kana's work until it is made public in the magic community. If you don't sign it, you will have to leave now. It is as simple as that."

Cassandra frowned at the paper. "And if we find ourselves in an abusive situation?"

"Abusive?" Professor White's eyes narrowed. "You expect that, do you?"

"It happens," Cassandra said. "So, what about it?"

"Paragraph 5," Kana said, pointing at her own sheet. "'In

the case any member of the team breaks the rules of Shipton University, the laws of the witch community, or any applicable laws of the non-magical community, the injured party, or those witnessing the event may speak to either the university administration or, if appropriate, the MLEA to deal with the situation."

"Ah." Cassandra looked over the paper again, still frowning. Jade shrugged, picked up her own pen, and pricked her thumb. A moment later she was blowing on the paper to dry the blood of her signature. Night did the same. Ian looked uncertain, and Vanessa's eyes were on Cassandra.

"If you don't want to sign it," Kana said to Ian, "then I'll pay you for this morning and you're done."

Ian looked at the page, shook his head, and grabbed his pen. "No. No problem."

Vanessa took a moment longer. Cassandra was the last to sign, and she looked troubled. Kana wondered at it— Cassandra had struck her as the reckless sort, if anything—but set it aside. She could ask her about it later. For now, it was time to pour a second round of mimosas, which Kana did. She raised her glass and smiled at them all.

"And now that you are all sworn to secrecy, let me tell you about the work of Akemi Wakahisa."

The entity forced the crying girl to stand up and move, leaving the broken phone behind. It ignored the girl's aching muscles and the way the skin on her face drooped on one side. The entity did not care about any of those things. It wanted the

Promised, and as long as the calling was still going, the entity could find where the spell was coming from, and then learn the identity of the Promised.

The entity forced the girl's body into a stumbling run.

"And if we can successfully duplicate Akemi's experimental results," Kana finished, "then we should be able to extrapolate from them the steps needed to create our ultimate goal, which is a stable wormhole that will allow mass to pass through both time and space."

The expressions around the lecture room ranged from stunned (Ian) to smug (Jade). Night wore a frown of concentration as he tried to work his way through the concepts. Vanessa looked thoughtful, and Cassandra, to Kana's surprise, looked wary. The young woman sipped at her drink and gazed back and forth from Kana to Professor White. Kana was about to ask Cassandra what she was thinking when Professor White stepped forward.

"I hope that you now grasp the enormity of what we are doing," the professor said, "and why we were so particular about having you sign the non-disclosure agreements."

"It's astonishing," Night said. "I don't know if it's possible, but it is impressive."

"I don't know, either," Jade said, her face shining with pleasure. "And I helped put together the proposal. But isn't it exciting?"

"What are you going to do with it?" Cassandra asked. "If you can create a stable wormhole through time and space? What do you want to discover or make happen?"

"That's a question we'll debate once we've reached the point where we know it's possible," Kana said. "I'm not even sure that's a question we can decide. The faculty will certainly have a voice, not only in approving it or not but in steering the research. Right now, everything is only theoretical."

"I'm going to go back and slap my past self until he promises to do better in school," Ian declared. "Because this is really cool."

"I take that to mean that you want to participate?" Professor White asked with a small smile.

"Hell, yes," Ian said. "Where do I sign?"

"And do the rest of you?" Professor White asked. Cassandra hesitated, but when everyone said yes, she added her assent. "Then I'll bring in the contracts while you go through the binding ritual and become a coven."

"Which leads us to the important question," Night said. "What do we call ourselves?"

"Experimental Group 2739 doesn't do it for you?" teased Jade. "I like it; it has a certain punk rock feel to it."

"You know punk rock?" Cassandra sounded skeptical.

"I had my rebellious youth," Jade said.

"When was that? Last year?" asked Vanessa.

Jade laughed. "I'm older than I look. I'm twenty-five, not seventeen. "

"We figured," said Ian. "Regardless of the zebra sneakers."

"And the Harry Potter glasses," Vanessa added.

Jade blushed. "They're ironic."

"More importantly," Professor White said, "as part of your NDAs, you cannot discuss your experiments in a public setting. So, naming your coven after the experimental group would lead to some difficulties."

Jade grinned. "How about 'Kana's Dragons.'"

"Definitely not that," Kana said. "Sounds like a football team."

"Worse, it sounds like the last team I played for," Night said.

"'Kana's Toads?'" Cassandra suggested.

"Nothing with my name in it," Kana protested. "And no toads, either."

"Traditionally," Professor White said, "It is the leader of the coven who names it."

"Me?" Kana shook her head. "I would have no idea what to…"

She stopped as a memory from her childhood blossomed. It had been a casual, ordinary day when she was seven. The type of day that would usually slip by and not leave a trace, except that, on this day, her father had begun talking about her mother.

They had been sitting beside the pool. Kana was lying on a towel, letting the hot California sun dry the water from her body. Her father was staring at her. She made a face at him, and he laughed. Then he sighed.

"My black dove," her father said. And when Kana tilted her head, he smiled. "That's what I called your mother. Her black hair would fan out like a dove's tail, just like yours is doing now."

"Oh," Kana had said, surprised because her father almost never mentioned her mother. "Do I look like her?"

"Sometimes," her father said. "Right now, you do."

"So, am I your black dove, too?"

"No," her father said. "Your mother will always be my black dove, but you can be my little black dove. What do you think?"

Kana shook off the memory with its exquisite tinge of longing and focused on the room of people waiting for her answer. "Little Black Doves. In honor of my mother."

Vanessa frowned. "How is that in honor of your mother?"

"My father used to call her his black dove, and me his little black dove. And since we're doing my mother's experiments, it seems like a good name."

The professor opened her mouth to speak, and then closed it.

"I've heard worse," Cassandra said. "'Sara's Sparkly Spell Spinners' leaps to mind."

"Wow." Jade's head cocked to the side. "Middle school?"

"How did you guess?"

"So," Kana agreed. "Do we do this now?"

"Yes," Jade said. "And then, more mimosas."

"An excellent idea," Professor White said. "Now, if everyone can stand in a circle and join hands. Kana, do you remember the ritual?"

Kana nodded. The others stepped into the circle. Ian caught Vanessa's hand first, of course, and held out his other hand to Cassandra. Cassandra took it, and Night stepped up beside her. Jade took Vanessa's other hand and left a space between her and Night. Kana felt Jade's small, warm fingers slip into her left hand and Night's oversized hand engulfing her right.

"The coven ritual we are going to use is an old one,"

Kana said. "One that goes back in history to the founding of Shipton. Professor White says that it is the single most effective ritual to enable sharing of power magic among the coven members. Is everyone ready?"

"Yes," all six chorused at once.

"And do you all, of your own free will, join me in the Little Black Doves coven?"

"Yes."

"Then let us be joined." Kana took a deep breath and began reciting. The spell was old, the words in Latin, English, and Gaelic. As soon as she began speaking it, Kana felt the change. It was like the blending of their magic in the experiment, only this time there was no build of power. She felt their magic merge and unmerge, weave in and out of each other, and separate only to come together again. And after the third verse of the spell, the magic changed subtly. When the magic separated again, it left behind six lines of magic, connecting Kana to each of the others. And from each of their chests sprouted six lines, connecting them to Kana and each other.

Warmth spread from each of them to Kana and a sense of camaraderie that had not been there before. It was not friendship, but rather a sharing of experience and magic that bonded them and made them stronger. Kana felt Jade's sweetness and Vanessa's strength. Ian's restlessness and Night's determination. Cassandra's fierce loyalty.

She wondered if they would all become friends. Or maybe more than friends, in Night's case.

Kana forced the thought from her head and focused on the spell. She spoke the last of the verses, and the lines of magic faded from sight. Kana could still sense them, could still feel the warmth of the contact with the others, but like her magic when it wasn't in use, the sense faded into the background.

"And it is done," Professor White announced. "Congratulations, Little Black Doves, you are a coven."

For two hours the entity stood across the street from the house. The girl's body shivered. Her head ached and her bladder threatened to empty where she stood. Still, the entity didn't move. The magic of the Promised was coming from the house. The entity could sense eight humans inside, though the shield around the house prevented it from knowing anything about them. But if one of them was the Promised, well, that could make all the difference.

Then the door opened, and six Promised stepped out.

The entity stared, the girl's eyes going wide with its disbelief.

It recognized the woman it had followed from the bar only days before. Two more it recognized as the man and woman whom it had tried to possess before it knew how a witch's power worked. The thought of the golden cat and raven slashing into it sent a shiver through the entity, and the girl's knees quivered with more than just cold.

The entity felt the magic of the Promised gleaming from each of them, calling to the entity like a human calling for their lover. It wanted the Promised. It wanted to take over and become one with its flesh.

But looking at the six, the entity had no clue whose flesh it needed to possess.

CHAPTER 11

V ANESSA WAITED UNTIL SHE AND Cassandra reached
their room to demand, "Where the *fuck* have you been?"

"Sorry," Cassandra rubbed her eyes. "I've been up to my
ass in classes, and I've got some friends in town and they've
been dragging me out."

"And you couldn't tell me?" Vanessa said. "You couldn't
leave a note?"

Cassandra's head tilted. "What are you, my mother?"

"I was worried, asshole." Vanessa sat down on her bed.
"Or did you not remember that two students have been
murdered?"

"I remember." Cassandra sat on her own bed and pulled
off her a boot. "I need food."

"We just ate brunch."

"That was barely breakfast. Want pizza? We can get the
cafeteria to send some up."

"Not really."

"Then I'll eat it myself." Cassandra tugged one boot off,
tossed it to the mat beside the door, and started working on
the other. "Got that bottle of vodka?"

"It's not even noon."

"Never stopped you before." Cassandra's other boot hit the wall. "And you really need a drink right now."

That gave Vanessa pause. "What do you mean?"

"I mean, pour a stiff shot for you and another for me. We need to talk."

Cassandra's tone sent a prickle of worry up Vanessa's back as she went to the small fridge and rescued the bottle of vodka. She poured two glasses high enough to make sure the drink would hit hard. After handing one to Cassandra, she sat on her bed and put her back to the wall. She raised a glass. "Cheers?"

"Fuck 'em all." Cassandra shot back the contents of her glass in a single gulp and shuddered.

Over the last two months, Vanessa had learned that Cassandra could put it away when she wanted to, but that most of the time she preferred to sip. For Cassandra to shoot back an entire glass of vodka meant something was up, and from the look on her face, it wasn't something good.

Vanessa shot back her own, letting the alcohol burn through her before asking, "Right, what is it?"

"My friend in the MLEA got back to me." Cassandra put her empty glass down on the nightstand. "About Rachel Meadows."

"And?" Vanessa demanded. "What did you learn?"

Cassandra crossed her legs and propped her elbows on her knees. "It's weird, all right?"

"Weird?" Vanessa frowned. "Is Rachel Meadows my mother or not?"

"Rachel Meadows and her daughter went missing twenty years ago."

"Okay…"

"No, not 'okay,'" Cassandra said. "Something screwy happened. Everyone in her family is rich, powerful witches. If she were alive, they'd have found her. If she were dead, they'd have found her corpse. Hell, they'd probably have brought her back to life long enough to know who killed her. Instead, she and the kid just vanished, and there is no record of her after that. Though I can assure you, the parents looked very hard and made sure the MLEA did, too."

Vanessa frowned. "That's… weird."

"It gets weirder." Cassandra took another breath. "You were found on the doorstep by Ambrose Levesque when you were two, according to his official report. You were never adopted, though he did become your official guardian. There is no record of your parents, no record of you in either the witch or regular foster system or orphanages. It's like you appeared out of nowhere."

"Fuck." Vanessa reached for the bottle of vodka. She had the top halfway off when the realization hit her. "Wait. I was two?"

"Yes." Cassandra stared at her, her eyes gleaming.

"Twenty years ago." Vanessa put down the bottle. "The same year that Rachel Meadows disappeared."

"Yes."

"Fuck." Vanessa slumped back against the bed. "Rachel was here, twenty years ago, visiting one of Professor White's students to help with a project. She brought a child."

"And then both vanished. And you appeared."

Vanessa frowned. "That is… weird."

"Yes," Cassandra agreed. "What do you want to do?"

"Aside from torturing Ambrose until he squeals out everything?"

"Yeah, aside from that," Cassandra said. "My friend in the police is curious about it, but can't do anything unless someone asks him officially."

"Officially?" Vanessa thought of sitting down with a police officer. "I don't... I don't know."

"I know you've had shitty luck with cops," Cassandra said. "And I told him you probably wouldn't be interested in it. But I thought I should ask. He might be able to get the Meadows' DNA and test you."

"Fuck." Vanessa fell back on the bed, her hands over her eyes. "I don't know. Maybe if we ask Professor White, she'll know who Rachel Meadows worked with. Then maybe we can ask them what happened, and maybe then we'll know something, and that's a shitload of maybes. Fuck. Maybe I'm not her kid; maybe I just look like her."

"Eat pizza with me," Cassandra said. "Get shitfaced if you want, call Ian if you want. Whatever works to get you through tonight. Then, take a day or two to process it and we can figure out what to do."

Vanessa nodded, grateful for Cassandra's support. The woman had a strength different from the friends Vanessa had in her past. Those had been the fast-living, drink-too-much type of girls looking for a quick laugh and a good time. Cassandra was hard-drinking all right, and certainly a party girl, from all the different bars she visited, but she was also smart, strong, and solid as a rock.

Vanessa passed her the bottle.

The entity remained in the girl's mind three days before the calling of the trap vanished. Its presence made the blood vessels in her head swell, doing more damage to tissues injured in the entity's sudden, brutal arrival. The girl wouldn't know it until she went back to school and tried to speak French again, and by then, the entity would be long gone. As it was, the girl lay in the dark, curled up in a ball, weeping and wishing the drugs her mother had given her were stronger.

The entity hated being hunted.

In its own world, the hunt was a way of life. The stronger ate the weaker, and the weaker ran and hid. But the entity had learned early that hiding only worked in the short term. It was far better to counterattack, to find its enemy and weaken them until they could no longer defend themselves. The entity had killed dozens who had thought it weak, and it would do the same to the witches who hunted it.

Slowly, as it fed on the girl's pain, the entity formed a plan.

Two days later, as evening fell, Kana visited Coven House Three.

After an afternoon celebrating with the coven and an evening of very athletic celebrations with Night, Kana had spent the last seven days immersed in data from the experiment and her studies. Jade had shown her how to read the data compiled by the computers and translate it into power input and output. All the numbers looked excellent, and Kana was certain that the group would be able to recreate the major experiments from Akemi's first two years by the end of the next academic semester. They might even get through her research by the middle of next semester and start discovering if her theories were actually viable.

None of which got her closer to finding out what happened to her mother.

Kana unlocked the door and stepped inside. The white sheets had been removed, the rooms cleaned and dusted. The entire place had a pine-scented cleanness. Kana left her boots at the door and walked around the main floor, thinking.

Her mother worked here before she disappeared. She walked these rooms. She cooked in the kitchen—which reminded Kana she needed to bring in a chef or organize a cooking schedule—she sat in the TV room, watching programs with her fellow students. She ran experiments in the labs and slept in the rooms above.

Did she have lovers here? Did they miss her?

Kana's father wasn't one of them. That was certain. He was California all the way and only went to the East Coast on business trips. According to him, it was in New York that he'd met Kana's mother.

But it was still before she'd finished her experiments at Shipton.

Akemi hadn't told Kana's father she was a witch; that was certain. She wondered how her mother could be involved with a man who didn't know the most important thing about her. Kana couldn't imagine it. Love, she supposed, but it made no sense for her mother to keep such a secret.

Kana went to the second floor, peering into the five meeting rooms. The table shone with polish, and the whiteboards waited for markers to obscure their gleaming white surfaces. She decided which one to use for their library, to hold all the records of Akemi's experiments for the team to read and review, and a second for meetings. The others could be used as study areas, so all of them—except Ian, of course—could work on their other classes.

Upstairs she went, peering into the bedrooms. Each had a neat double bed (which was nice) desk, fridge, chairs for sitting, and a small table for chatting. They even had small balconies for students to enjoy the weather when it improved. It made the graduate student rooms in the dormitory seem rather plain in comparison. The rooms were also fairly large, for which Kana was immensely grateful. At least she wouldn't have to hear Ian and Vanessa going at it. And that thought reminded her that she hadn't had sex with a partner in nearly three months.

She suspected Night would be willing to oblige, and the thought made Kana smile. She went back down to the main floor, slipped into the control room, and peered into the main laboratory. The circles and patterns were gone. Once the shield had dispersed, Kana had documented and erased them. Now the room was empty and ready for the next experiment.

Kana found the basement stairs and went down.

It was not nearly as far underground as the big labs under the university, but far enough. She opened the first door and found it led to the control room, with another door leading directly into the laboratory inside. The rooms were smaller in scale but built in the same style as the ones at the university—reinforced concrete with rounded walls and ceilings. The three labs—numbered two, three, and four, of course, stood along three of the outer walls of the hallway that ran around the solid base of concrete that supported the house, no doubt to minimize the possibility of catastrophic failure of the structure if something went wrong in one of the experiments.

Kana wondered if her mother had vanished working in one of the labs.

She made her way back upstairs, past Lab One and to the front door. Once they moved in, she could spend a few days collating Akemi's research notes. Then, she could start the next experiment. Kana stepped outside and saw Ian crouched by one of the corners, running his hand over the wall. He heard the door open and rose with an easy motion, smiling when he spotted her.

"It's our fearless leader," Ian said. "What brings you here?"

"I was just touring the inside, trying to figure out how to set up the meeting rooms. What were you doing here?"

"Looking for a safe place to tie up my baby." He pointed at his motorbike, parked at the end of the driveway. "Don't want someone driving off with it."

"And that side of the building looks particularly welcoming?" Kana teased.

He grinned. "No, this side of the house is particularly magical. Feel."

He squatted back down and pointed at a spot on the wall 5 feet from the corner. "When the professor told us about the crystals embedded in the house, I got curious. So, I put my hand on the wall and released a small amount of magic into it. Try it."

Kana's eyebrows went up, but she knelt, put her hand to

the wall, and sent some of the magic into the structure. She felt the building vibrating—a vibration as subtle as her own magic when she wasn't using it.

"Now, move your hand to the corner," Ian said.

Kana did, and felt the vibrations grow so strong it felt like her teeth were shaking. She took her hand away.

"Neat, huh?" Ian grinned. "Man, I would have gone to university if I'd known it was going to have cool stuff like this."

"Why didn't you?" Kana asked.

Ian shrugged. "My father never had the money. He was a mechanic. My mom actually worked here, in the administration building if you can believe it. But then she died, and my father never seemed able to keep his head above water."

"I'm sorry," Kana said and meant it.

"It is what it is." Ian headed down the driveway. "Want a ride back to the dorm?"

"No, thanks." Kana pointed across the common. "I can walk there in ten minutes, and it's not dark."

"All right. Say hi to Vanessa if you see her before I do."

Ian walked down to the end of the driveway, kicked at his starter until his bike roared into life, and drove off. Kana watched him go and wondered at the man. Night didn't like him much, though he'd never said why except that Ian was known to date the university students. There was something in Ian's behavior that felt off, as if he were always playing a role, but he hadn't done anything bad as near as Kana could tell.

Kana took her time walking across campus. She'd get some

dinner and plan her move. With luck, they could all be moved in by the end of the next week. Then, they could prepare for the next experiment.

The entity watched Kana—Promised four, it thought of her—walking through the campus. It couldn't touch her, not until it was sure she was the Promised, and even then, it didn't know if it could get past the golden animal that surely guarded her. The Reverend Marcus McCrae finished his sermon, the donation plate circled the room and came back full, and the entity sitting in the reverend's mind watched as most of the congregation slipped out into the setting sun.

Four men and two women remained behind.

The entity shivered in pleasure, sending a tingle through Reverend Marcus's flesh as the reverend led the six into the back room. He took them to the basement, where another altar had been set up. Instead of a cross, above this altar flew an angel, one that the entity had made the reverend himself paint, though the man could not remember it. All he knew was that he had dreamed of an angel visiting and woken up beneath it. After that, his dreams grew more intense, more insistent, and when a homeless man told the reverend a secret that no one else alive knew, he believed that the angel had indeed visited him.

The entity had done the same to the six that knelt with the reverend before the altar. It had picked them because it knew they were weak of mind, weak of purpose, and had secrets that none of them wanted shared. The entity had entered the minds of each, gleaning their deepest secrets. It had told them that God would take his revenge against those who oppressed them.

It had convinced them that great truths would be revealed to them tonight, and that, when God was ready, an angel would ride one of them like a horse, leading them to war.

The target was a witch named Glennis.

She was a third-year student at the university, studying business administration and magical physics. She was bright, eager, and having an affair with a married thirty-two-year-old man who ran a bar near campus. On Saturday nights his wife had her bridge club, which left him free to take Glennis to the empty apartment over his bar. The entity stalked Glennis, listening to her and her lover grunt and moan their way to finishing and after-cuddles. Now, it was ready to take her power.

The reverend and his followers rose to their feet and stood in a circle, facing in. The reverend's face was alight with excitement. His eyes gleamed as he said, "Tonight is the night, my brethren!"

The entity picked the largest of the men, Donald Calhoon, entered him, and made his body quiver. The others stared at him, fear, eagerness, and envy warring in their eyes. The entity could sense their hunger. It made Donald quiver more.

"I am Raguel," it announced through the man's voice. "I am the sixth of God's Archangels, as told in the Book of Enoch. I am an angel of justice, of harmony, and of vengeance."

"Tell us the secrets," Reverend Marcus said the words exactly as the entity had told him in his dreams. "Reveal our hidden truths, known to none other but ourselves, so that we may know who you are."

"I will," the entity said. "God knows your shameful secrets, and that tonight some shall be shared and forgiven, and with that forgiveness, you will be bonded together in the service of the Lord. Do you all consent?"

"We do," the other six said in unison.

The entity turned Donald to face Reverend Marcus first. "There was a girl named Lucy Adams. You aborted her child."

The reverend bowed his head, his face white. The entity put Donald's hand on his shoulder, drinking in the reverend's emotional pain. It did not say how the reverend had beaten her until she miscarried. It would save that for a time when the reverend's doubt surfaced and he needed cowing.

One by one it went through them. One woman had sold her body to have her father beaten. One man had slept with his stepmother. The second woman stole from her employer and had his mistress blamed for it. Another man had beaten a stranger half to death and ran before the police could take him. The third woman had disemboweled her neighbor's cats and left them on his doorstep. The last man had drunk himself into a stupor and cut open his now ex-wife's face with his broken bottle. These were not their worst secrets, but they were enough to convince them.

"We go now," the entity said. "Heed my instructions and follow them to the letter, and know that tonight, the true face of evil will be revealed to you."

The six listened, enraptured, as the entity riding Donald told them what to do. Then, it led them out into the night to take up positions. The entity took a spot in the alley, picking up the black iron pipe it had left there the day before for this very purpose. Across the street, another of the men waited, loitering in the streetlamp's light and looking intimidating enough to keep Glennis on the side of the road the entity wanted her. The others vanished to the places the entity told them to wait until Glennis came by, walking quickly and smiling to herself.

The entity grabbed her by the hair and threw her into the alley.

Glennis hit the ground hard. She scrambled to her hands and knees in time to receive a savage kick to her ribs that knocked the wind from her and sent her rolling down the alley. The entity walked Donald's body slowly forward. The woman stumbled to her feet, gasping for air that wouldn't yet come and grabbing at her ribs. The entity leaped forward and swung the pipe into Glennis's leg, cracking the shinbone and knocking her foot out from under her. She slammed sideways into the ground, landing on the ribs the entity had broken with its kick, the air rushing out of her lungs with a squeak.

"God has sent me to punish your kind, harlot," the entity said.

"Please," Glennis gasped, tears running down her face as she tried to crawl away. "Please don't do this."

"I will break your legs first," the entity said. "I will smash your pelvis so no other man will ever lie on it again."

Glennis raised a hand. Her voice broke as she begged. "Don't make me hurt you. Please."

"I'll shatter your ribs," the entity continued, raising its iron bar high in the air. "I'll beat your cow-sized tits until they explode, and then I will smash your hands so you can no longer befoul married men with your touch."

Fire burst from Glennis's hand and engulfed Donald head to foot.

The entity released control of Donald's mind. It reveled in the man's agony as he screamed and howled. Only when his knees gave out and he collapsed did it slip and fly into the woman, Angela, waiting at the far end of the alley. She was a drunk most of the time, but this night it had made certain she came sober and dressed respectably. The entity ran her body down the alley, calling, "Who's there? What happened?"

"Please!" Glennis begged. "Help me. Save me!"

"My word, child." The entity raised her up and dragged her away from Donald's burning corpse. Through the touch of her hand, the entity fed itself on the pain radiating from Glennis's broken shin and ribs. It hauled her to the far side of the street and into the alley beyond, saying, "This is the fastest way to the hospital."

"Stop, please stop," Glennis begged, but the entity had a tight grip, and try as she might the woman could not break free.

"Only a little further," the entity said, pulling her around the corner to the waiting arms of Reverend Marcus McCrae. He caught her and held her tight. The entity left Angela and entered his body.

"Please help," Glennis whispered. "Call the police."

The entity pulled a knife from inside the reverend's coat. "Burn in Hell, witch."

It shoved the knife into Glennis's kidney. The woman's body arched, her hands turning to claws. The entity grabbed her neck, drinking in her pain and magic until she collapsed in a heap at their feet.

"I am Raguel," the entity announced from the reverend's body. It waited until the others gathered. They were shaking with fear and exhilaration. The stench of Donald's burning flesh filled the air, even from across the alley. The fire department would be summoned soon. "Did you record it as I asked?"

"Yes," said one of the men.

"And me," said another of the women.

"Soon those recordings will be shared among our flock," the entity said. "We will show them the evil that threatens the lives of all good Christian folk."

"Amen," the others said, eyes wide with exuberance and fanaticism.

"And now," the entity gathered up all of Glennis's magic and held his hands over her body. "Let no one find this creature. Let her vanish from this world with neither mortal remains nor memorials to remember her."

And with those words, the entity released the magic, melting Glennis's flesh and bones into a puddle of noisome liquid that flowed down the alley to the drain. The reverend's followers gasped and stumbled back, their eyes wide. The entity smiled at them with his lips. "Be gone. Let no one see you. I will follow soon."

They ran away, disappearing into the night with panting, desperate breaths. The entity let the last of them go. Then, with the last of the magic from Glennis's body, it wrote a message on the wall with letters no one but a witch could see.

Give me the Promised.

CHAPTER 12

December

"I can't believe I'm going to miss this place." Vanessa put the last of her clothes into the ugly gray duffle bag and shouldered it. The room, stripped of the posters and Post-it notes, clothes piles, and half-empty bottles, looked sad and empty. Vanessa sighed. "I think I liked it here."

"Yeah, me too," Cassandra said as she struggled to stuff the last of her clothes into her suitcase. "But the new rooms are nicer, they're private, and they have balconies. And we actually have to cook or walk over here for breakfast, so I'm not going to get fat as fast."

"Yeah, there's that." Vanessa watched Cassandra force the lid of the case shut and led her out of the room. It wasn't a long walk to Coven House Three, at least, unlike the walk from the jail to the bus. The memory reminded Vanessa how angry she was at Ambrose, whom she called five times a week, trying to find out more about her mother. He never answered.

The snow had come, an inch falling overnight and gray skies promising more, though the temperature still wavered close enough to freezing that the chances of the snow being there by afternoon were slim to none. The paths and sidewalks on the campus were immaculately shoveled, leaving no worries of slipping as they trooped across the grounds to reach the house. A pickup truck stood in front of it, the back covered by a tarp. Ian stood behind it in a navy parka, his cheeks pink in the cold, pulling a rug out of the back of the truck. Vanessa called to him.

"About time," he said. "I was hoping for help."

"Good luck with that," Cassandra said, walking past him.

"Why the truck?" Vanessa asked.

"My dad loaned it to me," Ian said. "Just for the big stuff. Got to have my rug."

Vanessa looked at the rolled-up, beat-up Persian-style carpet. "I have no idea why."

"It's my rug." Ian did his best to sound wounded, but he was smiling. "Seriously, I've had it in every place I've owned."

"Yeah, I can tell," Vanessa said. "Have you thought of cleaning it?"

"Well, maybe if you help me carry it up the stairs, I will."

"Yeah, let me think about that." Vanessa walked past him. "No."

She dodged the half-hearted swat he threw her way and went inside. A lunch buffet sat spread out over the dining room table, with Kana and Professor White chatting behind it. Kana waved at Vanessa and kept talking. Vanessa went to the third floor, crossed to the women's side, (decided because the women's bathroom and showers were on that side) and found Cassandra staring from one room to the next.

"Kana took the one at the end," she said. "Closer or further from the bathroom?"

"Further."

"Well, there's six, so I'll take this one." Cassandra pointed at the door second from the bathroom. "Far enough not to smell it, close enough to run in a hurry."

"So classy," Vanessa said, heading for the middle room. The key was in the lock. Vanessa opened it and went in.

"Speaking of hearing, promise you'll only do Ian in his room?" Cassandra called. "Kana's far enough down the hall that I won't hear her or Night, but you're next door, and I need my sleep."

Vanessa poked a hand with a single raised finger out the door and looked over the room. The bed was a double, as promised, the desk was placed near the sliding door to the small balcony, the dresser beside it. It was small, well-appointed, and felt lonely to Vanessa. She shook her head. She'd only lived in the same room as Cassandra for two months; living down the hall from her wouldn't hurt at all. Vanessa put her bags on the bed, promised herself she'd unpack later, and headed down. She passed Ian and his rug on the stairs and got a mock glare from him. Vanessa blew him a kiss and headed for the dining room.

"Are you certain?" Professor White was asking as Vanessa stepped into the room. "Do you not need to do more work with the shields first?"

"You've spent twenty years perfecting the shields," Kana said. "They are as good as they are going to get. But I've never done this before, and since it's a key part of Akemi's research, I want to focus on that for the next experiment."

"All right," Professor White said. "When?"

"Next week, Monday. Hi, Vanessa."

"Hi." Vanessa picked up a plate and loaded it with meat slices and bread. Then, she remembered what Cassandra said about getting fat and added some vegetables and fruit before sitting down at the table.

"Move in all right?"

"Yeah. It's a nice room."

"Good."

There might have been more to say, but Vanessa was feeling awkward, as much because she just didn't like Kana as having nothing to say to her. She turned her face to her plate and managed to get a mouthful of food just in time for Professor White to sit beside her.

"How goes your studies?" Professor White asked.

Vanessa chewed mightily, swallowed hard, and managed, "All right."

"All right or good?" the professor asked. "Because if these experiments interfere with your studies, you might not be able to stay in the group."

"She'll be fine," Night said from the door. "As long as she keeps studying."

Vanessa rolled her eyes and pointedly looked away. His nagging was the last thing she needed.

"Night, welcome!" Kana said, her voice much warmer than it had been to Vanessa. "Are you moved in?"

Vanessa didn't listen to Night's answer. Instead, she turned back to Professor White. "Professor, can I ask you something?"

"Of course, Vanessa," the professor said warmly. "What is it?"

"It's about one of your old students."

"Rachel Meadows. The woman who might be your mother."

Vanessa's eyes widening in surprise. "How…"

"Professor Grindal has talked about it several times," Professor White said. "She said that Rachel was working on experiments with one of my students."

"Yeah." Vanessa swallowed against the dryness in her throat and asked, "Do you remember her?"

"I'm sorry, my dear," Professor White's voice filled with sympathy. "I don't remember her. I've had a thousand students of my own in the last thirty years. I'm afraid I don't pay much attention to other professors' students."

"Oh. Okay." Vanessa stared down at her food.

"Have you tried contacting her family?" Professor White asked. "Or the police?"

Vanessa shook her head. "I don't have any proof, except that I look like her. I don't want to go to her family until I have something more."

"And you'd rather not talk more to the police," Professor White's voice was soft enough no one else could hear it. "I do understand. I'm sorry I can't help you more."

"It's all right," Vanessa said. "I'm sorry to bother you."

"It's never a bother," Professor White said. "You are a student, despite the circumstances that brought you here."

Vanessa remembered what Night had told her about the cost of Shipton all those months ago. "Say, Professor, how did I end up at Shipton?"

Professor White's eyebrows rose. "I don't understand what you mean."

"Night told me at the beginning of the semester how much

it costs here," Vanessa said. "I'm nobody. I have no money, so why did they send me to Shipton?"

"I don't know," the professor said. "Perhaps someone on the Quebec Council of Witches has a connection here at the university?"

"Maybe." Ambrose had said the university had reached out, rather than the other way around. Vanessa shrugged. "Thanks, Professor."

Vanessa turned her attention back to her food, trying not to show her disappointment. As she ate, Ian, Cassandra, and Jade all arrived, loaded up their plates, and took seats. Ian sat beside her, which made her feel slightly better. Cassandra sat opposite, looked at the professor, and raised an eyebrow at Vanessa. Vanessa shook her head, and Cassandra's lips twisted in disappointment.

"Has everyone finished moving their stuff in?" Kana asked. When everyone nodded, she smiled. "Excellent. Tomorrow morning, I'll brief everyone on the next experiment and this Friday we'll do it."

"Can you give us a hint?" Ian asked.

Kana smiled. "We're going to open a magical portal and send something through it."

The Reverend Marcus McRae's audience had doubled in the month since they'd killed the witch. The entity had worked diligently, entering the minds of the humans that lived in the area. The poor, the mentally ill, the easily fooled, all were grist for the entity's mill. And every week, a few special followers were brought to the basement shrine to meet the angel Raguel and to witness the video of the witch burning poor Donald to death. They watched in horror as the man screamed and flailed and collapsed, and the entity, wearing the reverend's body, kept his hand on the new initiate's shoulders, drinking in their fear.

The entity had hoped for a response from the witches. The witch's police were investigating; men and women in suits came searching for the missing witch. The entity slipped into the body of one of the alley men and watched them. The witches searched the alley with magic long after the local police had given up looking for evidence, and looked grim at what they found. They stared at the wall and the message there and wrote in their notebooks. Then, they went back to the university where the entity couldn't follow them.

No one responded to its message.

And so, the entity sat back in the reverend's head and waited as the crowd of followers filled the storefront church to overflowing. They were not pretty people, but they glowed with faith, which was good. It would take all their faith and all the reverend's charisma to turn that faith into belief and that belief into action.

"Welcome, my brethren," Reverend Marcus began, and the crowd fell silent at once. "And I say brethren because I know that we are one and the same. We are all seeking for truth, for the love of God, and a sign that he has not forsaken us."

Heads nodded and a few folks muttered, "Amen."

"Donald Calhoon was a seeker, too," the reverend said. "He was a big man, full of physical strength, though inside he was as conflicted and sin-filled as any of us. But he fought against the dark voices in his head. He fought against the devil, and he was winning!"

More "Amens;" louder this time.

"But then the devil came for him with fire." The reverend bowed his head, sighed deeply, and when he raised it, there were genuine tears in his eyes. "Fire is an awful death. It is a slow and agonizing death and one that I would wish on no Christian. And when I learned that Donald, that this good Christian man, had died by fire, I knew then that the devil had caught him."

He fell silent, wiping at the tears in his eyes. Around the room, others did the same. They were imagining Donald's death, the reverend knew, and because he knew it, the entity knew it as well. Reverend Marcus let them imagine it, let them shiver and weep at the horror of it. And when their minds were full, he cried, "Donald, forgive me!"

The congregation raised their heads, eyes wide with surprise.

"I thought the devil caught you with drink, Donald," the reverend cried to Heaven above. "I thought that you spilled drink on your flesh and lit it by accident. Worse, I thought that the devil had so filled you with despair that you took your own life in the most painful way possible."

He lowered his eyes from the ceiling, and when he faced the congregation, those eyes burned with rage. "But now I know the truth. The devil murdered him and used the foulest tool at his disposal to do it."

The word 'murder' electrified the crowd. They whispered to one another, muttered under their breath, some cried aloud, "No!" And it was then that the reverend knew that he had them in the palm of his hand. He pointed to Angela, who flipped a new switch on the wall, making a screen lower behind the reverend.

He lowered his voice. "I must show you something shocking. Something horrible. Something so awful I tell you that, after seeing it, you may wish to run and flee from this room. But I tell you now: stay! Stay and face what you see, stay and help me face down this most evil of the devil's weapons. For it is only in the seeing that you will learn the truth of what evil walks God's fair earth."

The screen behind him lit up blue from the new projector the entity had made him install on the ceiling. The reverend pointed at it as the blue turned to black and commanded, "I say, do not look away!"

The screen lit up with an image of Donald standing above the prostrate form of Glennis. The bar in his hand and the rage on his face were barely visible in the dim light of the alley. But everyone could see Glennis raise her arm, and everyone saw the flames burst from that hand and engulfed Donald.

Several of the congregation screamed. Many cried out. The rest gasped in shock and horror.

"There!" The image on the screen froze, and the reverend pointed at the woman on the ground. "There is the devil's greatest weapon! For I tell you now, witches walk among us, and they seek to destroy us all!"

Kana looked through the thick glass window of Lab Two's

control room. The room beyond was empty save for a single post with a red globe balanced on the top of it. It was a simple, easy experiment and, if she was right, the first step in proving Akemi's theory of time travel. Kana nodded at Jade. "All right, let's do it."

"Excellent," Jade said, hitting buttons as she spoke. "Sound recording on. Video recording on... Seismic activity, air pressure, magic variability, and structural integrity monitors are all recording."

"Good." Kana straightened up and led them back up the concrete stairs to the main floor. Inside Lab One, the other five had already gathered around the circle Kana and Jade had put down. It was much smaller than last time but equally powerful. Kana nodded at them and turned to the thick glass window. "Everything is set up downstairs, Professor. Are you getting the feed?"

"I am," Professor White said. "And everything is ready here as well. All monitors on and recording."

"Excellent." Kana took her place at the head of the pattern on the floor. "Did everyone leave their phones on the dining table outside?"

When she got affirmatives, Kana continued. "This is a simple portal spell with two experimental sections. First, we're going to use the portal to transfer magical energy from this room to Lab Two."

"I've never done this before," Ian said.

"Neither have I, but the concept and execution are both fairly easy." Kana smiled at him and held up a small wooden ball. She tossed it to Night. "Then, in the second bit, we get to destroy something."

"Woo-hoo!" Cassandra called out. When the others looked at her, she grinned. "Oh, like you weren't all thinking it."

"The destruction of the ball is important," Kana continued, "because we can use it to measure the amount of energy that it receives when interfacing with the magical energy tunnel between locations. From there, we can extrapolate the shield power necessary to protect the ball during that transfer and whether or not it is possible to generate that energy with our magic. Make sense?"

"Make magic tunnel and burn stuff," Ian said. "After that, you lost me."

Kana's smile widened. "That's enough. Everyone ready?"

Everyone nodded, and Kana began the spell. Again, they summoned magic, and again, it wove together. The feeling was no less powerful than the last time, and Kana had to force her mind to stay focused and not revel in the magic flowing through the circle and her body.

Kana had read the process for creating the portal, of course; even so, it felt odd. The first step was not picturing the portal or the tunnel through the space that it created. The first step was fixing the *location* of a place in one's head. The coordinates were not just altitude and longitude, but elevation from the center of the earth and a series of magical coordinates that had to be calculated separately. It had taken a week to do the calculations, and Kana had both Jade and Professor White review her calculations to ensure they were correct.

Kana visualized the point in space—an abstract idea turned concrete by magic—and turned her attention to the portal.

Portals were easy to open, hard to direct, nearly impossible to maintain and, as far as all research but Akemi's showed, impossible to pass solid objects through. And if Kana did everything right, this experiment would demonstrate all those things. Then, she could work on proving Akemi right.

The spell in the circle, copied from Akemi's notes, worked perfectly. The portal opened as predicted. Kana willed the magic from the circle to travel from point to point, from the real world of the lab through magical space and into the lab below.

Ten feet above the circle the portal appeared: a small globe of glowing light, pulsing black and white and every color of the rainbow. Kana stared at it, stunned, and nearly lost focus. She felt the portal waiver and start to vanish and narrowed her eyes, willing it back to solidity. When it had stabilized, Kana breathed deep and sent the magic from the circle through the portal.

"Success," Professor White said. "The globe in Lab Three is glowing."

"Excellent work, everyone," Kana said. "Stay focused, please. Starting phase two."

Making the portal bigger was more difficult than creating it, but she managed it. Then came the hard part: hollowing it out. With as much energy as she could pull from the others, she forced a hollow space in the energy of the portal. It fluctuated, opening and closing like a small, round mouth, sucking at the air but unable to keep it. Then, for one brief second, it opened wide and stayed that way.

Night threw the ball into the portal. For one moment it

stayed intact in the magic tunnel, sliding down out of Kana's sight.

Flames burst from the portal, roaring with heat and blowing with such force it scorched the walls above the portal.

"Break!" Kana shouted, but the other six were already moving. The magic that had braided together in the circle tore apart with the force of a snapping cable. Kana's magic whiplashed into her, slamming her backward and onto the ground. She rolled into a ball and clutched her head.

"Everyone, freeze!" The professor's voice filled the room. "No one moves until I say."

The seconds that followed felt longer than the hours of work to make the circle around which they all lay. Above them, the portal flickered and flamed and faded to black, then to nothingness.

"All clear," the professor's voice filled the room. "Everyone answer when your name is called. Kana?"

"I'm alive," Kana said. "My head is killing me, though."

"You'll be all right. Night?"

"Here."

"Cassandra."

"Yeah."

"Vanessa."

"Fucking ow."

"Ian?"

"What she said. What the hell *was* that?"

"Questions later. Jade?"

"I'm all right."

"All right. Everyone, get up," Professor White said. "I am shutting off all recording devices for this room, then will do the room downstairs. Jade, come with me. The rest of you make your way to the lounge and sit down."

Kana rolled to her knees, nearly threw up, waited until her stomach stabilized, and rose to her feet. The others did the same. Ian looked the worst of them, his face pale and his entire body shaking. Vanessa let him lean on her as they staggered out of the room. Kana found a seat and tilted her head back, closing her eyes and watching spots dance behind her eyelids until she heard Professor White say, "Is everyone all right?"

An unenthusiastic chorus of affirmatives greeted the question. Kana opened her eyes. Her head still ached.

"Kana?" Professor White's voice was cool enough, but her expression was worried. "Are you all right?"

"Headache," Kana said. "But other than that, I'm fine. I think. What went wrong?"

"I don't know," Professor White said. "All the readings were fine, no major changes in air pressure or fluctuations in the magic circle."

Kana shook her head. "Then the ball should have gone into the portal and burned up in a cloud of smoke. That's what the manuals say. There shouldn't have been an explosion, and there shouldn't have been flames. Something had to have gone wrong."

"A drop in the amount of power, maybe," Jade said. "If the portal started closing earlier than expected, the ball would have connected with the walls of the portal before going in deep."

"And the explosion that should have occurred inside the portal occurred at the opening," Night said. "Makes sense."

Kana sighed and leaned back in her chair. "I'll check through all the readings once my headache clears. Maybe that will show what happened."

"Check them tomorrow," Professor White said. "For the rest of the day, everyone should take it easy and stay in the house. Keep an eye on one another for any problems other than headaches. I'll write up the accident report, then all of you will need to sign it."

"Right," Kana felt too weary to move. "Pizza's on me tonight, then. Everyone tell Night what they want, and I'll pay for it."

From the dining room, "Highway to Hell" played.

"Mine." Cassandra stood with a groan and headed to the dining table. "I want pepperoni, hot peppers, and mushrooms."

"I'll share," Vanessa said, but her voice sounded further away than it should. Kana closed her eyes and let the sounds of voices drift around her. Jade and Night argued about the necessity of anchovies, and Ian was trying to convince them all that pineapple was perfectly acceptable. Kana tried to tell them they could each order their own, but speaking felt like too much work.

"Fuck!" Cassandra's voice broke through the crowd. "Everyone, get your phones, now."

"What?" Night sounded concerned, but it wasn't enough to make Kana open her eyes. "Why?"

"Just fucking do it," Cassandra's voice was harsher than Kana had ever heard it. "And get on the video app. I'm texting you all the link. Hurry."

Kana opened her eyes and sat up. Her head still ached.

She watched the others get their phones and do as Cassandra said.

"Holy fuck," Vanessa went pale. "That's the girl who went missing, isn't it?"

"Glennis," Jade said. "What is she—"

"Holy fuck!" Ian's voice pulled Kana the rest of the way out of her haze. Ian was staring, his mouth open in disbelief. Jade was shaking, her eyes wide and her face as pale as Vanessa's. Knight's mouth was set in a grim line, while Cassandra watched them all, her eyes narrow and her face angry.

"What...?" Kana looked at Night. "What's happening?"

"It's bad," Night picked up Kana's phone and handed it to her. "Really bad."

Kana opened the text from Cassandra, tapped on the link, and watched. The missing witch lay on the ground of the alley, her arm extended. A large man stood over her, a pipe in his hands. He was shouting something, but there was no sound until the moment before flames exploded from the woman's hand and engulfed him. His screams, agonized and horrible, filled Kana's ears. She watched him stumble, arms flailing until he collapsed on the ground. The camera stayed on his burning corpse until sirens sounded in the distance.

"Read the description under it," Cassandra said, her voice flat.

Kana scrolled down the page. *Proof of the Devil,* the description read. *Witch burns a man alive in Shipton, Connecticut. STOP THEM BEFORE THEY KILL US ALL.*

"Fuck," Vanessa looked at Cassandra. "Is that real?"

"Yeah." Cassandra's face had turned a dark, angry shade of

red. "Glennis killed a man with magic and now everyone in the world has seen it."

"What does this mean?" Kana asked, seeing the fear in their faces.

"It means Glennis is dead," Cassandra said.

"But…" Jade shook her head. "She stopped him."

"But she didn't come back," Cassandra pointed at the screen. "She's in an alley. Not on the street. So how did whoever filmed this know she was there, and why weren't they helping her? And why does the sound go on only when she uses her magic? "

"Because they were with *him*," Vanessa said, anger filling the words. "The guy that burned. They knew she was a witch."

"How could they? I thought witchcraft was supposed to be secret," Kana frowned, trying to make sense of what she'd seen. "What happens now?"

"Damage control," Cassandra said grimly. "It's not the first time a witch has used magic to defend themselves, and it's not the first time it was caught on video. The MLEA and the MSA will be coming in and cleaning up the mess. Fortunately, most people will think it's special effects."

"What about the assholes who did this?" Ian demanded. "They've figured out that there are witches in Newlane. We're fucked."

"The MLEA and the MSA will be on it," Cassandra said. "It will vanish and so will they."

"They must have provoked her horribly to make her use fire," said Jade softly. "They must have really hurt her."

CHAPTER 13

THE PROTESTERS APPEARED THE NEXT day, shivering in a wet December east wind that brought a creeping cold to slip under the coats and hats of the crowd. They huddled together, waving signs reading, "Stop the Witches!" "God Watches Us All!" "Suffer Not a Witch to Live!" In front of them, standing high on a platform, preaching up a storm, stood Reverend Marcus.

And in the reverend's mind, scanning as far as it could, sat the entity.

The video had gone viral, according to the reverend's followers. Hundreds of thousands had seen it. Hundreds argued about its authenticity on websites and in chat rooms and on the video post itself. It was the talk of the town, the state, and possibly the country. The follower who'd posted it had linked Donald's obituary and coroner's report so all could see that the man had, indeed, burned to death. A pair of news crews from Hartford had come out to cover the crowd, and a dozen police stood at the gate of the university to keep the protestors out. Two witches wearing dark suits and too old to be students sat in the coffee shop watching the protest. The entity kept its senses on them, but neither did more than watch the crowd.

"You have all seen what was done to our poor parishioner!" Reverend Marcus bellowed the words loud enough that the sound echoed off buildings a block away. "Donald died screaming, died burning in the devil's fire, and there has been no justice for him! The ones responsible—the ones *truly* responsible—have not faced justice, have not faced the community, and have not stood before God to answer for their sins!"

It took a fair amount of mental gymnastics, helped by the entity's suggestions, for the reverend to be convinced that Glennis's death and disappearance were not his own responsibility. Even though the entity had controlled his body and mind, he still had felt guilty until the entity linked her to the university, to the rich, and to the witches. The web of frail threads and excuses the entity created gained strength from his hatred and prejudices and own desire for importance until they became cables of steel. Donald's death was not the reverend's fault; it was the girl's. Her death was her just desserts, but not true justice, because justice was perverted and would remain so until all the witches had been exposed.

Today, the reverend's voice rang out clear and confident and, if his words seemed mad to the news crews, who were likely to believe almost anything before the existence of magic, the entity knew it would frighten the witches hiding behind the gates of the university. Now, the witch students would stay on campus, hiding in their buildings with their magic shields. They would fear what was happening and maybe give the entity what it demanded.

For two hours, the demonstrators wept and prayed and sang. Then, the reverend led the marchers across the town to the alley where Donald died and gave prayers for justice and his soul. The wall still bore scorch marks where he had fallen, and the camera crews would eat up the visual, according to the members of the reverend's flock who knew such things. The entity rode in the reverend's head and listened as he preached, calling once more for justice before leading the flock to lay flowers where Donald had died.

And there on the wall, written in magical energy that no human could see, were the words:

Tonight. Midnight. Riverside.

Kana sat back in her chair, rubbed her eyes, and wished she had Vanessa's gift for swearing, because "fuck" just didn't seem enough right then.

She'd reviewed the video and audio from the experiment, read the printed out data for the seismic activity, air pressure, and structural integrity and all of it pointed to one thing: just before Night threw the ball into the portal, the magic power of the experiment had dropped. It had been a small drop, almost infinitesimal, but it had been enough.

Only there was no reason for it to have dropped.

The devices that monitored the magic in the room showed consistent output from all the participants. No one lost concentration until she'd called break. No one's magic diminished, which fit exactly with Kana's memories of how the magic felt when she held open the portal. There was no reason for the magic level to drop.

And yet, it had.

Kana rubbed her eyes and went through the printouts again. She examined the diagrams she'd used to make the spell and compared them to the photos of the diagrams she'd taken before the experiment. Then, she went back down to Lab One and went around the circle on her hands and knees, looking for something that would explain the discrepancy. She went down to Lab Two to the receptor she'd set up there—untouched since the experiment—and found nothing.

"Fuck" was nowhere near strong enough to express how irritated she felt.

On impulse, she summoned her magic, just a trace of it, and let it run through the patterns in the circle. It wouldn't be enough to open the portal, she knew, but it would allow her to follow the path of the magic and see where it had broken. The magic ran smoothly through the circle, flowed up into the air, and responded perfectly to Kana shaping it into the form that, had it been powerful enough, would have opened and become a portal for power to transfer to another location.

Something changed.

Kana held the magic longer, trying to understand. Something had happened, but she had no idea what. She ended the spell, took a breath, and started over. She paid closer attention to the flow of the magic through the circle and into the air above it. She focused her attention on the formation of the portal shape, watching closely.

Something changed again.

"Oh, for crying out loud!" Kana released the magic and leaned back from the circle, glaring at the air above it. The magic faded away, which was good because if it had stayed, Kana would have been tempted to hit it, which would do no

PLAGUE OF WITCHES

good whatsoever and would leave her waving her arms in the air like an idiot.

"Hey." Night's voice interrupted her angry thoughts. Kana turned and saw him standing in the doorway. He smiled at her. "What's up?"

"I don't know." Kana glared at the circle, suppressing the urge to pout. "Something is wrong with the magic, and I can't figure out what."

"Wrong how?"

"If I knew that, it wouldn't be a problem, would it?" The words came out sharper than Kana intended. She put on a smile and aimed it at Night. "Sorry. It's just annoying me. It's a simple experiment, right?"

"Yes. I created a portal in second year. And did the ball throw in third year."

"And did it ever close on you?"

"No."

"But this time it did." Kana frowned at the circle again. "The magic levels dropped during the experiment, and I can feel something happening when I cast the spell, but for the life of me I cannot figure out what."

"Give me your hand," Night said.

"Pardon?" Kana's eyebrows rose.

"Give me your hand and cast your spell again." Night held out his own. "I'll read your magic as you're doing it, and maybe I'll be able to see what's happening."

Kana felt slightly disappointed, which was stupid because they'd already broken in both their rooms, but on the other hand, holding hands with Night was always nice, and if it

209

helped her solve the problem, that would be even better. Kana took his hand, concentrated, and cast the spell.

When she finished, Night was frowning. "Do it again."

She did.

Night let go of her hand. "We need someone better at this. Is Professor White around?"

"No. She has classes to teach today."

Night frowned some more. "How about Jade?"

"I think she's upstairs."

Night pulled out his phone, texted, and waited. A few moments later, Jade came down the stairs. Night nodded at Kana. "Hold her hand."

"But I like blondes," Jade said without missing a beat. "Sorry, Kana."

"It's all right."

"Seriously," Night said. "Take Kana's hand and read her magic. Kana, cast the spell."

Jade's hand was nowhere near as nice as Night's, as far as Kana was concerned, but she took it and focused in on the magic. Again, she ran the spell, and when it was finished, Jade was frowning, too.

"One more time," Jade said. "And hold the portal spell until I tell you to stop."

Kana cast again and this time held the magic. It wasn't difficult since she was using only the barest fraction of her power. She risked a glance at Jade and saw the other woman staring into the room, her eyes unfocused. Jade breathed deep, closed her eyes, and a moment later said, "Release it."

Kana let her magic go. Jade raised her arms and spread her fingers wide. A haze of light appeared and spread from wall to wall. Jade stared at it, frowning at the patterns that spun through the haze. Kana watched too but had no idea what was happening. She glanced at Night, who wore an expression as confused as Kana felt.

"There!" Jade pointed at a spot in the haze, then another. "And there!"

"What?" Kana asked. "I don't know what you're seeing."

"Power sink spell," Jade said. "At least two in the house. That's what messed up the magic."

"What?" Kana rose to her feet. "But we compensated for that."

"No, you compensated for the power sink built into the house," Jade pointed at a third swirl in the haze. "I helped you design the spell. It took advantage of the power sink to draw power from it instead of putting power into it, right?"

"Yes…"

"But these are different power sinks. They're not built into the structure of the house, but they do leech power from the actual power sink."

"Wow." Night shook his head. "How the hell did you figure that out?"

"My masters is in magical interdimensional theory," Jade said. "Ninety percent of opening an interdimensional portal is figuring out what's interfering with opening an interdimensional portal. So, I tried the spell I use for detecting interference, and sure enough, something is interfering."

"What's the source?" Kana asked.

"That, I don't know," Jade brought her hands together and the haze vanished. "Both of the power sinks seem to feed off the main power sink of the house. They increase its energy pull by an infinitesimal amount, but it was more than the amount we planned on, and that's why it affected the experiments."

"I see." Kana frowned. "I'm going to go look over Akemi's notes and see if she encountered anything like that in the house before."

"Akemi's experiments happened twenty years ago," Jade reminded her. "It could have been something that happened since. Or something that's happening right now."

"I know." Kana sighed. "But I have Akemi's notes and I don't have the notes of anyone's other experiments, so before I search the entire house or go through the archives of the experiments done here, I thought I'd start with something easy."

"Fair enough," Jade said. "I don't have any classes today."

"I have an assignment to finish," Night said, "but I'll join you after that."

The river at night was a long, black line snaking through the landscape. The sky was clear and not even the reflected light of the city reached the water. The streetlights of the riverwalk barely touched the edge of the deep, flowing water. The entity remembered the months it had spent there, fighting to survive. It shuddered. If this witch was strong enough to hurt it, it might end up back in the water, fighting the current to stay away from the shield and feeding on the fish until it could climb out, assuming it even survived the battle.

The entity had exchanged Reverend Marcus's body for one of the larger members of his flock. The man was a retired marine fallen on hard times. He was still strong and could still kill a man with his hands (had done so, in a bar fight in another town, and that was why he was hiding in Newlane). The entity knew that if the witch used magic it would have scarce time for anything, but there was still a chance if it came to that. A dozen of the angel Raguel's followers waited nearby. If worse came to worst, the entity could switch to one of their bodies or summon them to kill the witch.

A block away, one of the streetlights went out. Then, across the riverside street, another went dark. The entity turned, peering into the night with the old marine's eyes, even as it reached its senses out in all directions. Another light went out, and then a fourth, like the dark itself was walking forward, extinguishing the light as it came. The entity tensed the marine's body, preparing it for a fight.

"So, it was you," a voice said behind it.

The entity tried to turn, but the marine's body didn't respond. It tried to override whatever magic was holding the muscles in place, but nothing worked. It reached out its senses again, trying to find the witch as it prepared to flee.

"Don't worry," the witch said. "If I wanted to kill you, it would have happened a long time ago."

The voice sounded neither male nor female to the marine's ears, and the entity could not sense the witch enough to guess which it was. It thought of leaving the body, but if another trap had been set to catch it, it would fly right into it.

"Your followers are similarly disposed," the witch said. "Or did you think I trusted you enough to come alone?"

The entity tried the marine's mouth, discovering it still worked. "Who are you?"

"The one you made a deal with."

"No," the entity tried to shake the marine's head, but it wouldn't move. "That witch is gone. I searched for her."

"Her body died," the witch said. "She lived on. Or did you forget what she learned, studying you?"

"Twenty years inside that shield made me forget everything about what I am," the entity snarled.

"And everything about our deal, apparently." There was disdain in the witch's voice. "Except the Promised."

"If you are the witch," the entity said. "Then *you* forgot our deal first and left me to rot in that prison."

"You weren't rotting. I made certain you were fed the entire time you were there, and when the time came, I was the one who released you."

"I broke free."

"From a cage that held you for twenty years?" The witch sounded amused. "Don't be stupid. I set you free in the city, to regain your strength so you could take the Promised when the time came."

"When?" the marine's voice came out harsh and angry. "When is the time? When do I get the Promised?"

"When you give me what I want."

"You are not the one I made that deal with," the entity said. "I have not detected her in this town."

"Magic is a thing of the body," the witch said. "When the body changes, the magic changes."

The entity pondered this. "If that is the case, then you have already gained what you want."

"Why would I want this body?" the witch demanded. "It

was old when I took it. Why would I want to look like this, to live like this? I would rather be in Hell."

"Then change bodies."

"I can't!" The words came out furious, and the entity felt the old marine's muscles spasm as if the witch's anger had spread through its magic. The entity took the moment to drink in the marine's pain. It gave it strength, but not enough to break free of the witch's grasp.

"Do you think I haven't tried?" the witch demanded. "Six times I tried, and all of them were failures. No, something happened that night, something that made it possible for me to switch bodies. So, I need to recreate what happened that night. Then, and only then, will I give you what you want."

"I can take what I want."

"You can't even tell which one is the real Promised."

"I can," the entity lied.

"Bullshit." The entity could hear the witch sneering at it. "You have no power to invade a witch. You'll be destroyed. No, you'll only be able to take over the body of the Promised and gain her powers if her soul is gone but her body is still alive. And only I can make that happen."

"I know the witches that are not the Promised," the entity put as much threat into the words as its frozen body could manage. "I can keep killing them until you give me what I want."

"Not anymore. Your video warned them. The MLEA is in the city in force. Do you really think you'll be able to hide from them forever?"

"If they catch me, I expose you."

The witch laughed, bitter and sharp. "I died twenty years

ago; you have nothing to expose. Whereas you, well, they are already searching for the one who murdered Glennis and the two young men. And they know it wasn't anything human."

"The waitress murdered those young men."

"That was you wearing her body. The MLEA has made an art of mind reading and knows that she has no memory of committing the crimes. And I know because the news has spread to the witches' councils around the world."

The entity seethed. The witch had it trapped, and she knew it. "What do you want?"

"The same thing you do," the witch said. "To complete our deal."

"And how do we do that?"

"I'll let you know."

"You'll let me know when?" the entity demanded. No answer came. "When?"

Any echoes the shout might have made died in the river's icy water. The entity raged inside the man's body, straining against its bonds until it could feel muscles tear and joints readying to pop. The human still couldn't move. In fury, it broke free of the man's flesh, leaving him gasping and wondering why he stood frozen in place by the riverbank. The entity rose into the air, searching. Two blocks away it caught a momentary glimpse of a bald man turning back to look at it. Light from a storefront caught on a pair of glasses. The entity raced toward it.

The streetlights lit up again. Behind the entity the marine fell to his knees, gasping with pain, and in front of it, the witch vanished from sight.

The entity hung in the air, seething. It would not allow the witch to control it, no matter what it thought, and no matter what the witch police thought. It would send its people to search and find the identity of the witch wanting to control it. And in the meantime, it would hunt again.

Kana sat back and glared at the papers spread out before her. She had spent the day going through every one of Akemi's portal experiments looking for any notes about the power drain. As far as she could see, none of Akemi's experiments had experienced it.

Jade put down the paper she'd been studying. "Nothing here. Night?"

"Nothing," Night tossed his paper on the pile. "No mention of power loss in any of the experiments I read."

"Which means that between then and now something changed in the building that causes a continuous drain on the power sink below the building." Kana shook her head. "So, we have to search the building from top to bottom in order to find what might be causing the problem, or go back over twenty years of experiments after Akemi's to see if any of them have problems."

"Bottom to top makes more sense," Jade said. "The labs are downstairs and so is the house's power sink. We're better off starting down there to find something."

"Wait a moment." Night's brow wrinkled as he thought. "What if Vanessa and Cassandra's bracelets caused it?"

Jade's head tilted as she frowned. "How?"

"Well, both of them are under a spell that controls their magic. So, what if that spell needs energy, and instead of just sucking it off the user, it also takes it from the magic around them?"

"I've never heard of that," Jade said. "But then, I have no idea how the bracelets work."

Kana thought about it. "Were they both in the house when I cast the spell yesterday?"

"Vanessa was," Night said, his voice dry. "I walked by Ian's room."

Kana rolled her eyes. "Are they both here now?"

"One way to find out." Night pulled out his phone and texted them both. Two minutes later the phone beeped. "Vanessa's here studying. Cassandra..." The phone beeped again. "She says she's at a bar, waiting for the band to start."

"At the bar?" Kana was appalled. "With all that's going on? She shouldn't even be off campus right now."

"Tell *her* that," Night said. "I'll ask Vanessa to come down. Jade, can you test her bracelet?"

"I can."

Vanessa came down, heard what they thought, and offered up the bracelet for inspection. Jade cast her haze around it and stared at it for a long time. Kana was starting to fidget when Jade finally spoke.

"The structure on this is absolutely amazing," Jade said. "It interlinks with the magic from all five casters and acts as a safety valve. As long as Vanessa's wearing it, the valve is open, allowing her access to her magic. If it comes off, the valves will snap shut and she'll have no access to her magic at all. It's wild. I'd love to meet whoever thought of this."

"Me, too," said Vanessa sourly. "So I can hit them."

"But is it what's causing the power drain?" Kana asked.

"Nope." Jade released the magic. "It's really cool and tricky, but it isn't causing the power drain."

"Which means Cassandra's probably isn't causing it either. Dammit."

"So, what do we do?" Night asked. "Go through the house and search it room by room, or go through the archives experiment by experiment?"

"Searching the house will be easier," Jade said. "I've seen the archives."

"When?"

"We may as well start now," Kana picked up the notebook she'd been writing in. "We'll hit the downstairs labs tonight and if there's nothing in them, we'll go through the main floors tomorrow." She stopped, frowning at the notebook. "That's odd."

"What's odd?" Night asked, peering over her shoulder. "Oh."

"Oh, what?" Jade asked. She also looked at the notebook. "Oh. Oh!"

"Anyone going to tell me?" Vanessa asked.

"Akemi used Lab Five for several of her later portal experiments," Kana explained.

Vanessa waited, but no one said anything else. "Well?"

"Lab One is on the main floor," Kana said. "There are three more downstairs. So where is Lab Five?"

CHAPTER 14

K ANA FLICKED THE SWITCH AT the top of the stairs, and the basement flooded with bright, white fluorescent light. She led the other three down the stairs and stared down the length of the white concrete hallway, frowning. Four doors were in sight on the outer wall, and she knew more were around the corner.

Jade smacked the concrete inner wall of the hallway. "This is the building core. It's concrete woven with spells to strengthen it and sits underneath the main lab. The power sink is below it and accessed through the door around the corner."

"And that," Kana said, pointing to a door behind the stairs, "is a storage room. Those two," she pointed at the door beside the stairs and the one at the end of the hall, "lead to the control rooms for Lab Two and Lab Three, which have doors to the labs inside them."

She led them down the hallway and around the corner. "Lab Four's control room was at the end. So where is Lab Five?"

"Maybe Akemi made a mistake in her notes?" Vanessa suggested.

Kana shook her head. "You haven't read her notes. The woman was meticulous to the point of being anal-retentive. She tracked everything in her experiments down to the dates of everyone's cycle and how much they'd eaten. She wouldn't have made a mistake about the lab number."

Kana led them around the last corner and looked at the lone door to Lab Four standing in the middle of the outside wall. She stared at it, frowning. "Why does the hallway go all the way to the end?"

"What do you mean?" Night asked.

"There's no storage room like on the other side." Kana walked the length of it. "No entrance to the power sink like on the middle wall, no window to let in light. So why do they need a hallway that goes all the way around?"

"Symmetry?" Jade suggested. "Easy access to the central structure for repairs?"

"Maybe." Kana ran her fingers over the end of the wall and tapped the concrete bricks there. "Jade, can you cast your spell here?"

"Sure." Jade closed her eyes, and a golden haze filled the room. She opened her eyes and stared at the patterns. The cloud swirled far more rapidly than before. "The house's power sink is skewing the results but... there."

Kana looked where Jade pointed but could see no changes in the pattern. Vanessa stepped closer and looked. "That's the problem?"

"That's one of them," Jade said. "It's smaller here, which is probably because the power sink is so powerful, or because the source is farther away."

"There," Kana pointed at a swirl near the wall. "What's that?"

Jade frowned at it. "It's a spell cast on the wall."

"Is it the power sink?"

"No." Jade pointed at a spot in the haze that to Kana looked identical to all the others. "That's the third power sink, and it's close to this swirl, but it's not the same." Jade peered closer. "That's an illusion."

"Illusion?" Kana stared at the wall. "What sort of illusion?"

"A good one." Jade put her hand on the wall. "Really good. I can't even feel a difference between this wall and the others."

"So how do we undo it?"

"Well, there're a lot of ways." Jade started counting them on her fingers. "We can analyze the spell and search for a weakness; we can look for the circle that's holding the illusion in place and break it; we can search for the caster and get them to stop it if we can figure out who cast it, or—"

"Or we could just break it," Vanessa suggested.

"Well, yeah," Jade said, "but you won't be able to if you aren't stronger than the caster."

"Vanessa's stronger than all of us except Kana," Night said. "I bet she can do it."

"All right." Kana looked at the wall one more time. "Vanessa, would you?"

Vanessa nodded and stepped past Kana to the wall. Kana moved back and watched as Vanessa closed her eyes and took a deep breath. She raised a hand and then slammed it against the wall, shouting, "Dispel!"

Pain, sudden and sharp, spiked through Kana's head, and everything went black.

The Reverend Marcus was in rare form for the last sermon of the day. He preached compassion and vengeance in the same breath. Love for poor deceased Donald. Revenge against those struck down true believers. Building a better world for those who followed God and Reverend Marcus and destroying those who worshipped Mammon and witchcraft. He was reaching the peak of his sermon, getting ready for the donation ask— and the donations had been flowing well these last few days— and readying his flock for the next set of protests against those who held them down.

His arm was high in the air, his congregation on their feet screaming, "Amen," when time stopped for them all.

The entity, coiled around the reverend's brain stem, felt the change instantly. It tried to move the reverend and couldn't. It was about to flee when the lights of the church went out.

"What are you doing here?" the entity called out. It couldn't see the witch, couldn't sense it, but knew it was there, nonetheless. "What do you want?"

"I told you I'd come find you," the witch said. "And now I have."

"Are you giving me the Promised?" the entity demanded, and even through the reverend's half-frozen vocal cords, it knew it sounded sulky.

"Not yet, but I will give you access to where the Promised lives."

"What good does that do me?"

"I told you, I want to recreate the circumstances of the

first experiment, and for that, you need to be occupying a witch's body."

"I can't. You said so yourself."

"I know." The witch sounded amused. "I lied. You can occupy a witch who gives you her body voluntarily or one who cannot access her powers. Of course, no one in that house will give you their powers voluntarily."

"So, what is the point of having access to the house?" the entity demanded. "If I cannot possess them, there is no point in watching them."

"There are two witches in the house that have limits on their power," the witch said. "Vanessa and Cassandra. They each wear a black bracelet. If either one loses her bracelet, she cannot use magic. So, watch them, learn their movements, and when the time comes, take one of them."

Which meant that neither of the two was the Promised. The entity kept the thought to itself, instead saying, "And how will I know when the time comes?"

"How else?" The witch's voice faded in the distance. "I'll tell you."

And then time resumed, and the Reverend Marcus finished his sermon as if he had not been interrupted at all.

Kana woke in Night's arms, which would have been nice if she didn't have a splitting headache. He held her head cradled in one arm, the other wrapped tightly around her body. He was looking across the room, concern on his face. She turned her head and realized she was lying in the common lounge, her legs sprawled the length of the sofa. On the other couch, Vanessa and Jade stared at her, worry on their faces. Ian sat on the arm of the couch, his hand on Vanessa's shoulder. Cassandra was there, too, glaring at Vanessa and Jade.

"She should be in a hospital," Cassandra was saying.

"She didn't hit her head," Jade said. "Night caught her when she collapsed."

"She's still unconscious!"

"She fainted, that's all," Vanessa said.

"And how the hell do you know that?" Cassandra demanded. There was real anger in her voice, and Vanessa winced at it. "She's been out for an hour."

"That's what used to happen to me," Vanessa explained. "Ambrose used the same spell on me whenever I'd use an illusion to hide from him. It would zap me hard enough to knock me cold."

"But it wasn't my illusion," Kana said. "So why did it zap me?"

"Kana!" Jade yelped the word as she spun away from Cassandra. "Are you all right?"

"My head hurts." Kana sat up. Night kept his arms on her, helping her until she was upright. She caught one of his hands and held onto it. "What did you do to me, Vanessa?"

"I shouldn't have done anything to you," Vanessa's eyes narrowed. "The spell I use only affects the ones who are attached to the illusion it disrupts."

"Which makes no sense," Jade said. "That spell has been there for years."

"How do you know?" Kana asked.

"Because the door and the circle drawn on it were covered in dust."

"Door?" Kana repeated. "What door?"

"The one to Lab Five," Jade said. "That's what the illusion covered. The door to Lab Five and the control room."

Kana stood up, ignoring the pounding in her head. Night rose with her and caught her as she swayed. She held on to him, but still told Jade, "Show me."

Jade led the way down the stairs and around the hallway to Lab Five.

"We didn't want to go in without you," Night said as Kana examined the door. Dust coated the entire door, including the circle. It was drawn in a red liquid so dark it was nearly black. Kana traced the pattern, wondering why it felt so familiar. Some of the red flaked off onto her hand. She stared at it, and then rubbed it between her fingers.

"Is that… dried blood?" She looked at Jade. "It looks like dried blood."

"Your guess is as good as mine," Jade said. "Using blood isn't unheard of, especially if the caster wants to have a stable connection with the spell. Which you would, I guess, if you want it to last a long time."

"OK." Kana put her hand on the door handle and tried to twist it. It didn't move, which didn't surprise her at all. Of course, whoever went to the trouble of casting an illusion spell to hide an entire hallway was going to lock the doors. "I don't suppose we have a key?"

"Don't need one," Vanessa said. She stepped up to the door, looked at it for a bit, then closed her eyes and concentrated.

The lock popped and the door swung open. Vanessa stepped back. "After you."

Kana pushed hard on the door. Like the one upstairs, it was heavy and air-sealed. Dust swirled into the room as the air from the hallway changed with the stale air inside. Kana sniffed at the air, half-expecting to start coughing like a tomb explorer releasing ancient spores, but the air was only stale. Kana fumbled for the light switch. The fluorescents above clicked and buzzed into life, revealing a room as neat as a pin, save the chair lying on the floor.

The controls looked similar to the ones in the labs upstairs, though they were twenty years out of date. Kana identified the sound and video recording switches and the switches to monitor the air quality and magic output. Kana stepped inside and peered through the glass to the lab. The room was pitch black, the glass showing nothing but the reflections of those in the control room. She looked down at the chair on the floor. Aside from its position, there was no sign that anything untoward had happened. It simply looked like the room had been closed off.

A set of six shelves stood on the wall opposite the control panel. On them sat six banker's boxes, each labeled with Akemi's neat writing.

Kana pulled the closest box half off the shelf and opened the lid. Stacks of research reports and papers filled it. Kana pulled the top report and read the title.

Examination of Interdimensional Being: Report 2.

"Interdimensional being?" Kana put the report back and pushed the box back into place. She grabbed a second and opened the lid. More papers, less organized. She picked the top one. It read: *Graph of Force Distribution on Interdimensional Portal Shields.* She put it back.

"Holy crap," Ian sounded shocked. "What the hell happened in here?"

Kana turned. Someone had turned on the lights in the laboratory, and on the other side of the control room glass, chaos reigned.

Charred piles of wood marked where tables had once stood, and a desk. Four metal chairs, twisted from heat, lay on the floor. Black smears of soot rose up the walls and burned shards of paper lay around the room where the heat of the fire had scattered them. And in the middle of the floor, surrounded by a half-burned magic circle drawn on the floor, sat a single large crystal, its white surface streaked with black. Kana, eyes wide, reached for the door.

"Don't!" Jade and Night said simultaneously. Kana jumped back guiltily like a child caught heading for a cookie jar. Jade leaned over the control panel and flicked the power switch. The board lit up and buzzed. Jade scanned it and pushed a button marked "Air Clean." From the other room came a loud whoosh as a fan, hidden at the top of the ceiling, roared into life.

"We don't know how old the burns are," Jade explained. "We don't know if the air in there is poisonous or what, so we need to clean out the room first."

Some of the burned papers in the room trembled and twisted from the force of the fan above them. A few became airborne and sucked up into the blades, vanishing from sight. Jade stared at the light on the board until one red light blinked green.

"Air exchange complete." Jade poked the button again, and the fan slowed to a stop. "It should be all right to go in there now, but if you smell anything funny or start to feel dizzy, you need to leave at once."

"All right." Kana opened the laboratory door a crack and sniffed. "I smell smoke and soot, nothing else." She stepped into the lab, her eyes on the circle on the floor. She stared at the lines, recognizing the pattern. "It's a shield like the one we were using, but different."

"It *was* a shield," Night said behind her. "The fire destroyed it."

"Or whatever destroyed the shield caused the fire," Jade said over the room's sound system.

Kana pointed at the crystal. "That's our power sink, I take it?"

"Should be, yes."

"Power sink?" Ian's voice came over the microphone. "The one for the house?"

"No, one of the two that messed up the spells," Vanessa said.

Kana tuned out the rest of her explanation as she squatted down beside the circle. "If this was like the one we cast, it should have absorbed whatever energy was thrown at it, from inside or out, right?"

"Yes," Night said.

"So, what was powerful enough to break it open?"

"No idea," Night looked over the mess in the room. "Maybe the power sink released?"

"Maybe." Kana reached out to it, thought better, and stopped. "Jade?"

"Yes?" Jade said over the speakers.

"Is it safe to move this thing? Is the spell broken?"

"Hang on. I'll come in." Jade stepped into the room and walked a circle around the power sink. She cast her detection spell and studied the swirls for a time. "It's still going. If you cast any magic in the room, you should feel it."

"So, what do we do with it?" Kana asked.

"Not sure." Jade flashed a smile at her. "Unless you want Vanessa to try to dispel it?"

"Hey!" Vanessa's voice came over the speaker. "I said I was sorry."

"We should tell Professor White," Night said. "She'd know what to do."

"No," Kana's voice came out sharp. "We can't tell her anything."

"Of course we have to tell her," Jade asked. "She's our advisor, and besides, she probably knows— "

"Exactly. She was Akemi's advisor, too." Kana looked at the scorched power sink. "There's no way she didn't know about this. So why didn't she tell us?"

The entity floated outside the house, sensing the shield around it and wondering if what the witch had said was true. There was no sign of the trap that had pulled it in before, no sign of any magic other than the power sink inherent to the house. The entity floated closer, examining the structure of the shield that surrounded the house. It felt different than it had the last time the entity had visited, but it couldn't tell if that meant it was safe.

The witch said that it would help the entity get the Promised, but not until it recreated the experiment that had allowed it to change bodies the first time. So really there was no choice, was there? The entity floated closer, stretching out its form to make minimal contact with the shield.

It passed through without trying.

The entity shivered with relief. It sensed the lines of magic floating through the building's structure and wove past them into the house. Inside, it sensed the six inhabitants and floated toward them. Each one had a box and was carrying it up the stairs to the second floor. All six were powerful witches, and each felt like the Promised. The entity immediately recognized the two with bracelets—Cassandra and Vanessa, the witch had called them, though it did not know which was which. The others it knew nothing about, other than that they all emanated power. The one in the front, a tall woman with long black hair and pale skin, led them to a large room with more boxes piled all around its perimeter. When they all put the boxes down, the woman gestured at them to sit. One of the men, muscular and tall, sat beside her. The Chinese woman sat on her other side. The other three witches took the other side of the table, the tall witch taking the middle seat, the black-haired man and short witch flanking her.

The entity had to fight the urge to swoop through each and see which one was truly the one it wanted.

The half-Asian witch looked from one to another of her companions, her face twisted with worry. She sighed, leaned

111111111111

back in her chair and said, "Remember the agreement you all signed when you joined this group?"

The other five looked confused but nodded.

"I wrote it. The Shipton legal department went over it, but I wrote it specifically so I could talk to everyone about my mother."

"Who?" The thin, black-haired man sounded confused. "Who is your mother?"

"Akemi Wakahisa." The witch nodded at the woman on the other side of the table. "She vanished after I was born, just like Vanessa's mother."

Vanessa—the taller of the two bracelet wearers, which made the shorter one Cassandra—leaned forward. "You think they're connected?"

"I think it's a hell of a coincidence that we ended up here together, especially given how different our lives are." The woman looked around the table. "I think it's weird that Professor White told me that Akemi did experiments here but didn't tell us about Lab Five. And I think it's incredibly strange that the room where the rest of her research is hidden is somehow linked to my magic, especially since I didn't even know Akemi existed until the beginning of the year." Kana shook her head. "I didn't even know I was a witch seven months ago, and now I'm doing research at the top magical institution in the country?"

"You didn't know?" The big man at her side blurted the words. "How could you not know?"

"Apparently I was put under a spell to hide my magic until I was twenty-one." The witch nodded at the Chinese woman. "Jade knew about it. Professor White knew about it, and I couldn't tell anyone else about it because in order to access Akemi's research, I had to sign a magical secrecy agreement about Akemi's work, and that included what she did to me."

"So, all the magic you know you learned since the beginning of the summer?" The big man shook his head. "Wow."

"I'm smart," The witch said, and bitterness filled the words. "Very smart. And apparently a super-powered witch. So, of course I ended doing this because it makes perfect sense to put a complete beginner in charge of experiments so dangerous that they could kill us all."

"Kana—" the Chinese woman started, but the witch cut her off with an angry slash of her hand.

"I may be a special snowflake, Jade, but I am not *this* special." The witch's voice was hard. "I can't believe I was stupid enough to buy the whole story. I *hate* being manipulated, and that's what's been happening from the beginning."

The table fell quiet. The entity above it quivered with excitement. It still didn't know what it needed to do to gain the body of the Promised, but now it knew which one was the real one. Kana, Akemi's daughter, was the Promised. It was she who the entity would take over and control, and when it did, it would have more than enough strength to deal with the witch who tried to control it.

"What does Professor White want?" the blond witch asked. "If it's not the research, then what is this coven about?"

Then, the short witch with the bracelet—Cassandra, the entity remembered—spoke up. "More to the point, Kana, what do you want to do?"

"First, I want all of you to promise me not to say anything about what we found to Professor White," Kana said. "At least not until I've gone through the files and figured out what is going on. Because I'll be damned if I'm going to be manipulated anymore."

The doorbell rang.

All six turned their heads, staring in surprise. A moment later it rang again.

"Did someone order pizza?" Ian asked.

Heads shook around the table.

"Is anyone expecting anyone?" Night asked, getting to his feet.

"If it was Professor White, she'd just come in," Jade said as she stood. "She has a key."

Night headed for the stairs, and a moment later the rest of them followed him. The entity floated through the floor and hung in the air above the foyer, watching as they made their way down. The doorbell rang a third time before Night reached the door and opened it.

The man on the other side was fat and bald, with a heavy face, downturned mouth, and round glasses that reflected the light from the foyer. The entity recognized him from the riverside and floated back, a tremor going through it. The man was a witch, and a powerful one from the energy emanating from him. He looked at Night as if the big man was an obstruction rather than a person.

"I am here to see Vanessa Lake," the man said. "Where is she?"

"Ambrose?" Vanessa turned pale and her eyes went wide. Disbelief and confusion filled her voice. "What the fuck are you doing here?

CHAPTER 15

THE ENTITY WATCHED VANESSA'S EYES first grow wider, then narrow with anger. Her nostrils flared, the hostility oozing off her. Cassandra moved up beside her and hitched her arm through Vanessa's, preparing to hold her back. The blond witch looked back and forth between them, and the black-haired witch just looked confused.

"I see being here hasn't improved your manners," Ambrose said, his voice cold and his eyes narrowing. "Considering I traveled from Quebec to see if you were all right, I would expect a better greeting."

"Bullshit you did," Vanessa snarled. "You've never come to see if I was all right. You only come if you're worried I'll embarrass you."

"Given the number of times you've embarrassed me, can you blame me?" Ambrose's gaze swept the room. "Who are these people? And how can you afford such large accommodations? You're supposed to be in the dormitories."

"She's part of my research team," Kana said, stepping forward. "We're living together as part of the project. And you are?"

"Ambrose Levesque, head of the Quebec Council of

Witches and Vanessa's legal guardian." He didn't ask Kana her name but turned back to Vanessa. "I cannot imagine how you managed to finagle your way onto a research team, but it will serve you no good at all if you fail your other classes."

"I am not failing my classes," Vanessa hissed. "I'm doing just fine."

"She is," Night said.

Ambrose looked Night up and down, and when he spoke there was a sneer in his voice that suggested Night was nothing better than what Ambrose might wipe off his shoe. "And you know this how?"

"I'm her tutor." Night's own voice cooled considerably. He put his hand on Vanessa's shoulder. "And Vanessa is doing just fine."

Ambrose's eyebrows rose as he looked at Vanessa. "Shall I ask how you're paying him?"

"The school is paying me," Night released Vanessa and advanced on the other man, his blue eyes sparking with fire. "And I don't like what you're implying."

"*Ian's* the one I'm fucking," Vanessa pointed at the black-haired skinny witch, who looked anywhere but at Ambrose. "Not Night. Why are you here, Ambrose?"

"Because witches are being murdered." Ambrose didn't acknowledge how close Night was to him. "The witch's councils have been alerted, and since my ward is one of the witches here, I have a special duty to make certain she isn't involved."

"Isn't..." Vanessa's face turned several shades of red. "You think I could be involved in the murders?"

"Given the amount of violence in your history, and your

tendency to lose your temper, yes, that is exactly what I think. Where were you the night the woman disappeared?"

"How the fuck should I know?" Vanessa demanded. "I have no idea when she disappeared."

"And no idea who recorded the video either, I'm sure," Ambrose turned away from her. "And would any of these people be able to vouch for you?"

"I could," Cassandra slid forward, her feet staying close to the ground, her knees slightly bent. Her hands stayed at her side but now were clenched into fists. "But I'm not certain I could vouch for *you*."

Ambrose looked at the bracelet on her wrist. "Another felon?"

Cassandra's smile made Night's expression look positively warm. "Yes, and one who is getting really, really irritated at you."

"Don't threaten me, little girl," Ambrose said. "I have friends on the MLEA who will have you behind bars so fast your head will spin."

Cassandra stepped closer. "No, you don't."

"Who was my mother?" Vanessa asked, the words tumbling out of her mouth like water released from a dam. "Why did you never tell me who she was? Why did I never ask you before now? What did you do to me?"

Ambrose turned his cold gaze back to Vanessa. "I don't know who your mother was. I never did. Nor did you care in the slightest to ask. As for what I did, I attempted to raise you properly and apparently failed miserably."

"Every adopted kid asks about their parents," Cassandra

said. "What did you do to Vanessa to keep her from asking about hers?"

Ambrose's eyes narrowed and his face turned dark red with anger. "I did nothing to her."

"Then someone else did," Vanessa said. "There's a hole in my memory, Ambrose. Who put it there?"

"You, most likely, with the amount of substances you abused."

"You son of a—"

This time it was Ian who caught her arms as she took a swing at him. Ambrose watched disdainfully as she struggled and said, "I expect you to meet me in the administration building tomorrow morning. Nine o'clock."

"I have class," Vanessa spat.

"It's not like you were going to attend it anyway," Ambrose said. "Don't be late or I'll have you arrested."

And with those words, Ambrose swept out of the door.

"Motherfucker," Vanessa hissed after the door closed. "Rancid, dumbass, piece of shit motherfucker!"

Vanessa tore free of Ian's grasp and stomped up the stairs, the staircase vibrating with every step. The entity felt the rage and emotional pain radiating off her and desperately wished to feed from her. The others looked at their feet, embarrassed.

Cassandra was the first to speak. "How did Ambrose know where Vanessa lived?"

"Maybe they told him at the dormitory?" Night suggested.

"They're not allowed to give out student information."

"Well, he is her guardian," Jade said. "He probably just asked."

"Hm." Cassandra looked back up the stairs. "Maybe."

Ian caught Vanessa when she reached the third floor. She threw his hand off her shoulder and tried to walk away from him, but he caught her arm. This time Vanessa spun and pushed hard, sending him off balance. He stumbled back against the wall.

"Leave me the fuck alone," she snarled at him. "Don't you try and stop me!"

"Stop you from what?"

"From…" Vanessa realized she didn't have an answer to that. All she'd wanted was to get away from everyone, to hide in her room and not have to deal with anything. "Just leave me alone!"

"If you go to your room, everyone is going to look for you there," Ian said. "If you're in my room, all I have to do is turn the music up and no one will knock."

Vanessa hesitated, knowing he was right but not wanting the company.

"And I have a fresh bottle of vodka." Ian jerked his thumb toward his room. "Come on, I'll pour you one."

This time Vanessa didn't hesitate. "Just give me the fucking bottle."

Two minutes later she was sitting on Ian's bed, her back wedged into the corner of the wall, pouring vodka down her throat.

What pissed her off the most was that this was exactly what Ambrose expected her to do: get shitfaced and fuck someone solely for the sake of spiting him, not that he ever cared enough for it to work. His only worry was that she didn't embarrass him, and with the bracelet on her arm, there was no way she *could* do anything extreme enough to cause him embarrassment.

Ian, to her surprise, seemed sensitive enough to the mood that he didn't come close to her. He sat on the chair at the desk, turned the stereo loud enough to keep the others away, and watched her closely. Occasionally he'd use magic to float the vodka bottle to his hand so he could have a drink, but he'd send it back a moment later.

Vanessa didn't stop him. In truth, she wasn't even drinking that much. After the first burning gulp of the vodka had seared its way down to her near-empty stomach and swirled there like a whirlpool, she barely wanted any more. She kept putting the bottle to her lips, but the booze would only go down in sips, not the gulps she wanted. She lit a cigarette and Ian opened the balcony door, letting a cold wind in and the cigarette smoke out.

"So," Ian said after a half-hour. "Your guardian is a right prick."

"No shit."

"I can see why you wanted to get away from him." He floated the bottle over and took a swig from it. "Seriously, these academics are too much for me. First the mystery room, then we learn that Kana's doing all this because her mother disappeared, and now your guardian comes along and is messing with you. It's too much."

Vanessa raised her eyes from the patch of rug she'd been trying to stare a hole into. "Are you thinking of quitting?"

Ian sat beside her on the bed and held out the bottle. "I'm thinking we should both quit."

"I can't quit, remember?" Vanessa held up her bracelet. "They'll erase my memory."

"I can get that off."

"So can I," Vanessa said. "That's not what it does. Without the bracelet, I have no powers."

"Oh. Shit." Ian took another drink. "There has to be a way."

"Yeah, I finish a degree and they let me go."

"I mean, a faster way. I bet I know someone who could break the spell."

"And then what?" Vanessa demanded. "We go on the run from the MLEA? How do we expect to survive that?"

"We get money," Ian said. "We rob a bank and we get out of the country before they know what hit them."

"Yeah, right." Vanessa took the bottle back. "And how are we going to hit a bank, Ian?"

"We're witches. We could walk in and out of any bank without being seen."

"And then the MLEA figures out what's happening and comes after us. No, thanks." Vanessa took another sip, but the vodka tasted wrong, thoughts of Ambrose turned the smooth liquor to acid that set her stomach and mind burning. "Wait a minute. Was that your idea all along? Hit a bank with magic and escape? That's your big illegal plan?"

"It will work," Ian protested. "I pay attention to these things—who gets in trouble and for what. How they're caught. I'm not naïve. I just need more power. And now there's a power sink in the basement with who knows how much power in it, just waiting for us to take it."

"No." Vanessa pushed off the bed and stood up. "No fucking way, Ian."

"Come on. Do you know how long I've been waiting for a chance like this?"

"What, you were just waiting for a power sink to fall into your hands so you could rob a bank?"

"No, I was waiting for enough power to rob a bank, and I'm nearly there, and with that power sink we'd have more than enough."

"Why the fuck are you telling me this?" Vanessa stumbled toward the door. "Why now? Just because Ambrose showed up? Is that it?"

"No, because…" Ian sighed in frustration. "Because it's all getting too complicated. This was just a job, right? Earn some money over the winter, build up power, and now… fuck."

"Build up power," Vanessa repeated slowly as if tasting the words and the meaning behind them. "Build up power, how?"

"What?" Ian's irritation faded, and he sounded worried for the first time. "No, that's nothing. I just don't need this sort of complication in my life, all right? That's all it is."

Vanessa stared at him, her mind racing. Jade had said there were two power sinks hidden in the building. They'd found the first and had been too distracted to think about the other one since. Vanessa took a long, slow look around the room. "Where is it, Ian?"

"Where is what?" Ian tried to sound confused, but when she met his eyes, he stared back a bit too hard, as if trying not to look away.

"There're two power sinks in the house," Vanessa said.

"The first one was down in the basement. You have the second one, don't you?"

"It's not…" Ian swallowed hard. "It's not like that."

"When you hit on me that first night, was it because you liked me, or because you could sense my power?"

"I liked you," Ian said. "You were the first one I've met here that I've ever liked."

"But not the first one you took home?" Vanessa held up her left hand, and a small flame appeared on her palm.

"What…" Ian's eyes locked on the flame. "What are you doing?"

"Jade's not the only one who knows how to detect a power sink." Vanessa blew on the flame. It swirled up into a small whirlwind that danced on her hand for a second before spinning apart. A small piece of flame dropped from her hand and vanished into the rug. Vanessa watched it and felt her skin grow hot with anger. "What does it do?"

"Vanessa," Ian began, but she cut him off with a shout.

"What does it do, Ian? Is that why I felt like crap every time I left your place in the morning? Because it was draining the strength out of me? Does it just suck away magic? Or does it charge with sex energy as well?"

Ian looked at the floor, his shoulders hunched.

"You son of a bitch." Vanessa headed for the door. "Do you have any idea how hard it's been to get through school feeling this bad? And I was blaming myself."

Ian stepped in front of her, his eyes wide and voice trembling with desperation. "Look, I'll make it up to you; I promise I will. Just don't tell the others about—"

Vanessa's fist slammed into Ian's jaw, twisting his neck and sending him stumbling back to the wall. She pulled the door open, stomped out, and slammed it behind her.

The entity hung in the air above Kana, watching as she, Night, Jade, and Cassandra sorted through the papers in the boxes. Jade seemed the most troubled; Kana, the angriest. The entity watched, hoping to learn more of what had happened and how to gain Kana's flesh and magic for its own to it.

Then, Vanessa stomped down the stairs. The woman didn't even look at her friends. Cassandra called after her but didn't get an answer.

"Wow," Jade said. "What the hell did Ian do?"

"No idea," Night said. "But she's looking mighty pissed."

The front door slammed.

"Shit," Cassandra stood up. "I'm going after her. Someone, check on Ian."

The entity followed Cassandra, floating through the wall to find Vanessa standing at the end of the driveway, arms swinging with unleashed fury. Cassandra stopped ten feet away from her. "Vanessa?"

"Fucking asshole," Vanessa spat the words, and when she turned to Cassandra, there were tears shining in her eyes. "That fucking asshole. I thought he liked me."

"What did he do?"

Vanessa shook her head. "Not yet. I'm not ready to talk about it yet. In need... I need to hit something, Cassandra, I need to break something. I need..."

She stopped, her eyes staring up the driveway. Cassandra

followed her look to Ian's bike, sitting under the shelter of the balcony.

"I need to steal something," Vanessa said, heading for the bike.

"Vanessa, no," Cassandra tried to get in front of her. "The roads are wet, it's cold, and it's dangerous. And Ian will be pissed."

"Ian being pissed is the last thing I care about." Vanessa walked around the bike and extended her hand. She closed her eyes. "He has magical protections on it. Dispel."

She slammed her hand on the motorcycle's seat with the last word, and from Ian's open window above came a yelp loud enough to be heard over the music. Vanessa pulled the bike upright, swung her leg over, and put her fingers by the keyhole. Something clicked. Vanessa jumped on the starter and the bike roared into life.

Cassandra stood in front of it. "Vanessa, you can't do this."

"Watch me."

"Goddamnit…" Cassandra hesitated a moment longer, then stepped around the bike and hopped on behind Vanessa. "If you're going to be stupid, you're not doing it alone."

"Good." Vanessa kicked the bike into gear and opened the gas. "I want the bar furthest from campus and still in town. I need to get shitfaced. Then I'll tell you what happened."

The entity followed them across the town, staying high above until it saw them pull into a roadhouse on the edge of town. Then, it winged back to the Reverend Marcus, dropping into his mind and pulling his body from sleep in the same moment. The entity rolled him out of bed toward the phone.

If it could get his people together, then it could get ahead of the witch that manipulated it.

And maybe, it could take the Promised for its own before the witch expected and no longer have to concern itself with the others.

Kana was still sorting through papers when Night came back into the study room. Before she could ask, he said, "That was a heck of a lover's quarrel."

"How bad was it?"

"Vanessa hit Ian hard enough that he was only half-conscious when I got to his room. I was getting him onto the bed when he convulsed and screamed in pain. That's when I heard his bike outside. So, I look out, and Vanessa is driving off on his bike with Cassandra behind her. And by the time I turn around, Ian's sitting up and swearing. Apparently, Vanessa broke the magic lock on his bike before she took it."

"Wow." Kana put down the paper she was holding. "That's impressive."

"Yeah. I promised Ian a bag of ice for his face." Night looked over at the papers. "What do you have?"

"A large pile of weird," Kana said. "Twelve papers, written over two years. And a ton of notes, and what looks like a diary. It's all out of order like Akemi was packing it all up in a rush."

"Fun," Night said. "I'll get the ice, then I can help you sort through the mess."

"Thanks."

Kana set the diary aside and put the pages of notes and diagrams into piles to sort later. The papers she laid out in front of her by date. The earliest was the one labeled, *Graph of Force Distribution on Interdimensional Portal Shields,* and Kana opened it first. She looked at the list of contributors and stopped, staring, until she heard Night's heavy footsteps on the stairs.

"Night, come here," she called, and when he was standing beside her, Kana pointed at the paper. "Look at this."

Night looked over the list of contributors. "Holy crap."

"Yeah," Kana said. "There's Rachel Meadows, Vanessa's mother, and Ambrose Levesque."

"Not that." Night's finger shook as he pointed at the name *Caroline Robertson.* "That. That's my mother."

"Your..." Kana shook her head. "Get Jade and Ian. Drag them here if you need to. I want to know if their parents are in here, too."

It took Vanessa three shots and four beers before she was ready to tell Cassandra what happened. When she did, it came out mixed up in a torrent of swearing, insults at Ambrose, Ian, and every other man she'd ever dated or slept with, and a long tirade against the universe itself. She was not being at all coherent, she realized, but that didn't seem to faze Cassandra in the slightest. The other woman waited until she was done swearing before she spoke.

"Three things," Cassandra said. She put down her own beer—her only beer since she'd come in—and raised a finger with each point. "First: Ian is an asshole of the grandest kind. Second: Ambrose is also an asshole of the grandest kind. Third: you need to decide what you're going to do about them both."

Vanessa knew Cassandra was correct, but that didn't make her any happier. "Maybe I can get Ambrose and Ian to have a bragging contest and they'll both vanish up their own asses."

"You're not that lucky," Cassandra said. "Want some advice?"

Vanessa looked at her beer. "No."

"Sleep on it. Tell Ian in the morning he has to confess by the end of the day, or you'll tell everyone. That way, he gets a chance to fix his own mess and fuck off before they throw him out or charge him. Also, tell him to fuck off and never come back."

"I was planning on that last one." Vanessa poured the rest of her beer down her throat. "Know something funny?"

"What?"

"I haven't drunk this much since the first night I came here," Vanessa said. "Even when I was celebrating a good grade, or just killing the evening. And the further we've gone in the semester, the more I cut back."

Cassandra shrugged. "Maybe you like being a student."

"Yeah," Vanessa sighed. "Maybe I do."

"Speaking of which, we should get back." Cassandra stood up. "I'm driving."

"Fair." Vanessa fumbled in her coat, but Cassandra caught her hand. "I'm buying tonight. You buy next time."

Vanessa let her, mainly because she was too drunk to figure out what she did and didn't owe. She rose from her seat, staggered a bit, and righted herself. Most of her outrage had burned off with her stream of invective, leaving her feeling slightly guilty for dumping it on Cassandra. She focused on her friend, who was already heading for the door.

"Hey," Vanessa called, stumbling slightly. "Hey, wait."

Cassandra stopped.

"I wanted to say sorry," Vanessa said as she stumbled closer. Cassandra smiled at her with the condescending look reserved for the fairly drunk. Vanessa frowned and put more sincerity into it. "No, really. I shouldn't have dumped all that on you. I'm sorry."

"It's all right," Cassandra said. "Someday, I'll dump all my secrets on you to get even."

Vanessa had to think through that before decided it was a good thing. She frowned. "Promise?"

"I promise," Cassandra said. "Think you can stay on the bike?"

"Yeah, no problem."

"Good."

A thought made Vanessa stop. She smiled. "Hey, Cassandra?"

"Yes?"

"You should have seen the look on his face when I punched him."

Cassandra smiled back at her. "I wish I had. Now come on, we need to get back. They're probably worried about us."

"Oh, yeah." Vanessa muddled through the alcohol in her brain until the thought came, "Should I text them?"

"No." Cassandra put an arm around her waist and pulled her toward the door. "Let's just get home."

"Good idea."

They stumbled out the door, the cold air slapping Vanessa's face hard. She breathed in a deep lungful, and the chill of it cleared her head just enough to help her find the motorcycle, parked on the side of the bar. She focused on walking in a straight line, which made Cassandra giggle. Vanessa pushed her away with a grand gesture and walked to the motorcycle with only the slightest of stumbles.

"Did it!" she declared as Cassandra laughed at her. "Now, are you going to start this bucket of bolts, or am—"

Someone smashed into her from behind, driving the air from her lungs and sending her to the ground. Her head bounced against the concrete, making her eyes water. Through the blur of the tears, she saw Cassandra, falling under a pile of men.

CHAPTER 16

V ANESSA SHOOK HER HEAD, TRYING to clear it. More
bodies piled on top of her, pinning her arms and legs.
She flashed back to the Trois-Rivières police station and the
six cops who'd pinned her. She didn't have her magic then.
This time was different. Vanessa pulled her magic together
and hissed. "Freeze!"

The men holding her down stopped moving, their grips
going slack. Vanessa took the moment to breathe and blink
her eyes clear. In the middle of the parking lot, Cassandra
struggled hard against the men pinning her. Every time one
of them grabbed a limb, she broke free of it and struck out
with fists and feet. Even so, they were going to overwhelm
her. Vanessa tore one hand free and pointed it at the closest of
Cassandra's attackers.

"Freeze!" Vanessa shouted, and one of the men stopped in
mid-motion. She pointed to another. "Free—"

A fist came out of nowhere and smashed into her jaw,
sending her head to the pavement again. Someone shouted,
"Get their bracelets, idiots!"

More men poured into the fight. One grabbed Vanessa's
head and slapped his hands over her mouth. Two more seized

Vanessa's arm and tugged at the bracelet. Vanessa screamed into the hand covering her face and twisted, trying to break free.

"Got it!" someone shouted from on top of Cassandra. "She's helpless now!"

The air around Cassandra exploded, and men flew in all directions. She gained her feet in a single smooth motion and shouted something in a language at once singsong and guttural. The men on Vanessa flew from her, slamming into the cars around her or skidding off into the distance. Vanessa scrambled to her feet. Cassandra's hands glowed white and lightning poured from her fingers, shocking anyone close enough to touch them.

She wasn't wearing her bracelet.

"Cassandra?" Vanessa struggled to clear her head. "What the fuck?"

"I'll explain later!" Cassandra shouted. "Get your bracelet back! Hurry!"

Vanessa looked down at her bare arm. The black bracelet was gone. She looked around wildly but couldn't see it.

Something slammed into her stomach and pain blossomed from it like a follower of fire. At first, she thought she'd been shot, but she could see no damage. The pain raced up her chest and neck and into her head. Vanessa screamed and fell to her knees.

"Get up!" Cassandra shouted. She yanked on Vanessa's arm, trying to get her to her feet. Around them, a dozen men lay moaning in pain or unconscious. "Up! Get up!"

"It's all right," the entity slurred. The alcohol in Vanessa's body affected it far more than it had when it possessed the drunk in the alley. The entity staggered up, struggling to take full control of Vanessa's body. "I'm all right."

"Get on!" Cassandra dragged her to the motorbike. "Behind me, hurry!"

The entity dragged Vanessa's body to the bike, put her hands on Cassandra's shoulders, and swung her leg over the seat. "I'm on."

Cassandra pulled Vanessa's hands down to her waist and clasped them together. "Hold tight!"

She made a gesture and the bike roared to life. Cassandra stomped it into gear, and they roared off, leaving the bleeding men in the parking lot behind them. She took the first turn so fast that the entity feared they would get thrown from the bike.

"Lean into the turns," Cassandra shouted. "Stay tight to my body and move with me!"

She didn't slow down once through the town. They blew through three red lights, skidded around corners, and dodged in and out of traffic as if the cars were holding still. At one point, Cassandra slammed the brakes, sent the bike nearly on its side, and dragged her foot on the ground to change directions. She gunned the throttle, righted the bike without stopping, and raced to the coven house. She skidded to a stop in front of the driveway and grabbed Vanessa's hands from her waist.

"Get inside," Cassandra said. "Fast."

She shoved the kickstand down as the entity clambered Vanessa's body off the bike and stumbled up the walk.

Cassandra grabbed her around the waist with one hand and hauled her up the driveway. She fumbled with her keys in the lock, got the door open, and shoved Vanessa's body inside. She slammed the door behind them and shouted, "Help!"

The entity didn't resist as Cassandra dragged Vanessa's body to the lounge and forced her down on the couch. It sat there, listening to the footsteps clattering down the stairs, and took stock of Vanessa's body. The woman's head hurt and was swelling with bruises where she was hit and where her head hit the concrete. Her arms and legs were scraped, and her ribs ached where the man had slammed into her. Her body was shaking with shock, which suited the entity fine. It meant answering fewer questions. It reached for her memories…

And couldn't find them.

It searched her mind again and found, where her consciousness and memories should be, a glowing, golden raven wrapped in wires of magic. The entity didn't dare touch it for fear that the magic being that must be caged within could lash out at it.

The entity growled in frustration. It had none of Vanessa's knowledge, no way to imitate her. At best it would be able to use her body, but not well.

"Vanessa!" Night's voice, filled with alarm, echoed in the foyer.

"Get the first aid kit from the control room," Cassandra snapped. "Hurry."

"What happened?" Ian knelt beside Vanessa's body. "Vanessa? Are you all right?"

"No," Cassandra's voice was hard. "Help Night with the first aid. I need to make a call."

"Cassandra, wait!" Kana said. "What happened?"

"We were jumped," Cassandra said as she pulled out her phone. "Dozens of them. We fought them off, but they got our bracelets."

"Shit," Jade said from the door. "So, you can't do magic? How did you fight them off?"

"Vanessa can't do magic." Cassandra put the phone to her ear, waited, and then said, "Sarge? Ten-six-six, Ten-one-oh-eight. Ten-five-two. My location."

"Wait, what?" Ian stood up, his eyes wide and wary. "What is that?"

"Go help Night, Ian," Cassandra said. "You aren't in trouble, *yet*."

"Can someone *please* tell me what is going on?" Kana said, her eyes going back and forth from Cassandra to Vanessa.

"I'm a cop," Cassandra said as she collapsed into a chair. "Detective Cassandra Grace, MLEA. I'll tell you everything later, but right now, I really need some help."

The entity stared at Cassandra through Vanessa's eyes, its thoughts whirling.

Kana retreated upstairs to the study room as chaos descended on the house. Outside, six unmarked MLEA cars parked in and around the driveway. A large van pulled up as well, with four witch paramedics fully trained in physical medicine as well as in removing curses and healing magical damage. They examined Cassandra and Vanessa and informed both they were lucky not to have concussions. Then, the women paramedics took Cassandra and Vanessa up to the shower room to treat their injuries.

Ian, Kana noticed, retreated even faster once Cassandra told the other officers to leave him alone. She wondered what exactly he'd done to earn the ire of the MLEA, and then set it aside. She had enough problems already. She worked through the piles of paper, not reading anything other than the dates that Akemi left in the top right corner in her neat, tight writing.

Half an hour later, she heard Cassandra groaning her way down the stairs from the showers. She wore shorts, a T-shirt, and bandages on her knees, elbows, and face. She pressed an ice bag to one eye and moved gingerly down the stairs. She spotted Kana and waved.

"Hey," Cassandra said. "How are you doing?"

"A little stunned," Kana admitted. "Are you really a police officer?"

"Oh yeah." Cassandra eased into one of the chairs with a groan and a wince. "Ugh, I skidded on my ass when they tackled me. Hurts like hell to sit, hurts worse to stand."

Kana winced in sympathy. "That's awful."

"I've had worse," Cassandra said. "But no, it's not fun."

"How did you end up at Shipton?"

Cassandra shook her head. "I'll tell everyone tomorrow, all right? Tonight, I just need a drink and to lie on my stomach. But I've got to talk to my sergeant first. We've got the bastards now."

"How?" Vanessa asked from the stairs.

Cassandra turned, wincing. "My bracelet tracks my movements and magic use for official police record. So, if they've got it, we can track it down. That's not the big problem, though."

"No?" Vanessa moved unsteadily down the stairs until she reached the second floor. "What is?"

"They knew about the bracelets," Cassandra said. "No one outside the magic community knows about the bracelets, so how did they?"

Kana looked down at the piles of paper. She shook her head. It was all too much at once.

Cassandra groaned and stood up. "No rest for the wicked. Got to talk to sarge."

"Can I ask you something first?" Kana reached for the list of names she'd gathered from the reports. "Did your mother or father go to Shipton?"

"Nope." Cassandra limped to the door. "All my family are cops."

"OK, thanks. Vanessa?"

Vanessa stopped her slow progress to the stairs. "Yes?"

"You were right. About your mother, I mean. She did work with Akemi."

Cassandra turned back. "Rachel Meadows worked with Akemi?"

"And Ambrose Levesque," Kana said. "Both of them were part of her project."

"That's…" Vanessa looked confused. "Fascinating?"

"Your mother and your guardian both worked with Akemi, Professor White lied to you, and all you've got is 'fascinating?'" Cassandra frowned. "How hard did you hit your head?"

Vanessa put a hand up to her chin. "Pretty hard. Honestly, I can barely stand."

"Then go to bed," Cassandra said. "You don't have a concussion, so you don't need to stay awake. Get sleep and feel better. We can talk about it in the morning."

"I want an ice pack first," Vanessa said. "Then I'll go to bed, I promise."

"Sure," Cassandra said. She held out an arm and let Vanessa lean on it as they limped down the stairs together.

Kana watched them go, sighed, and stared at the piles of paper before her. She sighed and kept putting them in order. With luck, she could spend the next day going through it all and finally make some sense of what was going on.

The entity spent an hour on the main floor, listening to the police. It learned nothing new, save that Reverend Marcus's followers were about to have a very bad day. Fortunately, the entity had instructed the reverend not to participate, so there was little chance they would trace the event back to him. The followers of Raguel were fanatically loyal, though the entity didn't know how long that would last. When it realized it couldn't glean any more information out of Vanessa or the police, it put her to bed.

Had she been a normal host, it could have waited until she slept and explored the house.

Instead, the entity floated in Vanessa's mind, staring at the golden ball that held her memories and magic. It could sense Vanessa hiding inside the magic, bound by the same threads that bound her power, and glaring back at it. The entity didn't dare reach in to grab at her and her memories. The golden raven that lived in Vanessa had her wrapped in its wings and was itching to attack the entity, to render its form into nothingness. The entity knew for certain that the moment it left her body, Vanessa would rise up and tell the others. Instead, it stayed on guard all night, doing an inventory of Vanessa's body as it waited. The woman was hurting and stiff, but not damaged, as near as the entity could tell. It made her rise, took her to the shower to wash off the dirt and blood from her flesh, and returned to put on clean versions of the clothes she wore the night before. Underwear, tight jeans, tight T-shirt, and boots. It didn't bother with a bra. It took her downstairs and stopped outside the study room. Kana had laid out the papers in perfect rows, just like her mother would.

The thought caught the entity off guard. It circled around it, trying to pry out more memories. Nothing came, though. It snarled silently in frustration. Maybe if it went through all the papers, it would remember what happened.

"Hey," Cassandra said behind her. "We're meeting in the dining room this morning. You coming?"

The entity stared at the papers a moment longer, then sighed. "Yeah. I'm coming."

It took Vanessa down the stairs, being sure to move gingerly so it looked like it cared about the body's injuries. The others were already in the dining room. Steel containers arranged down one table wafted the scents of sausages, eggs, and pancakes. A large urn filled with coffee stood beside them. A bowl of fruit, a plate of bread and cheese, and another of pastries finished the buffet.

"I figured we could all use a good meal," Kana said from the next table. "So, I got the cafeteria to deliver. Dig in."

The entity, not sure what Vanessa would take, filled its plate with some of everything and ate while it covertly watched the others. Jade sat beside Kana. Night and Ian were at another table. Night looked shell-shocked from everything that happened, and Ian kept shooting glances toward Vanessa as if waiting for her to speak. Cassandra watched Ian, the smirk on her face saying she knew what was going on. The entity wished it did.

"So," Cassandra said when all six plates were empty. "I'm a cop."

"You said so last night," Kana said.

"Yeah." Cassandra stood up and took another cup of coffee. "And now I'm going to tell you what I'm doing here. And it's a secret, so I need you all to keep your mouths shut about it until we get this mess resolved, all right?"

Heads around the tables nodded. The entity made Vanessa's head nod as well. Ian, it noticed, just narrowed his eyes and said nothing. The entity reached out to sense the emotions in the room. Jade and Kana were both curious and wary. Ian was frightened, and Night was both shocked and curious. Cassandra was pissed off more than anything, with a bit of embarrassment on top of it, mostly when she looked at Vanessa.

"Three years ago, the president of the university came to the MLEA," Cassandra began. "High-powered witches have been vanishing from Shipton University for the last fifteen years."

"What?" Jade sat forward in her chair. "I've been here for six years, bachelors and masters, and I've never heard of that."

"It's not something they make public," Cassandra said.

"And it's not always a typical disappearance. Some suddenly drop out. Some move to another school without reason. Some go home."

"That happens," Kana said. "It happened all the time at UCLA. Promising students would just disappear."

"True," Cassandra said. "But when the president followed up on them, all the ones he found had been subjected to magical interference."

"What sort of magical interference?" Jade asked. "Like, their memories were erased, or their grades dropped or what?"

"We're not sure." Cassandra shook her head. "The investigators the president sent all detected magic, but none of them could figure out the source of it or what it actually did."

"But it was enough to make them drop out?" Jade shook her head. "That's weird."

"Wait a minute." Night was frowning. "You said, 'All the ones he found.' How many couldn't he find?"

"Three vanished without a trace," Cassandra said. "None of them from rich families, of course, or they would have raised a stink all over the witch community. They were scholarship students like Vanessa and Night, only without any family at all."

"And the university didn't look for them?"

"The university spent more than $3 million looking for them," Cassandra said. "On top of the police investigations. There was nothing. They vanished off the face of the earth."

"Like Rachel Meadows and Akemi Wakahisa," Kana said.

"Exactly like them." Cassandra took a drink of coffee. "Only we didn't know about them until you found them."

Kana folded her arms and sat back, thinking. "At least two of the papers upstairs talk about dealing with an interdimensional being. Do you think that it has something to do with it?"

The entity inside Vanessa nearly spoke up to protest its involvement. It hadn't been anywhere in twenty years and most certainly had not been attacking witches. It managed to keep its mouth shut and settled on looking attentive.

"I was sent in last year as bait," Cassandra said. "My detective sergeant arranged my admission, and I've been here ever since. Then, when we heard Vanessa was coming, the president suggested we room together, both to make a more tempting target and for me to keep an eye on Vanessa. Sorry."

The last word was directed at Vanessa. The entity managed a smile and said, "It's all right."

"Are you sure?" Cassandra asked. "Because if it was me, I'd be pissed."

"I'm… a little shocked," the entity decided on, cycling rapidly through its memories of other young college students talking in the bars and cafes. "And I may get angry later, but right now, I want to know what happened to the others."

Cassandra sighed. "We still have no clue. Literally. Two years I've been here and nothing has happened."

"Was your cover blown?" Ian asked. "Maybe they know you're here?"

"We thought so, and I was going to leave, but then those boys were killed." Cassandra shook her head. "The murders made no sense. And when we examined the waitress, we found she had no memory of the crime, which was weird. We checked for magic interference, and it was there but different from the other students. Something played inside her brain and made her do it all."

"So, what happens to her?" Kana asked. "If she didn't really do it?"

"She won't be charged, but she can't stay here. We have to take a huge chunk of memory and relocate her," Cassandra shrugged. "Anyway, that's when I started going to bars in the hopes of luring the murderer out. Then, Glennis disappeared, and that seemed more like the original disappearances until the video showed up."

"So... what are you going to do about it?" Ian sounded concerned, but the entity felt the fear radiating from him.

"Well, this morning I'm going on a raid," Cassandra said. "We're going to track down the bracelets and everyone who knows about them. Maybe then we'll find the murderer."

"Do you think they'll talk to you?" the words slipped out of Vanessa's mouth before the entity realized it When the others looked at Vanessa, it cursed itself for the question. It was safe as long as it was in the witch, and by the time the others gave any useful information, it would have the promised for its own. The entity said, "I mean, they didn't look like they'd be cooperative."

"They don't have to cooperate," Cassandra's voice became cold. "I'll read their memories the way I did yours and see what happened. Once we're finished, I'll come back and let you know if I've found anything."

"So, what do the rest of us do?" Ian asked.

"Stay on campus." Cassandra's voice stayed cold. "Especially you, Ian. Stay here. I have some things to talk about with you."

Ian's fear blossomed even larger, and under it, anger grew. "Of course."

"I'm going to go through Akemi's notes," Kana said. "Maybe I can find something in there."

"I have classes to go to," Night said. "But I'll be back after."

"Same." Jade stood up. "And I need to spend some time working in the library."

"I'll help Kana," the entity said.

"Don't you have a meeting with Ambrose at 9?" Jade said. "He sounded like he'd be pretty angry if you missed it."

"This is more important." The entity wanted to avoid Ambrose until it was sure what was going on. It was certain Ambrose was the witch it had seen. Did that mean that Ambrose was the witch searching for immortality? He had been part of Akemi's team, so it was certainly possible. But if it learned what happened at the end of things, maybe the entity could figure out how to take over the Promised by itself and wouldn't need the witch at all. "If we can find out what Akemi was doing, maybe we can stop whatever is going on."

"I'll have a detective meet him at the administration building and tell him you've been delayed," Cassandra said. "I'll have them question him while I'm at it. He was part of the team when Akemi disappeared, so maybe he knows something."

"Are they going to read his mind?" the entity asked, trying to sound curious instead of worried that the investigation might lead them to it.

"No. We can't do that to a witch without permission or a court order."

"But you can with regular people?" Kana sounded disturbed.

"Only in cases where the witch community is being threatened." Cassandra stood up from the table. "Don't worry, they won't remember it. I'll see you tonight, most likely, and maybe we'll be able to tell how all this connects back to Akemi."

Cassandra left. Kana finished her breakfast with a distracted air and went up the steps to the library room. Jade and Night finished their own meals and headed for class. Ian was the only one left, and he stared at Vanessa like she was at once his lifebelt and the shark pulling him under. The entity stared back as it finished eating the food and drinking the coffee. Vanessa's body needed fuel to function, and the entity wanted it functioning for a bit longer at least. Ian rose from his chair and sat across the table from her.

"I know you're upset," Ian kept his voice low and quiet, "but I wanted a chance to explain before you tell everyone. Can you give me that chance?"

The entity once more wished that Vanessa's memories were not locked up in the back of her mind. It hesitated and said, "Why should I?"

Ian stared at the floor. "Because I care about you, all right? Because I wanted you to help me and I know you can't, but at least let me sort this out. I'll tell everyone at supper tonight, all right?"

The entity nodded. Hopefully by supper it would learn what had happened. Or maybe it would be in the Promised already and it wouldn't need to care. "Fine. Tell them at supper tonight. Or I will."

"I promise." Ian leaned in to kiss her mouth. "Thank you."

The entity pulled back from the kiss because that's what angry women did. Then, it headed upstairs to the library room. Kana was already seated at the table, her hands resting on either side of the thick diary. She stared at the first page, not moving. The entity cleared Vanessa's throat. Kana blinked several times and turned her head, her eyes coming back into focus. She managed a smile.

The entity stood alone in the room with the Promised; the one that it had wanted for twenty years. The pull of her presence almost made the entity rip free of Vanessa and dive inside the sun that was Kana, but it knew that the woman's magic, even stronger than Vanessa's, would destroy it in an instant.

"Hi, Vanessa," Kana said, her voice small as if speaking was an effort. "Are you better?"

"A little." The entity made sure to move stiffly as it pulled up the chair beside her. "Are you okay?"

Kana shook her head. She looked back down at the diary. "No, I'm really not."

The entity leaned forward and looked at it. "What is it?"

"It's an experiment diary. From the last two years of my mother's life, I think. And it's...." Kana shook her head, unable to talk.

The entity reached out and put Vanessa's hand on Kana's arm. It was meant to feel reassuring, but inside, the entity was reaching forward with all its senses, trying to find a weakness that would allow it to break into the Promised and take her body for its own. It could feel her magic, sensing its investigation and responding.

But instead of preparing to attack it, the magic opened up and *welcomed* the entity to her body.

The entity didn't know why, and it didn't care. It raced forward down Vanessa's flesh, preparing to transfer into the Promised no matter the consequences. It would be able to kill Vanessa before the other broke free, it was sure. Then, it could do the same to the others, and using its magic body, open a gate for the rest of its kind to come. It could rule them and break them, eat as much as it wanted, grow ever more powerful—and all it needed was to enter this woman's body.

It ran into a barrier, invisible and stronger than steel, that sent it flying back into Vanessa's body, the shock almost knocking Vanessa out of her chair, except the entity clamped down on her muscles to freeze her in place. It removed the hand from Kana's arm, the fingers feeling cold and damp. The entity roiled with anger and frustration, sending shivers through Vanessa. The entity waited until it had her body once more under control before it spoke.

"Can you tell me," the entity said, "what's so special about the diary?"

For an answer, Kana turned the page. There, in Akemi's neat and tidy writing, were the words:

Studies in the Use of Body Transfer by an Interdimensional

Entity as a Method for Human Immortality

CHAPTER 17

Studies in the Use of Body Transfer by an Interdimensional
Entity as a Method for Human Immortality
By Akemi Wakahisa
Diary 1

Purpose: To record the experiments leading to the discovery of the formula for human personality transfer and immortality without informing the university authorities.

NOTE: This will be the strangest experimental record I have written, and there are still parts of me that doubt whether it should be written down at all, but I believe that if I am successful I will need to be able to duplicate the event in the future, and to do that I will require a complete record of the experiments. I cannot share these experiments with either the university or my colleagues to ensure the security of the information, and so, in addition to the proper research papers that I will develop for the university, I will use this book to record the other experiments on the entity as we move towards immortality through body transfer.

Background

The entity arrived in our world as a result of our late-stage interdimensional portal experiments. These were the last experiments before we begin inter-temporal research. We were testing the shields I created for use in interdimensional as well as interspatial work (see paper: Force Distribution on Interdimensional Portal Shields for results of the experiments). The shields held as expected, and the objects sent through have been recovered. In this test, we sent organic matter through (plant: dwarf fern; maidenhair spleenwort; Asplenium Trichomanes) to see if it could survive the interdimensional portal. This was to be the first step toward human interspatial/interdimensional portal travel and eventual inter-temporal travel.

The plant was sent into the portal as per the experimental parameters and returned in the time expected (all information is in the above-cited paper). We were preparing to close the portal when A.L identified something else coming through.

"A.L." Kana frowned. "Ambrose Levesque? Your guardian?"

"I suppose so," the entity said, though it kept Vanessa's eyes on the paper. It did not remember who had been there when it came through, but then, it had lost so many memories over the years. It kept its eyes on the page.

As per protocol, all witches put their energy into the shield and allowed the portal to collapse. The entity slammed repeatedly against the shield walls before stopping. At that time, there was no way to see the entity, and it was only through the recording of its energy presence that we could detect that it was still there. We informed P.W., who suggested we maintain the shield and inform the university council. Fortunately, the shield could be attached to the building power sink and maintained without effort.

The entity then began what appeared to be a series of explorations of the shield holding it, prodding the energy field as if looking for a point of weakness. This went on for a period of hours, during which we noticed that the energy signature of the entity appeared to weaken. Finally, it floated in the middle of the shielded area, apparently resting. At this point we decided to perform a series of experiments to determine the creature's nature and whether it posed a threat. Below is a list of experiments:

Kana flipped over the page, looked at the next two pages, and flipped past them as well.

"What are you doing?" the entity asked. "I was reading that."

Kana shook her head. "Akemi was redundant beyond all measure. Everything listed here will have a full copy somewhere else, and there's going to be a summary at the end of it... Here."

Summary of Official Experiments

Entity determined to be an energy-based creature of extra-dimensional origin, needing the input of organic energy to survive. Though it survived with plant life (used ferns from previous experiments), animal energy proved more useful (use laboratory mice from biology labs). It was determined that the entity could move in and out of the bodies of the rats, appearing to take over control of them until the rats died. Autopsies done on the rats determined that they all suffered brain aneurisms that resulted in their deaths. The entity seemed unchanged by the death of its hosts, leading to questions concerning the life span of the entity.

Out of curiosity, I trapped one of the stray cats in the area and put it within the entity's shield. The entity immediately entered it and used it to hunt the rats. It seemed to adapt to its new form without difficulty as if in taking over a creature it absorbed the knowledge of how to use it. Of note was that, the greater the pain of the rats, the more the energy of the entity increased. Even so, it maintained a much lower level of energy than it had when it first appeared, which suggests it must be used to living in a larger creature and eating larger prey. I put this idea to A.L. and R.W., who agreed, but were unsure what size creature should be used for the experiment. Obviously, neither would agree to the obvious, which is to bring in a human to host the creature and see if we could begin communications.

Fortunately, I am not so squeamish.

Unofficial Experiment 1: *Entry of Extra-dimensional Entity into a Human Body and Communication*

Host: *Jonathan Phillips, age 22, 5'9" in height, pale skin, dark hair. Strong and in good health. At Shipton for business administration.*

Process: *I seduced J.P., a non-witch student, brought him to the building for a tryst, and took him down to the laboratory. It was an easy matter to lure him into the room and lie to him about the nature of the experiments. My mother had long ago taught me how to erase a human's mind, so I had no concerns about him remembering the evening's events. I pushed him into the energy circle to see what would happen.*

Results: *The entity immediately entered his body. J.P. clutched at his head and went stiff. For a time, he didn't move, and when he did, his movements were different from how J.P. had moved before. He circled the shield again, putting his hand against the surface of it. He winced and pushed his hand through it, then pulled it back, rage on his face. At last, he turned to face me.*

"Who are you," he said. "Where am I?"

"You speak English very well," I said, mainly to confirm what he told me next.

"I am in this man's mind," he said. "I can read his thoughts, feel his muscles, and use the memory of how they work to make him walk and talk. Where am I?"

"A different dimension than your own," I said. "You came through as we were closing the experiment."

J.P. frowned, or more correctly, the creature within him frowned using his body. "Are you going to send me back?"

"Perhaps," I said. "It is not often that the university gets interdimensional creatures that are not a direct threat to human survival. The fact that you are an energy-based entity is fascinating. Though it appears you are not entirely energy-based. Am I correct?"

"Yes." The entity walked around its space, again checking the energy field as it spoke. "We can survive separately from a physical entity, but it leaves us vulnerable to attack and makes feeding difficult. So, we take a physical body."

"What do you feed off?"

"Pain, you would call it. Specifically, the energy

a creature gives off when it is in distress." The entity paused and J.P.'s head tilted. "Interesting. The creatures in your world are capable of being in distress without being in physical pain. The taste is... different."

The entity seemed excited by the idea. I asked, "Why did you come here?"

"Because I sensed the energy in the world. It is everywhere. Even in this prison, I can feel the energy in the world, ripe for the plucking."

"So, you came to feed?"

"I came to rule," it said. "There are many of my kind in my world. The strong devour the weak or oppress them. The weak kowtow and plot against their masters. It is a constant struggle to survive. Here, I could populate the world and rule it. Or gain enough power to bring others through to serve me."

"How can one creature populate the world?"

"You would call it asexual reproduction through fission. We grow strong enough to let others exist to serve us. Sometimes those grow strong in their own turn and try to kill the one that created them. I did."

"And the physical bodies that you possess. What happens to them?"

"They live their lives out possessed, and when they die, we possess the strongest of their offspring. It is a dangerous time for us."

"Why?"

"Because our power is invested in the bodies of the body that we possess. When we switch bodies, we lose that power. It is vital when one switches to immediately feed as much as possible, usually on the other offspring of the creature in which we live."

"So, if I leave you in that body, you'll stay in it gathering power?"

"No. This body cannot hold power. It can barely hold me. Already I can feel it rebelling against my presence. Long enough and it will die, though not as soon as the cats." At that point, the entity stared at me and asked, "Why is it different from you?"

"How do you mean?" I asked.

"Why is it your body can hold power but this one cannot?"

It was at this point that I realized that when the creature spoke of power, it did not just mean strength from feeding. Instead, it meant magic. I told it, "I am a witch. We have power. That one is only human. He doesn't."

"What is a witch?" The entity asked the question,

then frowned. "There is information in this one's mind about them. It is... odd."

"It is inaccurate," I said. "Unless it says that I have power enough to destroy you in an instant."

"So you say." The entity held up its hands. It approached the edge of the shield. "And will you destroy this body? I think not."

I walked up to the shield, grabbed J.P.'s shirt, and hauled him through. As I expected, the creature could not pass and had to leave J.P.'s body so as not to be destroyed. I took J.P. upstairs while he was still dazed, erased his memory of the laboratory, and had sex with him.

Kana sat back from the book, shaking her head. "Wow. That's... cold."

The entity agreed, though its thoughts were more admiring than repulsed. It was a pity Akemi had not been one of its kind. She would have been incredibly powerful. As it was...

"What happened next?"

Kana turned the page.

Three times in the next week, I had similar "trysts" with J.P. while I interrogated the entity. In between these times, it continued to live in the bodies of cats. The stray that I originally brought died within a week. I procured a second cat from the local animal shelter—much healthier, and therefore more likely to have a long lifespan.

Needless to say, the entity was furious at me for pulling it from J.P.'s body and tried to get revenge, which is how I learned that it could not possess a witch. Right after I put J.P. in the ring, it immediately reached his arm through the shield and hauled me inside, gritting J.P.'s teeth in pain the entire time. It then left J.P. and attempted to enter my body. Even before I could muster a magic defense, my totem was already attacking it. The entity was heavily damaged and fled to hide in J.P.'s body, where it sat shaking. I told it to leave his body or it would receive worse damage. The entity did as I asked and returned to the cat. I took J.P. upstairs, made sure he had suffered no damage, and again erased his memory of the lab and had sex with him.

The second time I brought J.P. down, the entity was calmer. It sat down in the middle of the floor and said nothing. I offered it food, but it refused, saying that dead matter had no energy for it. It asked what I wanted. So, I asked the question that had struck me the night it revealed it changed bodies. "How long do your kind live?"

"Until we are killed," the entity said. "Usually that is by being absorbed, though occasionally one of us will fade from existence from lack of energy. The latter is rare, though, because there is almost always a corporeal to possess."

I tried to ascertain the creature's age, but it lived

in a world where there was neither night nor day, only a gray, unchanging sky. I tried calculating by the lifespan of the creatures it possessed and learned only that the entity had possessed six so far.

On the third visit with J.P., the entity asked, "How often do your kind change bodies?"

"We don't," I said. "We are attached to our bodies and die with them."

"Why?" The creature seemed actually curious. "You are creatures of energy, like I am. Why do you not leave your bodies when they weaken?"

It was a very good question and one that I had not thought to ask before. So, we left it at that for the day, and I took J.P. for our usual tryst. After he left, I spent the night thinking about the possibility of mind-to-mind personality transfer, and what it would mean for a witch.

I did not sleep that night as I thought of the possibilities. I would need far more information to understand how the entity moved from body to body, and to learn how a human could do the same thing.

Unofficial Experiment 2: *Measurement of Energy Flow in Body Exchange*

Before bringing J.P.to the entity again, I needed a way to see what happened during the entity's possession of his body. I used the standard spell for measuring energy transfer, inscribed on a small stone, which I gave to J.P. as a good luck charm. He accepted it and had it in his pocket when I sent him into the experimental chamber.

As soon as the entity entered his body, it knelt on the floor and banged J.P.'s face against the concrete. I immediately stepped inside the shield and used magic to freeze it in place.

"What are you doing?" I demanded.

"I'm hungry," the entity said. "You do not feed me enough."

"And smashing Jonathan's nose will help that?"

"I can feed off my host's pain as easily as the mice," the entity said. "Easier, in fact, since I have to make contact with the mice to feel their pain. I can drink Jonathan's pain directly from inside him. It is much better."

"Do not do that again or I will not bring you another body."

"Yes, you will." The entity sounded very certain, which was irritating because it was correct. "Because I have something you want. Several things, it seems."

"And what are those?" I asked.

282

"First, I am, as you say, an other-dimensional creature, and your colleagues are most anxious to study me. Second, you are desperately curious about the nature of my existence. So much that you are willing to risk this man's life to get information. And third…"

It didn't say more, but stared at me, smiling. I knew it was baiting me but chose to ask anyway. "Third?"

"Third, I can teach you how to change bodies," the entity said. "And even through the shield, I can feel your desire to learn it."

The entity was correct. I did desire it, more than anything else. More even than my time travel experiments, which I needed as a cover for what I was now working on.

"Yes, I do," I said. "Will you teach me?"

"What do I get out of it?" the entity demanded. "Why should I teach you when you leave me here half-starved? I am trapped in a small cage in a world full of energy and power. First, feed me, and then I will consider it."

"And if I do not?"

"Then I'll smash his face against the floor until his own mother wouldn't recognize him."

"Given that you can't move," I said, "That is an idle threat. However,"

I have a pain spell that affects the muscles and nerves. It is excruciating, as if one's entire body is on fire but does not cause any actual damage. I cast it on J.P. and watched his body roll around on the ground, arching and twisting, for the better part of fifteen minutes. When I released it, he fell limp to the floor.

"That is acceptable," the entity said. "Though I should warn you that this one's mind will soon suffer permanent damage if you keep allowing me to host in him. I suggest finding a new sex partner."

"I will have to anyway," I said, "Thanks to what you've done to his face. I can convince him he tripped on the stairs, I suspect. So, do we have a deal?"

"I will consider it," the entity said. "For now, I suggest you use your power to observe what happens when I leave this body and return to the cat."

I did, detecting all the magical and physical energy that I could without casting a major spell. I watched it leave J.P.'s body, saw how it disentangled itself from his mind and left him lying there as it went into the cat.

The rest of the night was spent tending to J.P. and erasing his mind.

"Vanessa!" Ambrose's voice echoed through the room. Kana slammed the book shut and spun in her seat. The entity, as surprised as she, was halfway to its feet, fists balled. It was a futile gesture, of course. Ambrose's magic could destroy it in a moment if he so chose. So, the entity unclenched Vanessa's fists and turned to face the man. Ambrose's head shone red from anger, almost glowing in the morning light. He stomped across the room until he was nearly nose-to-nose with Vanessa's body.

"How *dare* you." The words were low and angry. "You were supposed to meet me in the administrative building an hour ago."

"Was I?" The entity leaned close to Ambrose, Vanessa's mouth to his ear, and whispered, "I think you have me confused with Vanessa, *witch*."

Ambrose's face turned a darker shade of red, his mouth opening to shout. Then, his eyes widened and his face turned pale. The entity could see the comprehension in his eyes and horror with it. It made Vanessa smile at him, which made Ambrose shake.

"Um..." Kana began. "I'll leave so you two can be alone."

"No need." The entity took Ambrose's hand in Vanessa's and pulled him toward the door. "My *guardian* and I will talk upstairs. Won't we, Ambrose?"

The entity kept pulling, and Ambrose stumbled behind. It led him up to the third floor and Vanessa's room. Only when the door had closed behind him did the entity let go. "And how are you doing, dear Ambrose? Did you truly come to yell at poor Vanessa or just get her ready for my presence?"

Ambrose stared at him. "How did you get in there?"

"Massive attack on this one and the other bracelet-wearer," the entity said. "Fortunately, we got this one's bracelet first, or I might have ended up trying to take over Cassandra, which would have been unpleasant."

"It will be unpleasant for you either way," Ambrose said. "Get out of her. Now."

"No." The entity sat on the bed. "I'm rather enjoying her body. I've learned so much in it. Things that I suspect you don't have the faintest idea about, *witch*."

"This is not part of the plan," Ambrose said.

"Yes, it is. You told me I could take over her body."

"When the time is right." Ambrose's hands flexed into fists. The entity felt his magic gathering. "This is not that time."

"She's aware, in here," the entity said. "Unlike the humans, she still has control over her mind. When I leave this body, she will remember everything, and what do you think she will say?"

Ambrose's fists stayed clenched, magic pulsing from his hands. The entity waited. At last, Ambrose spluttered, "What do you want?"

"The same thing I have always wanted," the entity said. "Freedom in this world. Power. The Promised. And yet I have none of those things because you kept me a prisoner, starved me nearly to death, and would not keep your end of our bargain."

The last words were a guess as much as anything else.

The entity still didn't know what the full bargain had been, though it could guess: immortality for the Promised. And Kana was definitely the Promised, but something still blocked the entity from entering her. It would be damned if it was going to allow that to continue.

"You did not keep your end," Ambrose snapped. "The experiment was not replicable. We tried."

The word 'we' caught the entity's attention. "How unfortunate for the young women you experimented on."

Ambrose's mouth pressed into a thin line. "You should have obeyed us."

"You should have given me the Promised," the entity said. "Then, none of this would have happened."

"You idiot," Ambrose raged. "Do you know what we had to go through to create the Promised? Do you understand the sacrifices we made?"

"The murders you committed?" the entity suggested. "I don't care. Give me the Promised."

Ambrose stepped away from the entity. "Wait for further instructions. Do not try anything without us."

"Don't worry," the entity said. "I'm exactly where I need to be."

CHAPTER 18

"MOTHERFUCKER," VANESSA SCREAMED AT AMBROSE'S retreating back.

He didn't hear it, of course. Her words echoed in the darkness that surrounded her. Gold wings wrapped around her, hugging her tight and protecting her from the entity's continuous probes at her memory. Vanessa snarled and slammed her magic against the cage that held her and her magic. Nothing happened. The totem held her tighter, and Vanessa, still raging, slumped into its warm embrace.

There had to be a way to escape, she just needed to figure out *how*. The entity had firm control over her. Even when her body slept, the entity stayed awake, patrolling her mind and scheming. Vanessa knew that her magic could drive it off in a moment, probably destroy it if she wanted, but she couldn't use the magic at all thanks to the tight cage the Shipton president and faculty had woven. Once she was out, though, she would kill it herself.

She would kill the entity first, Vanessa decided. Then Ambrose. Then she would kick Cassandra's ass for not telling her she was a cop and Ian's ass twice for plotting stupid shit.

But first, she had to escape her own mind.

The entity took her back down, where Kana sat staring at the diary. With her mouth, it asked, "Learn anything new?"

"Not yet," Kana said, not even noticing that the voice was different, to Vanessa's irritation. "Most of the rest of the book is about experiments that Akemi ran on the entity and the bodies she used to give it to possess. Apparently, Jonathan fell sick about a month into the experiment and had to be hospitalized. Brain injuries."

Vanessa suspected she'd have the same if she didn't get the entity out. She snarled at it from within, but it ignored her the way Ambrose had every time she'd wanted attention as a child.

"Akemi apparently had five lovers between the beginning and end of this diary," Kana said. "It looks like they didn't make any progress on human mind transfer for the rest of the year."

"I see," the entity said. "How about after that?"

Kana shook her head. "That's where the diary ends."

The entity frowned—Vanessa could feel her face responding to its command and it drove her mad—and said, "Are there more diaries?"

"Not in the boxes." Kana sighed. "She might have destroyed them or hidden them somewhere else. Or maybe they're down in Lab Five and we missed them."

"Let's look," the entity said eagerly. "I really want to know what happened."

"I'll get Night and Jade to help us," Kana said. "The more, the better."

Vanessa growled in frustration as the entity followed Kana down the stairs to the lab. She couldn't close her eyes, but she could turn her attention away from what her body was doing and look inwards. It was a technique Ambrose had taught her years before as a way of keeping her quiet. Now, she applied it with all her might, focusing her attention not just inward, but on the wires of the cage that bound her magic. She felt them as if she were running her fingers over them, feeling the way the magic of the wires interwove and how the spell came together....

Seamlessly.

Vanessa gave up on the cage, gave up on controlling her body, and let the golden raven within embrace her. She turned her mind to her own magic, feeling its shape and size and studying its power. She'd never *seen* it before, after all. Maybe if she stayed focused and calm and looked hard enough, she could find a way to break free. The professors were experienced and powerful witches, but they didn't have nearly as much at stake as she did.

"Here!" Night's voice broke through Vanessa's concentration. She watched the entity turn and look, the feeling as horrifying as a childhood nightmare. Night lay on his belly with one arm stretched deep beneath the bookcase, saying, "I think I've got something here."

"Or we could move the bookcase," Jade suggested, smiling down at him.

"Where's the fun in that?" Something small dragged across the concrete floor, and a moment later Night pushed a mousetrap, fortunately empty, out into the middle of the room. He sighed and stood up. "Well, so much for being the hero."

"The attempt is noted," Kana said. She looked around

the room and sighed. "Too much to hope that it would be somewhere easy."

"But it has to be somewhere," Jade said. "You said Akemi is massively anal-retentive about her notes. She wouldn't have left one of her notebooks with her notes and not the others."

"So then, where is it?"

"Could it be protected by an illusion?" Night asked.

"Good idea. Jade?"

Jade cast her detection spell and watched the clouds. "No. There's no illusion on the bookshelves."

"Dammit."

The entity looked around the room but offered no solutions. Vanessa felt momentarily smug that, whatever else, the entity was useless at searching.

"Maybe she put them in another room?" Jade suggested.

Kana shook her head. "No. If they exist, they should be with the rest of her research. She would have kept them together if at all possible."

Night gestured to the ruined room on the far side of the window. "Maybe it wasn't possible."

Maybe." Kana did another turn around the room. "No, that's too easy."

"What?" Night followed her gaze and her finger pointing at the control desk.

"Jade," Kana said, "Cast it on the desk."

Jade did. "Yep. Two illusions, and since Vanessa can't do it…"

A moment later, six drawers appeared on the control desk. Kana started on one side, Night on the other. From the second drawer, Kana pulled out three thick diaries, holding them up for all to see.

"Number four, number two, and number three." Kana shook her head. "Well, I feel stupid."

"Not stupid! You found them!" Jade said. "Yay. What do you want to do with them?"

"Take them upstairs and start reading," Kana said.

"Hey." Night raised a cloth bag out from the bottom drawer on the other side. He shook it and the contents rattled together, sounding like dried sticks. "What's this?"

He opened the bag, looked in, and then reached inside and pulled out a disk the size of a tea plate. He held it up. "See the pattern?"

"It's a spell circle," Jade said. "But I can't tell what type."

"Here." Night tossed it to her. "There's at least a dozen more."

Jade looked it over. "It looks a lot like the professor's shield research. But why is it on the disk?"

"No idea," Night said. "Do you think it's important?"

"I think we should take it all upstairs," Kana said. "Then, we should order some dinner and get to work."

They trooped back up the stairs to the lounge, arguing over what to order for dinner. In the midst of it, Cassandra came in, wearing black jeans and a T-shirt but with a bulletproof vest with "POLICE" written in large letters across the front between them and her flannel coat.

"We've caught them all." Cassandra sounded both grim and pleased. "Twelve of the bastards, hiding in the basement of a storefront church."

"What did you do with them?" the entity asked, and for the first time, Vanessa heard concern in its voice.

"They're in a secure holding facility, chained to the wall with bags over their heads. Interrogations start tomorrow."

"That seems... extreme," Kana said.

"They assaulted two women, one a police officer, and took magical bracelets that they were not supposed to know existed," Cassandra said. "Some of them may have helped kill Glennis. It's an extreme situation, especially since we can't take them to the regular authorities."

"So, what will you do?" the entity asked.

"Read their minds, learn whether or not they present a danger, and then erase their memories of the last forty-eight hours."

"And if they do present a danger?" Kana asked, sounding both appalled and intrigued.

"They vanish."

"Oh." Kana's mouth opened again as if she had thoughts on that, but the expression on her face made it clear she didn't know what those thoughts were. She closed her mouth and fell silent.

"What about the bracelets?" the entity asked. "Did you find them?"

"We found what was left of them," Cassandra said. "They cut them to pieces. We've already informed the president, and you'll have a new bracelet by tomorrow."

"Good," the entity said, and Vanessa could feel the lie in the words. "I'm growing tired of not having magic."

"What about you?" Cassandra asked. "How goes the research?"

"We've found the rest of Akemi's diaries," Kana said.

"She had diaries?"

"Four. Vanessa and I finished the first one. And we found the others in the desk downstairs."

"I'd very much like to read them." Cassandra picked it up. "Vanessa, how are you doing?"

"All right," the entity said.

"Have you talked to Ian yet?" Cassandra asked, her eyes boring into Vanessa's.

The entity ran Vanessa's hand through her hair. "Not yet. I've been working with Kana and, well, what she's discovered is a lot more important."

"That's not me!" Vanessa shouted into her own mind. "Come on, Cassandra, ask more questions. Figure it out."

Cassandra frowned and said, "All right."

"I'll talk to him soon," the entity said. "I promise."

"Goddamnit, Cassandra, this isn't me!" Vanessa said to the image in her eyes. "No way I'd think this was more important than telling Ian to go fuck himself. Come on!"

"Where is he?" Jade asked. "Last I saw him was last night in his room."

"As far as I know, he hasn't gone anywhere," Night said. "At least, I haven't seen him."

"I'll text him about dinner. That should bring him." Jade pulled out her phone and then stopped. "Or do you want to do it, Vanessa?"

The entity shook Vanessa's head. "No. He's still upset with me."

"Fair enough. He'll get over it."

Vanessa was fairly certain that he wouldn't. Especially

after she got through kicking his ass. Twice. And Cassandra's twice, the second one for being so dense. That assumed she could escape the prison of her own brain before it damaged her beyond repair, of course. That thought made Vanessa shudder.

Across the table, Cassandra's eyes narrowed. "You will talk to him, though, right?"

"After dinner," the entity said. "I promise."

Vanessa watched the suspicion on Cassandra's face. She would have held her breath if she had control of her flesh. As it was, she hung in the Raven's embrace, desperate for Cassandra to do something, anything that might reveal what was happening.

Jade's phone beeped. She read the screen, and a half-smile grew on her face. "He says he's not feeling well just yet, and to go on without him. How hard did you hit him, Vanessa?"

"Harder than I thought," the entity said, putting on a smile.

"Not nearly hard enough," Vanessa muttered inside her own head. "I should have taken his head off, the bastard."

"I'm going to start going through the next diary," Kana said. "Can someone yell at me when the food gets here?"

Summary of Previous Academic Year's Learning:

- *The entity is made of living magical energy and requires a physical host to survive. It can last for a period of time without one but cannot feed.*

How the energy became cohesive and conscious is unknown.

- *Now that we know how the energy exists and what energy it uses, we can detect it and maintain knowledge of its whereabouts within its confined space.*
- *Pain is the entity's food. It can live off its host's pain or the pain of those the host touches equally effectively.*
- *The entity gains strength by having its host absorb magic. Since most hosts on Earth cannot use magic, it has no way to increase its power.*
- *It cannot enter a witch, as the witch's own power will destroy it. This suggests that witch magic is in itself alive, which may be a place for further study.*
- *Projecting power into a human host gives the entity limited use of magic, but it starts to drain at once, as regular human flesh cannot hold magic for any extended period of time.*

On another note, it has proved a most interesting summer for the experimental group. Linda Simcoe is engaged to a young man and has announced that she will be leaving the group after she completes her degree this academic year. Rachel Meadows has also found a beau but is keeping the name quiet, as her parents would not like him in the slightest. This much she confessed while drunk at our opening party, but she has not revealed the name as of yet.

This is irritating to say the least, as I will need to recruit new members for the time travel team.

Kana's eyebrows rose at how bitter the woman sounded. Given how many lovers she had gone through in the first year of her diary, Kana was surprised that she begrudged the others some affection. Of course, those lovers had been part of her experiment, not threatening to get in the way of it. Kana felt a surge of distaste and disappointment. The more she learned of her mother, the less she liked the woman. She had been brilliant, certainly, but far from a stellar human being. She shook her head and kept reading.

Despite this, we have made major strides forward in our time travel work, as well as much lower levels of success in the examinations of the interdimensional entity in Lab Five. The university has approved our team doing the joint investigation, with the inspection of the entity being led by Rachel Meadows.

The entity has become less frustrated with its confinement now that I understand its dietary requirements. We are still using cats and mice as primaries, only now I am regularly feeding it the pain of the various men that I have brought home— and women on occasion, though that is rarer, as I am not naturally inclined in that direction.

In order to reduce suspicion of how dangerous it is, the entity has agreed to spend most of its time outside the body of the cats that we use for experiments. As a result, we have only lost one cat since the first. As well, I have been certain to rotate the humans I bring to feed it, as I do not wish to damage any other students, either from the entity's presence in their mind or the pain spells that I put on their bodies.

Of equal misfortune is that Ambrose has discovered what I have been doing.

In retrospect, I am surprised I managed to get away with it for as long as I did. Be that as it may, Ambrose came in while I was feeding the entity the pain of a third-year economics student. He was horrified, of course, and I had to stop what I was doing to explain what exactly was happening. He was still horrified, but when the entity and I explained to him the nature of the experiments, he became intrigued. We have now entered into an agreement to work together.

Last year's work has given me an understanding of the entity's nature and how it moves from body to body. This year, we will focus on moving our own consciousness in and out of our flesh and then on how to move consciousness from one person's flesh to another.

The concept of "astral travel" was long ago proven to just be a variation on farseeing, where the witch remained in their flesh while their magic collected information for them from distant locations. If we can succeed at the moving of consciousness in and out of flesh, we may be able to create astral travel in truth.

We will also search for ways for the entity to be able to move around within the building, then within the city. My suspicion is that the anti-magic shield around the city will contain it, but we do not want to risk that without testing it here first.

Experiment 1: *Body Consciousness Shifting*

Kana skimmed through the list of experiments, reading only the title, abstract, and results. As near as she could tell, Akemi had been stunningly unsuccessful at moving human consciousness for most of six months. The entity, meanwhile, was growing more temperamental and demanding, often refusing to perform in experiments until it was given some semblance of control, which led to a shift within the experimental process.

Experiment 6: *Expansion of Entity Territory.*

Purpose: *To give the entity a longer range of movement without losing track or control of it.*

The key to the experiment is to develop a method for containing the entity within a physical body. To do so, A.L. and I studied the specific magical structure of the entity (see diagram 6) and developed an appropriate mechanism for trapping the entity within a body using the body's own electrical field to power the minimal magic required to maintain the shield.

We first tried using the cats, but their electrical fields were not strong enough to power the shield. We then used our own bodies for the experiments to ensure the human body could, in fact, hold the magical power. The final steps were, of course, human testing.

We tried and discarded several methods and discovered that the best device for our purposes was a ring, as it would always maintain contact with the flesh and generate the necessary power source. It took a great deal of time to carve the ring with the precision needed to make the spell effective, as well as a spell that prevented the wearer from removing it. We then put the ring on a girl who A.L. brought home and put her inside the shield with the entity (we used several mind control spells to do this). As expected, the entity was not able to enter her body. We removed the ring, at which point the entity entered her body.

Stunned, Kana looked down at the ring on her finger. The professor had said it was from her mother, and she hadn't taken it off since the professor had given it to her. Could it be the same ring? If so, that would mean her mother was still worried about the entity when she died. But why wait twenty years to give it to her? Kana reached to take the ring off, but her fingers stopped moving before they touched the metal. She was desperately curious about the ring and wanted to examine its designs, but at the same time, she didn't want to take it off at all. That realization, more than anything, made her suspicious. She reached for it again but stopped. She couldn't do it. She thought of asking someone else to do it, but the idea immediately felt *wrong*.

Kana skimmed the rest of the experiment. By the end of it, Akemi and Ambrose had found a way for the entity to go outside its shield at night to examine the world around it. It was always accompanied, never tried to escape, and always returned to its room after. It seemed to be enjoying living off the pain of the victims Ambrose and Akemi supplied it.

"Kana!" Jade's voice echoed up the stairs. "Food's here!"

The entity shoveled food into Vanessa's mouth as it listened to Kana describe what she had found and show off the ring on her hand. Jade cast her spell and showed that, yes, the ring was magic, though she could not say more than that without studying it closely. She offered to remove it, and Kana refused so forcefully that everyone's eyebrows rose high on their faces.

"Well, that answers that," Kana looked embarrassed at first, but her expression hardened. "I'll talk to Professor White about it tomorrow."

The entity watched the ring, feeling its power, then with an effort, looked away. All it needed was a way to get the ring off. It just needed to figure out how.

"So now we know Ambrose is involved up to his neck,"

Cassandra said. "I'll pay him a visit tomorrow morning and grill him."

"You think the entity is still around?" Night asked.

"I don't know," Kana said. "It's been twenty years. It might have died, or it might have gone back or…"

"Or it could be here killing people," Cassandra said. "I'm going to need to read those diaries."

"I'll give them to you as soon as I'm done," Kana said.

"I'll sit with you again," the entity said. It wasn't letting Kana out of its sight if it could help it. All it needed was the right moment, and it could take the Promised. "There might be something about what happened to my mother."

"I'll let you know what happens," Cassandra said. "I'll need to talk to my superiors first. And *you* need to talk to Ian."

"I wouldn't bother right now," Night said. "I checked in on him, and he's pretty drunk."

Cassandra snorted. "Not surprised at all."

"I'll work with Kana some more," the entity said. "Then I'll go check on him."

Cassandra looked askance at Vanessa, which the entity noticed. Something had happened with Ian, but it still had no clue what. It was frustrating as hell. The entity followed Kana up the stairs, aware of Cassandra's eyes on its back. It kept its mouth shut and kept walking.

Kana led the entity into the room. "I'm done with Diary Two," she said. "So, we'll be looking through Diary Three, unless you want to review something else?"

The entity shook Vanessa's head. "You told us what you learned from Diary Two. We should keep going. I want to find out what happened to my mother and I think the diaries are probably the best bet."

"All right," Kana said. "Grab a chair and let's read."

Once more, the entity sat down beside Kana. This time, though, what they saw brought both of them to a stop.

Shit. Shit. Shit. Shit. Shit were the first words written in the diary. *Linda Simcoe is pregnant; Rachel Meadows is leaving at the end of the year, and I think I've solved the time travel problem.*

Kana's eyes went wide. She clutched at the table in shock. The entity sat back, staring in surprise. It had not expected that such a thing was possible.

"How…" Kana sounded stunned. "How could she have done that? It's not possible, is it?" She shook her head. "Nothing that Professor White gave me suggested that she might have solved the problem. As far as Professor White was concerned, it was a mystery."

"Maybe Akemi was hiding it from her?" the entity suggested.

"But why?" Kana read the next paragraph, and her mouth formed a hard line. "Oh. Of course."

> *I know I should be thrilled for that last one, but I am so close to understanding the entity's mechanism for moving consciousness from body to body, and if I reveal that the time travel equations have been solved, we are going to be inundated with reviewers and examiners and any privacy that we have managed to maintain is going to be gone.*

Fortunately, the equations are complex enough that no one will be able to see the errors that I inserted to slow down the process. With them, and with the success of the interdimensional and interspatial work, we should be able to buy another year, but time is running short.

Kana looked around the room at the piles of paper and boxes that surrounded them. "It wasn't in any of the papers that Professor White gave me, so that means…"

Kana stood up and went to the piles of paper, sorting them into fresh piles.

"What are you doing?" the entity asked. "Aren't you going to read anymore?"

"Don't you understand?" Kana said. "She figured out time travel. *Time travel.* Do you know what that could mean?"

The entity did not know but nodded anyway.

"The answer is in here somewhere," Kana gestured at the pile of papers. "She wouldn't have succeeded and not written it down. I have to find it."

"Oh." The entity looked down at the book. "Can I keep reading?"

"Go ahead," Kana said.

The entity turned the page of the book and kept going.

The entity itself is much more content to be subject to our experiments now that it has gained mobility. We have tested it and know it cannot get past the shields around the city, which means we can offer it more freedom without worrying about escape. We have still not solved the problem of how it can stay in a body long-term, nor how a human can change bodies, but we are growing closer on each. Our next experiment will involve whether or not the entity can survive in a witch's body.

Experiment 32: *Transfer of Interdimensional Entity Into Consciousness of a Living Witch.*

Purpose: *To determine the damage caused by the entity in a short-term occupancy of a witch's body.*

This experiment proceeded after much discussion. Ambrose and I were both loath to try it but knew that allowing the entity entry into a witch's body might give us the information we need for human consciousness transfer.

After much discussion, we decided A.L. should be the guinea pig. I have more power than he does, in case something goes wrong. First, Ambrose and I cast a spell on him, suppressing his magic and making it impossible for him to access it. It is a difficult spell for one witch to maintain, so if we ran into trouble, we assumed Ambrose could break it. We then attached Ambrose to a series of magical gauges for heart rate, blood pressure, and other physiological changes, with a failsafe to release his magic if any of his symptoms became dangerous. Then, we went into the entity's chamber and had it take him over.

The results were strange, indeed:

- *The entity took control of his body rather easily and maintained control for the length of its stay in his flesh (eight hours).*
- *During the time the entity was in his flesh, A.L. was completely aware and conscious but unable to respond or control his body. His magic protected him from the entity, but the barriers on him meant that he could not communicate at all.*
- *When asked to do so, the entity was able to absorb magic from an external source (a small power sink I created) and hold that energy within A.L.'s body for as long as it remained inside it.*
- *The entity's presence did not cause any damage to A.L.'s body or mind.*
- *The entity was able to use the magic it absorbed to perform magical feats, though it could not access Ambrose's magic itself.*

The entity sat back from the book and looked at Kana. The woman was feverishly separating papers, practically throwing them away from her. The entity went over the last words it read in its mind and finally knew how it was going to take over the body of the Promised.

But first, it needed power.

The entity stood up and gave Kana a rueful smile. "I should go upstairs and talk to Ian before he gets too drunk to speak."

"All right," Kana said, though it was obvious she wasn't paying attention.

"Tell me what you find," the entity said. "I'll be back soon."

And with luck, it would take over Kana's body when it returned.

The entity walked up the steps, went to Ian's room, and knocked on the door. "Ian," it called. "We need to talk."

CHAPTER 19

V ANESSA SCREAMED INTO THE VOID that held her. The golden raven, her totem, reached out to wrap its wings around her, but she threw them off and hurled herself against the cage. In frustration, she slammed her magic against the wires that bound her, screaming, "DISPEL!" again and again. The wires did not even bend, let alone begin to fray. Vanessa howled, wordless and agonized, as the entity used her fist to pound on Ian's door.

"Ian, get your drunk ass out of the bed and come to the door or I will kick it in!"

"Why don't you just magic the lock," Ian shouted back. "Like you did with my bike!"

"Because I don't have my power right now, you idiot," the entity shouted. "Now open the fucking door!"

"Don't open it," Vanessa shouted into the darkness, knowing it was hopeless "Please, don't open it."

There was stirring inside the room, and grumbling, and the sound of feet crossing the floor. The lock turned and the door opened a crack, letting out a waft of cigarette smoke and stale air. Ian glared sullenly at her. "Leave me alone."

The entity shoved Vanessa's shoulder against the door,

driving Ian back. It shoved into the room and slammed the door behind it. Ian stumbled backward and landed on the bed, staring at her. The entity locked the door, crossed the room, and opened the balcony door. It stepped out and looked down at the ground below.

"You're not throwing him out the fucking window," Vanessa growled into the darkness. "You're not."

"You're right," the entity said back to her. "I have other plans."

"You can hear me?"

"Of course," the entity said. "We're sharing the same head. I can hear everything."

"Leave Ian alone," Vanessa begged. "Please. Don't hurt him."

"Oh, I'm not going to hurt him," the entity said. "I'm going to kill him."

"Why did you open the balcony?" Ian demanded. "It's freezing out there."

"Yeah, well, it stinks in here." The entity stepped back inside the room. "You trying to fart yourself to death?"

"Fuck you."

"Not likely." The entity advanced on him, scanning the room as it did. It looked down at the carpet. "This is what it's all about, isn't it?"

"What?" Ian looked confused.

"You're draining everyone's power without them knowing it." The entity raised Vanessa's eyes to meet Ian's. "That's why I'm pissed at you."

"I know why you're pissed at me," Ian growled. "You going to tell that fucking cop?"

"The fucking cop already knows," the entity said. "What she doesn't know is what to do about it. That's up to me."

Ian frowned as he tried to puzzle his way through it. "So, what are you going to do?"

"First, get rid of this."

The entity knelt on the rug and placed its hand on it. Inside her body, Vanessa could feel the entity searching for the source of the power, feel it understanding the nature of the power sink.

"Hey, wait," Ian said. "I thought you said you didn't have your power anymore."

The entity ignored him and absorbed the magic from the rug. Vanessa could feel the power pouring in. She reached for it, but the wires that held her magic in place kept the magic from her.

"How long have you been collecting?" the entity asked as it absorbed more power. "You have enough here to destroy half the town."

"Five years," Ian said sullenly.

"Well, you did good." The entity sighed as it absorbed the last of the power from the rug. "Now, let's get out of here."

"What?" Ian stared at Vanessa, confusion, made more potent by alcohol, spreading over his face.

"I said, let's get out of here." The entity stood up and kissed him full on the mouth as Vanessa raged helplessly within. "Unless you're too stupid drunk to drive your bike?"

"Never," Ian declared. He stood up and grabbed his coat. "I've been twice this drunk and not had a problem."

"Good." The entity unlocked the door. "Because I want to be somewhere else for a while. Understand?"

"Yeah," Ian said, though from the haze on his face, Vanessa knew he didn't. "Leave it to me."

They went down the stairs, the entity dragging him past the dining room where Night, Cassandra, and Jade were picking over the remains of the Chinese food. Cassandra looked up and watched them go. Vanessa tried to make her body pause, tried to wave or gesture at her, but she couldn't do anything. The entity led Ian out to his bike, waited until he started it, and got on behind. Ian had neglected his helmet, and Vanessa could feel the entity's glee as it put on the spare.

"Are you fucking insane?" Vanessa screamed at the entity. "You're going to get us killed!"

"Not both of us," the entity gloated. It pointed to the darkness behind the university, where the town petered out and the woods still remained and said to Ian, "Take us that way."

Ian gunned the engine and popped the clutch. The entity clung to him as the bike raced out of the driveway. True to his word, Ian seemed in total control of the bike, but Vanessa could feel the difference in the way he drove. His shifts were slower and sloppy and his turns wider than they needed to be as they went from the broad street that the coven house stood on to the narrow laneway behind the school.

"You know where the pond is?" the entity yelled over the noise of the bike. "I want to go there."

"No problem!" Ian sped up, racing the bike down the back road.

Vanessa had no idea where the pond was but didn't care. She wanted to save Ian. She was furious with him still, but she didn't want him to die. She wanted to slap the shit out of him and not speak to him ever again, sure, but not kill him. But all she could do is watch as they reached a sharp turn and a signpost saying, "Pond Road."

Ian downshifted the bike, skidding slightly to slow down for the turn. The entity leaned into the turn with him at first, then pushed off the bike, sending Vanessa's body into the air as it fired a spark of magic into Ian's front tire. The wheel locked and Ian pitched over the handlebars, his drunken body floating a moment before landing hard against the gravel of Pond Road. Then, Vanessa's body hit the ground rolling and spinning, the gravel abrading her flesh. The helmet protected her head, but nothing protected the rest of her. By the time she stopped moving, her elbows and knees were raw, her back and legs scraped and bloody.

The entity lay there, and Vanessa felt it drink in her suffering. It was an awful sensation, as if an oversized leech had attached to her flesh and was draining her dry. Then, it rolled to a sitting position, pushing her bloodied palms against the earth without regard for the damage it might do. It stood lurching to the side as one of Vanessa's ankles gave way and staggered forward to where Ian lay in the dirt. Vanessa could feel her ankle swelling and the bruises and abrasions but didn't feel anything broken. Ian had not been so fortunate. One of his legs stuck out at the wrong angle, and he clutched one arm to his chest.

"Vanessa," he moaned the word. "Vanessa, are you all right?"

Vanessa screamed and slammed into the cage holding her power with every ounce of her magic, trying to do with brute force what she had not managed with skill.

"I'm fine," the entity said. It limped along the edge of the road, its eyes on the gravel. "I just need to find…. There it is."

"Leave him alone!" Vanessa screamed. "*Stop it!*"

"I noticed before that people tend to dump their empties on the side of the road on their way back from a night at the pond," it said to Vanessa. The entity reached down into the grass and came up holding a half-bottle by the neck. The jagged bottom of it where the glass had broken away gleamed in the darkness. "Such a pity."

"Sorry," Ian slurred. "I'm sorry. Does your phone work?"

"It doesn't matter," the entity said, pushing the bottle against his throat. "Nothing matters for you anymore."

Blood, black in the darkness, sprayed from Ian's neck, coating the road. Vanessa screamed in her head and the entity drunk her pain, both physical and emotional, as it pinned Ian's head to the ground, watching him struggle and convulse.

"Do you know," the entity said to Vanessa, "that your spirit dies before your magic? That in the moments when the last of your life slips away, your magic is still there, ripe for the taking?"

"Fuck you! I will kill you!"

"Oh, I don't think so." It watched Ian's struggles slow. "After all, I still have use for you."

Ian's struggles stopped. His eyes stared, unseeing, into the distance. The entity drank all the magic from Ian's flesh. And when the last of that was gone, it stood up and limped away without a single backward glance for Vanessa to see one last glimpse of Ian's bloody corpse lying in the road. Vanessa screamed, howled, raged against the magic that held her in place and kept her from tearing the entity to shreds.

The entity took Vanessa's phone out of her pocket, activated it, and punched in a number. A man said "Hello" on the other end of the line.

"This is Raguel," the entity said. "Gather your followers, Reverend Marcus. The final battle is going to begin, for I have found the witch's lair, and we will destroy them all."

It limped back toward Coven House Three, giving the reverend specific instructions while Vanessa raged helplessly inside her own mind and the wings of her raven wrapped power and warmth around her.

Kana sat at the long table. Across from her Cassandra, Night, and Jade all stared, their eyes wide, as Kana held up the paper titled: *Effective Use of Interspatial and Interdimensional Portals to Enable Temporal Travel.*

"You are shitting me," Cassandra said. "She did it."

"She did," Kana said, "Inanimate objects, plants, animals. She never made it to human testing, but that was the only thing she didn't do. And look…"

She spilled the bag of disks onto the table. "Each one of these is a miniature version of the shield we created before. You attach it to whatever is going through the portal, and it protects it."

"How?" Night picked one up. "There's no way that generates enough energy."

"It doesn't need to," Kana said. "Remember, the shield absorbs the energy it receives and uses it to strengthen itself.

So, the disk just needs enough power to cast the shield. After that, it takes care of itself."

"That's…" Jade's eyes went from the paper to the pile of disks. She opened her mouth and closed it. It took her three more tries before she managed, "That's insane! Why didn't she tell anyone about it?"

"Because she was after immortality," Kana said. "She hid her success with the time travel because it would bring more scrutiny upon her other research."

"Really?" Night said. "Because I'm thinking time travel is cooler."

Kana shook her head. "Akemi was obsessed. She wanted immortality more than anything, and that meant working with the entity."

"Which brings us to the question," Cassandra said. "Where is the entity now?"

"I don't know," Kana said. "I thought maybe it had left or been destroyed."

"Or maybe it's responsible for the disappearances of all the witches over the years." Cassandra sounded grim. "I need all the research about the entity, Kana. I need to turn it over to the MLEA and we need to start hunting it."

"I don't think it was the entity," Kana said. "We know it can't enter a witch."

"But we also know it *can* enter this building," Night said. "You said that Akemi modified the shields to let the entity in and out. Is that still the case?"

"I don't know." Kana looked at Jade. "Could you tell?"

"No. It's too subtle a difference to the magic." Jade frowned as she thought about it. "But we could do a reset."

"A reset?" Cassandra sounded skeptical. "It's not a computer."

"It's close," Jade said. "And all the shielded rooms come with resets in case of damage to the building's shielding. If we reset it, we should be able to keep the entity from entering the building again."

"What if it's already here with us?" Night asked.

"Then we'll keep it from getting out and murdering anyone else," Cassandra said, her voice grim. "And the sooner we do that, the better."

"It will set off an alarm," Jade warned her. "Alerting the university authorities that something is wrong."

"That's fine." Cassandra tapped her chest. "I'll take full responsibility."

"We need to tell Vanessa," Night said. "And Ian."

"Ian can go fuck himself," Cassandra said firmly. "Vanessa's the important one."

Night frowned. "What did he do?"

"That other power sink?" Cassandra said. "It's in his room. He's been using it to drain magic to pull off some sort of big score. A bank job or something similarly stupid."

Night's face turned red. "How long has he been collecting?"

"Years, according to Vanessa. Mostly from the women he sleeps with, but once we all moved in here, he modified it to collect magic from us all."

"That son of a bitch," Jade growled. "I'll turn him inside out. Twice."

"So why is Vanessa with him?" Night asked. "Where did they go? They took off an hour ago."

"I don't know," Cassandra said. "She's been acting weird. I've been trying her phone and she isn't answering."

"Should we go look for her?" Night asked.

"She's a grown woman," Kana said. "He's not going to hurt her; we already know she can knock him out."

"True." Cassandra didn't look convinced at all.

"Help." The quiet call from the floor below froze everyone in their spots. All four fell silent, unsure of what they heard, until the voice called, "Help me, please."

"Vanessa." Cassandra was the first out of her seat, Night right behind her. Cassandra's feet clattered on the stairs, and a moment later, she shouted, "Holy fuck! What happened to you?"

"Ian," Vanessa said as Kana and Jade followed the other two. Vanessa leaned against the front door, blood dripping from scrapes up and down her legs and back. One of her ankles swelled dangerously large, and both her elbows were ragged and dripping with blood. Vanessa looked up at them, the pain etched clearly on her face. "He shoved me off the bike while we were moving."

"Fucker!" Cassandra looked at Night. "First aid kit, now. Jade, call an ambulance."

"No, please," Vanessa said. "Not an ambulance. I just need to rest."

"Half your skin looks like raw meat," Cassandra snarled, "and your ankle is bigger than your head. Sit the fuck down and wait for the ambulance. Jade, magic ambulance. Now."

Cassandra wrapped her arm around Vanessa's waist and guided her into the lounge. Night reappeared with the first aid kit moments later and started applying it. Jade got on the phone and started calling. Kana watched it all, unsure of what she should do, or even could do for that matter until Cassandra solved it for her.

"Kana, go to the kitchen and get a bowl and some water," she said. "We need to clean the gravel out of these scrapes."

"Right." Kana left the foyer and went to the kitchen. She found a bowl, filled it with water, and put it and some clean dishtowels on a tray. She headed back through the dining room and froze in place.

Car lights shone in through the window.

"What the…" Kana went over and peered out. Four cars sat in front of the house, perpendicular to the street, their lights shining in the window. A dozen more were pulled up on the grass behind them, and more were arriving. She squinted through the lights and saw a crowd of men and women forming a line behind the cars. Then she saw what they were carrying.

Kana ran to the lounge. "Cassandra! There's a crowd of people out there. With guns."

"What?" Cassandra handed the first aid kit to Night. "Take over."

She ran to the other room and looked out. Kana put the bowl of water down on the table beside Night and went to join her. Cassandra already had her phone out and was swearing as she lifted it to her ear.

"Sarge, we got a riot," Cassandra said into it. "A hundred, maybe more, firearms outside Coven House Three. Get backup and get here. Fast!" She lowered the phone. "Jade!"

Jade came running.

"Get down to the power sink," Cassandra ordered. "Do

the shield reset. Can you change it so no humans can enter the building?"

"I can," Jade said. "But I'll need another witch."

"Take Night. I'll guard the door until they come. Kana, can you look after Vanessa?"

"Yes, of course."

"No," Vanessa said from the doorway of the lounge. "We should go upstairs, away from the crowd. If they get in, there's no telling what they'll do. We have to protect Akemi's work."

"Christ, there's more of them coming!" Cassandra swore vociferously and held her phone to her ear. "No firing yet. I can see that damn priest we couldn't catch out there among them."

"Will they send the regular police?" Kana asked.

"No. This is a witch matter. Too many police means too many questions. We have a squad of MLEA in town, thanks to the murders. That should be enough to stop them."

"Unless the entity is out there," Kana said. "Then it will just keep switching bodies and attacking."

"Maybe," Cassandra said. "But there's ways to freeze a hundred people if we need to. Get Vanessa upstairs and get her cleaned up."

Kana put the strap of the first aid kit over her shoulder, picked up the bowl and towels, and let Vanessa lead her upstairs. Vanessa's ankle was badly swollen now, and every step looked painful and awkward. "Are you sure you don't want to stay downstairs?"

"No," Vanessa said. "I want to read Akemi's last diary."

"All right." Kana thought it was strange and suspected the woman was in shock, but Vanessa was still walking and didn't sound like she'd hit her head. Kana promised herself that she'd do as thorough an examination as she could before the ambulance came.

Vanessa limped into the library and sat down near the stack of diaries. She reached for the first, saw the state of her hand, and pulled it back. "Maybe you should read it while I clean myself off."

"Let me clean you first. We can read it later."

A flash of anger crossed Vanessa's face, then faded. "You're probably right."

To Kana's surprise, Vanessa didn't utter a sound as Kana washed the gravel from the wounds on her hands, knees, and elbows. She'd known Vanessa had a tough girl act, but it had not occurred to her that it might be real. The dishtowels turned red as the blood flowed. Kana applied gauze and tape to each one but ran out before they got to the big scrapes on Vanessa's back. She cleaned those out as gently as she could and settled for laying the remaining clean towels over them.

"That's as good as I can do," Kana said as she put the last towel in place. "We just need to wait until the ambulance arrives."

"From the size of that crowd, I think we're going to be waiting a while." Vanessa gestured at the books. "Shall we?"

"You've really become interested," Kana said.

"In there, I can find out what happened, I hope," Vanessa said. "It might have answers to everything."

'Everything' for Vanessa would be quite different than it was for herself, Kana realized. Vanessa might find out what happened to her mother without knowing that the woman was an absolute psychopath, like Akemi. Kana felt a flash of jealousy, which was stupid considering the circumstances, as she picked up the fourth book. She opened the cover and skipped past the title page and background pages. She already knew what was in those. But when she turned the page over to examine the experiments, her breath sucked in sudden and fast.

> **Experiment 48:** *Entry of Entity into an Infant Body to Examine Relationship to Strength of Magic and Strength of Entity.*

"Oh, my God," Kana whispered. Vanessa, beside her, just leaned closer to the book.

> *After the great strides of last year, we are still unable to give the entity its own body. Though we have managed to do some "spirit-walking" ourselves, we have not been able to enter the body of another individual, especially not a witch, as the witch's totem attacks any spiritual invader.*
>
> *With that in mind, we have taken the entity to visit Linda Simcoe, who has given birth to a boy. The child is healthy and strong, but it is not until a witch hits puberty that their full strength comes into being. And so, while we visited (with the entity controlling Ambrose's body), the entity attempted to enter into the child and take over its flesh. The results were mixed, unfortunately. The entity was able to enter the child's body, and to control it for a time, which it showed us by engaging in behavior that no young child could do while the babe's mother*

was getting us tea. It could not talk—the baby's vocal skills were not developed enough—but it did manage several hand gestures before returning to Ambrose.

As we analyzed the event later, we learned that the entity had been fighting with the child's totem the entire time it possessed him. The totem was weak enough that it could do only minor harm to the entity, but it was relentless, and the entity could not control it.

So, we arranged for Rachel Meadows' birth control to fail.

She was upset, of course, when she fell pregnant, especially to a man her parents did not like. Fortunately, the father, after his initial shock, was delighted. He had also finished his law degree and was employed at a prestigious magic law firm in Boston. They agreed to keep the child and arranged for Rachel to finish her degree. Her parents objected, but when the father settled her in her own townhouse near the university, paid her tuition, and arranged a maid and future childcare, they relented somewhat.

For most of this year, the entity was allowed freedom of the area. It went out at night, usually in the bodies of unsuspecting students or street people. Knowing both that we can now detect it at will and that it cannot break free of the shields that protect Newlane, we have allowed it freedom of the city on nights and weekends as long as it was back in its place by morning. Meanwhile, we have been working on spells to make Rachel's child more amenable to the entity.

I suspect it will not work and have prepared a second plan. We need a witch child that we can manipulate in the womb, and for that, we cannot rely on someone else.

Kana stopped reading and stared at the page. She had been appalled from the beginning of the experiment, more appalled that Akemi would allow the entity to enter an infant, and what they had done to Rachel Meadows was unconscionable. But this?

I explained my idea to Ambrose, and he was not opposed to the idea, especially since it meant he would be having sex with me regularly for the next few months.

"No." Kana breathed the word. "No, that can't be the…"

Experiment 49: *Body Exchange as a Means of Consciousness Transfer.*

Since the last experiment, we have made excellent strides forward in spiritual travel and have learned two things of import:

- *As long as the witch's body is alive, the witch's*

spirit will remain anchored to it and will return to it at the first available opportunity, no matter what the witch desires.

- *A totem attacks a spirit entering its body, not because it wants to prevent a second spirit from entering the flesh, but because it cannot serve two masters.*

Our next obvious step was to attempt spirit exchange, in which both Ambrose and I would leave our bodies at the same time and go into each other's. It was a success, again within the limitations above. Each of us was able to maintain our presence in the other's body so long as the other's spirit was gone. It took concentration but allowed each of us to experience what it was like to be the opposite gender, which was fascinating. We also learned that when a witch transfers bodies it takes on the power of the witch whose body it took. In my case, I became significantly less powerful when I took over Ambrose's body.

The next question, then, is how to make the change permanent. For that, we have no answers.

***Experiment 50:** Pre-Birth Magical Alteration as a Method for Allowing the Entity to Engage in a Physical Form.*

Rachel Meadows was seven months pregnant by the time Ambrose succeeded in impregnating me.

CHAPTER 20

"**O**H FUCK." KANA SAT BACK from the table, her eyes wide. "That's not possible."

Night was two years older than she, Vanessa a year older. The timing was perfect, except that Akemi had not yet met her father. She had not even mentioned him in the entire diary. So that meant... Kana shook her head, trying to find a way to refute the evidence before her, but unable. If Akemi had been pregnant with Ambrose's child when Rachel Meadows disappeared, she might have miscarried, but that was a slim possibility. More likely she carried Ambrose's child to term, and that would mean that...

"No," Kana whispered the word. "It can't be true."

> We continued our plan to expose Rachel Meadows' child to the entity as soon after its birth as possible but suspected that it would not work. Rachel Meadows spent less time at Shipton, and less time working with the entity as her pregnancy progressed, and by the time the child was born, she had already moved to Boston. We managed to arrange visits, and during those times, we cast certain spells on the

child we thought would make it easier for the entity to take the place of the child's spirit.

It was sheer misfortune that, when Rachel came to visit, she discovered what we were doing.

In retrospect, I am not surprised she figured it out. Rachel had spent years attempting to understand the nature of the entity. Though we had successfully masked its absence when it had gone out into the city, and successfully fed it without anyone being the wiser, it was not enough. Rachel had grown more and more suspicious of our activities over the last year, and in her last act before leaving to give birth, had set up a separate monitoring system to watch both the entity and the research team that was replacing her.

When we visited her in Boston the last time, she demanded the truth. So, we told her about the entity's true abilities and the possibility that it unlocked a key to immortality.

Needless to say, she was horrified.

She informed us of her intention to put in a complaint to the ethics committee, including all the evidence we had gathered of inhumane treatment of those we had the entity possess and that we tortured to feed it. We pleaded with her not to do so, but she would not listen. Instead, she insisted we turn over all our research records and results.

I agreed and arranged to meet her at Coven House Three for the handover. I also arranged for Ambrose to cast a spell on the child so that Rachel would bring it with her.

Needless to say, Ambrose was almost apoplectic. He raged at me all the way back to the Newlane and kept raging at me. I reminded him that he was as culpable as I and that I had a way out of the mess if he would just trust me. He quieted down, at least, but remained furious for the next three weeks, as I refused to share my plan with him.

This was an act of caution on my part. If he knew what I planned, and things went wrong, there would be no way for him to hide that knowledge from the MLEA.

On the day Rachel came into Newlane, we had the entity possess a high school girl from one of the schools near the campus. It was sitting in the middle of the shield when she arrived.

"Hello, Rachel," the entity said when she entered the control room. "Please come in."

"No," was Rachel's reply. "Who the fuck are you?"

The exchange that followed lasted rather longer than we expected. Rachel was disgusted at the entity's choice of hosts but fascinated by the creature itself. For its part, the entity had learned much over the past three years and used that knowledge to keep Rachel Meadows talking. It answered her questions and told her all about its world and its abilities with complete honesty, just as I had asked. Rachel was torn between her intellectual curiosity and her revulsion for what we had done. Ambrose sat beside her the entire time, also just as I had asked. That allowed me the freedom to make my final preparations under the guise of gathering all the information that Rachel requested. And when she was done talking to the entity, I asked her if she would reconsider and join us.

Of course, she refused.

The entity left the girl's body. The high school girl, finding herself in an underground concrete room with no knowledge of how she got there, started screaming. That noise gave me the distraction I needed to put the shield disk on Rachel's back. Rachel demanded we open the room, but would not go in carrying her infant. As she shouted at Ambrose to help the poor girl, the entity possessed her child. It used the prearranged signal to show us that it had done so. A moment later, it was back in the schoolgirl.

"The child is not suitable," the entity said.

Rachel realized what that meant and tried to run out of the room. I caught her before she could escape.

I warned her that she needed to keep her mouth shut or things would get out of hand. It was then that she told me she had already sent a preliminary report to Professor White.

I let her go, and she ran straight into the time portal I had opened in the hallway.

"Oh, my God." Kana's hand went over her mouth. "Oh, my God. No. No, she didn't."

"Kana!" Cassandra's voice rang up from the hallway below. "The professor says she needs to talk to you."

"Yeah," Kana whispered. "Of course she does."

Vanessa stood up. "What are you going to do?"

Kana shook her head, closed the book, and left it on the table. She rose slowly and made her way down the stairs, everything she had learned falling together into a picture that horrified her even more than what she had read. She was aware of Vanessa limping behind her, of Cassandra glaring at Ambrose and the professor. She watched the professor and Ambrose both look at her, and then switch their gaze to Vanessa. Kana wondered at it, but said nothing. She reached the main floor and walked to Professor White. The professor's eyes shifted, and the woman put on a concerned expression.

"You look terribly pale, my dear," the professor said. "Are you all right?"

"No." Kana realized her hands were shaking and clasped her fingers together to still them. "I'm not all right at all. Cassandra, where are Jade and Night?"

"Still downstairs," Cassandra said. "Finishing the reset."

"Reset?" The professor's voice held a note of alarm. "What do they need that for?"

"Because there's a riot outside," Cassandra said. "In case you haven't noticed."

The professor ignored her and reached for Kana's elbow. "You should sit down, Kana."

Kana stepped back. "Don't touch me."

The professor's expression flickered, but she turned the irritated frown into a look of concern. "Kana, you do not look well."

"I'm fine," Kana lied. "I was reading Akemi's fourth diary."

Again, the professor's expression changed, but this time, the frown stayed. And the words came out a shade too late to be truly surprised. "What diary?"

"Her diaries of experiments on the entity," Kana said. "The experiments she was doing that Rachel Meadows told you about."

The professor's face smoothed out. "I don't know what you're talking about."

"Yes, you do." Kana glared at Ambrose. "Rachel told Akemi that she'd sent you everything just before Akemi sent her through a time portal."

Professor White put on a condescending smile. "Akemi did not manage time travel."

"Yes, she did," Kana said the words through gritted teeth and had to force her jaw to relax before she could continue. "She documented everything, including what she did to sabotage her own experiments so she could study the entity longer. And don't tell me that you don't know what entity I'm talking about, because we all know that you were the faculty advisor for its study."

Professor White's eyes grew as cold and calculating as a serpent readying to strike. "And what else do you all know?"

"They know the entity was trapped here," Kana said. "They know about the time travel, and they know you were in charge of the study of the entity. They didn't know that Akemi shoved Rachel through a time portal to keep her quiet and that Ambrose helped her do it."

Now it was Ambrose who turned pale. Cassandra's lips turned up into the smile of a predator whose prey had come within reach. Ambrose looked at Professor White, his eyes wide and pleading.

"I did not know about Rachel," Professor White said. "Not until much later, and by then, Akemi was dead."

"Dead?" Now it was Kana who looked shaken. "You said she disappeared."

Professor White drew in a slow breath. It came out as a sigh. "Kana, there is so much you don't understand—so much I don't understand. But I think now is the time to share what information we have."

"No. Tell me what happened."

"I'm not asking, Kana," Professor White's voice became sharp. "I am your faculty advisor and the one responsible for this building. There is a riot starting outside and you're telling me that the time travel project I have been waiting to complete for twenty years is already finished and accusing me of being complicit in a murder. Now, I know for a fact the last is not true, and as for the rest, well, first show me where you found the evidence of the entity. And have Night, Jade, and Ian join us. Then, I will share what I know."

"We don't know where Ian is," Vanessa said. "He threw me off his bike and drove off."

The professor frowned at her but nodded. "Then just bring Night and Jade. Now."

"Once they finished the reset," Cassandra said. "Not before."

Professor White's eyes narrowed. "Young lady, I will remind you that you are a student and on probation. So, I suggest you get them, now, or you will be in a great deal of trouble."

"Then I'll be in trouble," Cassandra said. "Because I'm not getting them until—"

A buzz, sudden, sharp, and purely magical, echoed through the house. A vibration shook them all, and the smell of the air changed, becoming drier and more sterile.

"—they're done," Cassandra finished. "Which is now. Kana, do you want to go downstairs?"

Kana looked from her to Ambrose and the professor. Ambrose was near panicking, which was worrisome, but the professor still looked unperturbed. Kana thought about refusing, but more than anything, she wanted to know what had happened. She nodded at Cassandra. "Yes, we should go downstairs."

The entity fell in behind Cassandra as Kana led them downstairs. They ran into Jade and Night coming up, and both of them froze at the sight of the professor. Kana told them to follow, and the entire group went to Lab Five. She opened the control room door and held it. The professor and Ambrose stepped inside, flicking on the lights as they went. Ambrose whistled in surprise at the destruction on the other side of the window. The others filed in behind, Kana coming last. The entity stayed close, wondering when its chance would come.

It had the Promised within its grasp. It just needed to get the ring from her finger, and it would be able to drive her out of her body and make it its own. It felt the power it had taken from Ian's power sink and his bleeding corpse. It was a great deal, greater than any of the witches in the room, but it was non-replenishable. One it was gone, the entity would be helpless and trapped in the building, easily destroyed once it was detected.

And with six witches surrounding it, its chances of surviving outside of the Promised were almost none.

The professor stepped through the heavy door into the laboratory, surveying the state of it. Ambrose stayed on her heels, and after a moment, Cassandra, Jade, and Night followed her in. Kana remained in the control room, and the entity stayed with her. Professor White's eyes lingered on the twisted chairs and the piles of charred wood. She took in the soot on the walls and the burned shards of paper before stepping into the center of the circle. She reached out with one hand to touch the power sink crystal, closed her eyes, and smiled.

"I can still feel her," she said. "Her magic was always unique."

"Her?" Jade asked. "Akemi, you mean?"

"She had childhood leukemia; did you know?" The professor opened her eyes and looked at Kana. "And of course, magic can do nothing against that. That experience, the weakness of it, so close to death, left Akemi terrified of being helpless and of dying. She worked so hard to make her magic the strongest it could be, just to prevent that from happening again. Foolish woman."

"What happened that night?" Kana asked. "The night Akemi vanished? You know, don't you?"

"Yes," the professor said. "I know what happened. I killed her."

Kana gasped in a breath, horrified. Her mind tried to wrap around what she had heard, but could not. Professor White had asked her to come to the university; had asked her to investigate what happened. And while Kana had long suspected that something was wrong, this was too much. She looked over at Jade and Night. Both had gone pale. Both had known the professor for years, and though they knew Kana's suspicions, to hear the professor admit to murder was beyond what they could accept. Cassandra's eyes had narrowed, and Vanessa frowned as if thinking hard.

"What do you mean, you killed her?" Cassandra demanded.

"It wasn't my intention," the professor whispered, eyes cast down. "But she was going to sacrifice Kana and I couldn't allow that."

"Sacrifice her?" Cassandra's eyes narrowed. "To who?"

"She was going to give me to the entity," Kana said evenly. "She created me for it."

Professor White nodded. "She bragged about it when I confronted her. It was ten months after Rachel had vanished. We had no proof of what happened to her, of course. She was simply gone. The MLEA and the private investigators her mother hired tore the entire campus apart, including this building, looking for any sign of her. They found nothing. But when the dust had cleared, I found the package she had sent me."

"Why didn't you tell anyone?" Cassandra asked.

"Because I couldn't believe it," the professor said. "An entity from another dimension that could inhabit a human body? It was unheard of. And when I came to this laboratory, I found it empty. The entity was gone. I thought it had been destroyed or gone back to its own dimension. I didn't realize that Akemi had given it the freedom of the city. But I reviewed all the data and the recordings, and when it looked to be true, I prepared a report to send to the ethics committee and the MLEA. Akemi had left campus to give birth three months before, so I thought I had plenty of time to deal with it. Then, she came back."

The professor looked over the room again and sighed. "Akemi was far more powerful than I, of course. But she was occupied when I arrived. She and Ambrose had brought the entity back into the shield. It was wearing a tall man's body, I remember, and had laid out Kana on the table. Akemi was casting a spell that I had never heard before. It was the final step of what she did to Kana: it loosened Kana's soul in her body so it could be easily pushed out by the entity."

The professor's eyes grew unfocused, as though she was back in time with them. "Ambrose had traced a pattern on the floor to act as a shield to protect the child while Akemi finished the spell. I knew it was my one chance to stop them, so I did."

"How?" Kana demanded, cold anger filling her voice. "How did you kill my mother?"

"Fire." The professor's voice grew angry. "A very long time ago, I served in the witch military, and they taught me that it doesn't matter how much power you have, it is impossible to cast a spell when your entire body is on fire."

Ambrose looked at the floor. His body trembled and his hands shook. Kana watched, sure he was reliving Akemi's death. She felt only the smallest sympathy for him, and far less for the mother who had tried to kill her for her own immortality.

Professor White stared at Ambrose, a half-smile quirking up one side of her face. "The entity fled, taking its body with it. Ambrose was too busy dousing Akemi's flesh to fight me, and by the time he was finished, I had already summoned the university authorities. Isn't that so, Ambrose?"

Ambrose nodded, not speaking.

"And that is what happened," Professor White said. "The university covered it up, of course, with the MLEA's assistance, and this room and the research in it were locked and hidden until you found it."

"Jesus," Jade said. "You... you really killed her?"

"I really did," the professor said calmly. "And the worst part is, she never did understand the entity's secret."

"No matter how many times she repeated the experiment," Kana said.

Everyone turned to look at Kana. The professor's head tilted to one side, while behind her, Ambrose began trembling even harder. The professor cleared her throat and said, "What?"

"Every time she repeated the experiment, it failed." Kana walked across the control room and into the lab. Vanessa followed behind her, which gave Kana a sense of comfort. If nothing else, Vanessa could handle herself in a fight. "Every couple of years, she tried again with a new girl, hoping to make the jump to a newer, younger body. And every time, she failed. That's why she summoned me to Shipton. She wanted my help."

"Kana," Jade shook her head in confusion. "Akemi's dead."

"No, she isn't. Professor White is dead. She's been dead for twenty years." Kana raised a finger and pointed at the professor. "She's Akemi."

CHAPTER 21

KANA GLARED AT AKEMI, WHO stared back with the look of an animal choosing between fight and flight. No one in the room spoke for the space of half a minute. Night and Jade stared, shocked. Cassandra's head went back and forth between Kana and Professor White. Vanessa stood silently beside Kana, her eyes narrowing. Ambrose looked sick and ready to flee.

At last, Akemi raised her chin and broke the silence, her voice at once irritated and admiring. "And what brought you to that conclusion?"

"Too many lies," Kana said. "Beginning with asking me to come here and find out what happened to my mother. The whole thing was too good, too convenient."

"And that all added up to me being Akemi?" Akemi shook her head.

"No, what added up to you being Akemi was that you isolated me from the other students to keep me from seeing what a normal course of study was like. You put me in charge of a major experiment so you could confine me to this building where the lab that held the entity was sealed off using my blood. That's why it hurt when Vanessa broke the spell."

"I see."

"The power sink which held the entity for the last twenty years is still at full power," the words tumbled out of Kana like a dam had been released. "Which means you must have been getting the magic to charge it from another source: me. That's why I had no power until you released the entity and allowed it to go on its killing spree. Add that to the girls disappearing for you to try to become younger, your claiming no knowledge of Vanessa's mother, despite her being one of Akemi's assistants and in charge of the entity experiments and that, if you really killed Akemi after she used a spell you'd never heard before, you would still have no idea what that spell did."

A smile spread slowly over Akemi's face. "Oh, very well done, Kana."

The door from the hallway to the control room clanged shut, making the five students jump. Ambrose slid behind Akemi. Cassandra, in response, moved to a place where she could see them both.

Kana swallowed hard before asking, "Is Ambrose really my father? Not Wayne Klausen?"

"He is," Professor White said. "I married Wayne Klausen so the child would appear legitimate. He was easily enspelled and rich, which suited my purposes. He paid for the birth, and when I said I wanted to return to my work, he had no difficulty with it. My parents would have been horrified if they were alive."

Kana felt her heart ache for her father—for the man she thought was her father—at how he had been so horribly betrayed. She would have to tell him when she saw him again, and her heart ached worse for the thought of it. "And Professor White figured it out?"

"Yes. She tracked my activities, monitored the behavior of the entity, and created a massive dossier to take to the MLEA. Only, I returned early." The professor ran her hand over the crystal, rubbing away the soot that covered it. "Magic is a thing of the body. It resides in our flesh, and as our flesh ages and weakens, so does our magic. This body is quite old now. I have to take extraordinary measures to keep it healthy: special diet, exercise, vitamins, and even with those, I feel my strength and magic failing. I was running out of time, so I brought the one thing the entity wanted back here to help me."

"Why didn't you do it earlier?" Vanessa asked. "Why did you wait so long?"

Akemi glared at her, hatred blazing in her eyes. "Because the *entity* didn't know how it changes bodies. It had no idea how to make it possible for humans. It only wanted a body it could permanently inhabit. I found that out in the two years after my body died. So, I left it here to rot while I pursued other means."

"By murdering those girls," Cassandra said.

Akemi waved away Cassandra's words like a buzzing fly. "Magic lives in the body after the spirit leaves. Not for a long time, but long enough. When those girls died and their spirits left, I should have been able to take over their bodies. I should have been able to leave this old shell and move into their bodies once they were empty. Only it *never worked!*"

Akemi glared at the five as if it was their fault. "I did it once. I switched bodies permanently, but instead of ending up in someone young and strong, I ended up in *this.* And I haven't been able to do it since!"

"Why did you let the entity out?" Kana asked. "If it can't help you, why did you set it free?"

"Because last time it was here," Akemi said. "And so were you. So, I am going to recreate that moment with all of you and see if it will work this time."

"Except the entity isn't here," Kana said. "We changed the shields to keep it out."

"Oh, Kana," Akemi laughed, then, and when she finished, her eyes went to Vanessa. "The entity is standing right beside you."

The world went white.

The entity opened Vanessa's eyes, blinked the dryness away from them until it could see. Vanessa's body was immobile. The magic that had knocked them all out had paralyzed them as well. It reached inside and found Vanessa herself still fully conscious, protected by the same cage that held her magic in check. The entity felt the shape of the magic that held it in place, compared it to the magic that it held from taking Ian's power sink and his life.

"Pull Jade here," Akemi said. "We'll use the power sink to help us."

"Jade?" Ambrose said. "I thought you would use Vanessa. She's more powerful."

"That was my plan," Akemi said. "But the entity went into her instead of into Cassandra, so I'm forced to use Jade."

The entity watched Ambrose pulled the small woman across the floor by one arm. It tried to shift its gaze, but Vanessa's eyes didn't want to move. But there, on the edge of its peripheral vision, it could see Kana, lying on her side, the hand with the ring under her body.

"If it works, you can change into any of them," Ambrose said. "Except for Night. I want him."

"Hoping to be taller?"

"Hoping not to be charged with murder." Ambrose carefully lowered Jade down at Akemi's feet. "This had better work."

"It will work." Akemi knelt, keeping her hand on the power sink. "Everything is in place, everything is the same as last time, and with the power sink, I'm as powerful as I ever was before I ended up in this body. It has to work."

The entity watched, waiting. Akemi caressed Jade's face, then looked up at Ambrose. Ambrose stepped back and started casting. A shield rose up around them and expanded slowly out to cover the entire room.

"Everyone is inside," Ambrose said. "Just like the first time."

"Then there's only one step left, isn't there," Akemi said. She smiled down at Jade. "She was a good student. Too bad."

Akemi touched Jade's chest, and a single spark of magic leaped into the woman's chest.

And at that moment, the entity tore the spell paralyzing it to pieces.

They didn't use a spell, just a burst of raw power that tore through both the magic and its caster. Akemi screamed and clutched at the power sink for balance. The spell shredded, bringing all the students to groggy consciousness at once. The entity, once more able to control Vanessa's flesh, scrambled across the floor and grabbed for Kana's arm. Kana moaned in surprise, shaking her head and trying to see. The entity rammed Vanessa's shoulder into Kana's back, pushing her onto her stomach. It caught hold of her hand and yanked at the ring.

Ambrose's blast of magic tore into Vanessa's body, sending electric shocks through it and into Kana. The entity ignored them and pulled hard on the ring that clung stubbornly to Kana's finger.

Another blast of magic sizzled through the air as Cassandra fired at Ambrose. Ambrose screamed and fell, his arm smoking. The entity redoubled its efforts. Kana rolled over, grabbing at Vanessa's hands and kicking her midsection. The entity gave one more mighty pull and fell away from Kana, the ring clutched tight in Vanessa's hands. Kana's eyes went wide in terror.

"Mine!" the entity screamed as it tore free of Vanessa and dove into Kana's body.

The entity poured into Kana's body like boiling water. She screamed and fought, but the flood of pain drove her into darkness, deep inside her own mind. In a single moment of lucidity, she saw inside herself, saw the glowing gold spider that was her magic hanging in the darkness between her and the bright red blob of malice that was the entity. Kana reached out, a spectral hand floating in inner space, desperate to connect with the spider that was her power. The entity pushed against her, shoving her further and further from the source of her power. Kana attempted to push back but could gain no purchase. She felt her strength slipping away, felt her grip on her body fading.

And then Kana was in the air, floating above her flesh.

Kana's scream of horror was soundless, her cries for help unheard. She spun in the air, looking for help. Vanessa lay on the ground, gasping; Night had staggered to his feet and was stumbling in front of Kana's still prone body, hurling up a magical shield in a misguided attempt to protect her from Ambrose's magical attacks. Cassandra fired blast after blast at the shield around Ambrose and Akemi. Akemi herself sat down on the ground, her eyes closed, with one hand still on the power sink, the other on Jade's head. Jade lay still, her eyes staring sightlessly at the ceiling.

Kana rushed back to her body and was rebuffed not only by the entity but also by her own magic. The great golden spider, a symbol of her strength and skill, had become an immense and terrifying entity, glowing red with the entity's power and protecting her flesh against the invading spirit. She tried to grab at the entity, tried to force it out, but it brushed her off with a thought and shoved her out again. Kana hung in the air, desperate. Her strength had already begun fading, as had her urge to stay grounded to the earth. She felt something, half-calling, half-pulling, trying to carry her away from the earth, away from the physical world. Kana fought against it, not ready to go, and once more caught sight of Jade's lifeless body.

And at that moment, Kana realized what Akemi had missed.

The shock of having her body back shook Vanessa even more than the paralysis of the recently broken spell. She pushed her arms against the floor, trying to sit up, but they skidded across the concrete and left her on her face. She tried to put her legs under her, but they kicked and jerked like young colts being fitted for bridles. Turning her head made the world spin. Vanessa growled and strained, forcing control back over her flesh. At once, her limbs erupted in tingling as if they had all fallen asleep at once. It burned through her nerve endings along with pain from when she hit the floor and when Kana's feet slammed into her stomach. But with every jolt of pain, Vanessa felt her control returning. She sat up to her knees and a bolt of energy blasted at her. She could do no more than cringe as it came, but Night's shield held against it, splattering the energy harmlessly off the walls around them. Cassandra answered back with a blast of her own.

Vanessa reached for her own magic, then cursed. Even with all that had happened, her magic remained constrained behind the cage that Shipton University had woven for it. She swore and went to the ground again as Ambrose's magic smashed Night backward. Ambrose was channeling the energy sink's power, gathered from twenty years of feeding off Kana's magical energy, into his shield. It had more power than all of them put together, Vanessa suspected, even if Kana herself joined the battle.

Except Kana couldn't because Kana no longer resided in that body.

Vanessa growled her anger and looked above them. The walls and ceiling were concrete, reinforced, and spelled against magic. There was nothing they could do to bring them down on Ambrose.

"We have to get out!" Vanessa shouted to Cassandra. "They're too powerful as long as they have the power sink."

"I'm open to ideas how," Cassandra shouted back, spreading her arms and casting a shield that blocked the next round of magic bolts from Ambrose. "Can you drag Kana out of here if we cover you?"

"That's not—"

"She doesn't need to," Kana said from the ground. She extended a hand, and a blast of energy, far greater than what Cassandra had managed, smashed into Ambrose's shield. For a moment, the world glowed electric blue as Kana's magic shattered and smashed into the walls.

At Akemi's feet, Jade's body twitched.

Ambrose's shield was built to block magic, not spirit, and Kana slipped past it as if it weren't there at all. She hovered in the air above Jade's body, hesitating. Jade was her friend, her mentor, and her guide. The woman's joy and love of research had been more than a match for Kana's own. Her eagerness to help Kana study, her ready smile and quick laughter had helped Kana get through when the work felt overwhelming. To invade her body in this way was horrifying. It made her no better than Akemi or the entity to take another's body from them.

Except Jade was no longer *in* her body.

Jade was gone; her body was dead, and Kana could feel the magic in it starting to fade, even as it tried to fight off Akemi's invasion. Akemi smashed her own magic, reinforced by the energy sink, into the fading golden cat that resisted her presence.

Kana summoned the last of her courage and, resisting the call that cried for her to leave the physical world behind, dove into Jade's flesh.

Immediately she was engulfed in the flashing magic as Akemi attacked Jade's totem. Akemi had to walk a fine line, attempting to beat the cat into submission without destroying it and, with it, her only chance to take over Jade's flesh. Kana's spirit raced between the blasts, charging at the cat totem.

"You!" Akemi's voice filled the space around her. "How did you get here?"

"The entity threw me out of my body," Kana snarled as she dashed for the cat. "So, I'm throwing you out of Jade's."

"You can't!" Akemi hurled magic at her. "This body is mine."

"Magic is a thing of the flesh," Kana let magic pass through her. "It can't harm spirit."

She was nearly at the cat. The beast's glowing eyes faced her. Its head tilted as it recognized what she was. Akemi sent another blast at the cat, sending it skittering backward through the void like a kitten pushed across a tile floor. Kana charged forward, and Akemi dashed between her and the cat.

"You cannot take her!" Akemi screamed in the void.

"Wrong," Kana said and shoved her away. Akemi's spirit flew back. She tried to come back, but Kana shoved her again, pushing her away from the cat, whose golden glow faded with every second. "I can."

Kana raced forward, nearly making contact with the golden cat, but Akemi pushed back using a strength of spirit Kana had not suspected the woman of possessing. She felt her hold on Jade's flesh slipping, felt her spirit slipping out of the woman and answering the call that demanded it fly from the world.

A single golden paw, claws extended, hooked into her spirit and hauled her back inside.

The cat pulled her close, and Kana could almost feel it purring as it gathered her into its paws. Akemi's screaming filled the darkness as the cat's ethereal form glowed brighter and brighter. Kana felt the cat's magic, strong and bright, though not as strong as her own had once been, fill her. She felt Jade's limp body grasping at her spirit and knew that, if she weren't careful, she would still die.

The cat lashed out, and Akemi's spirit flew from Jade's body. Kana used the cat's magic to send a spark of life into Jade's heart and air into her lungs. Jade's heart stuttered and stopped again. Kana sent another spark, stronger, and Jade's heart sputtered like an old engine getting barely enough gas. Then it began pumping, strong and steady, and Kana spirit merged into Jade's body and mind as if it were her own.

Kana's magic flowed through the entity's flesh.

And this time, there was no question that the flesh belonged to the entity. Kana was gone, pushed from the flesh as easily as if she'd been water brushed from its skin. The entity felt the golden spider of Kana's totem embrace it and merge its magic with the entity. It felt power surge through its body, and it reveled in it. It was whole at long last.

Ambrose's magic splattered against Night's shield, nearly breaking it.

Instinctively, the entity fired back. The blast of pure magical power that pulsed from its flesh made it gasp with delight. It smashed against Ambrose's shield, but the power sink gave it too much energy for the entity to break through, even with Kana's immense power. The entity sent another spell, this time measuring the shield's power and searching for weaknesses. It was more powerful than anything Kana could break, and she suspected more powerful than the three of them put together.

Behind Ambrose's shield, Akemi heaved in a breath and screamed in fury. She broke away from the power sink and scrambled back, pulling her feet to her chest. Bracing her hands behind her, she launched a vicious double kick into Jade's ribs. Jade let out a mighty groan as the air burst out of her lungs. Akemi pulled back her legs for another kick.

"We need to get out of here," Cassandra yelled. "As long as they have the power sink, we can't touch them."

"Jade's alive," Night protested. "We need to help her."

"We can't if we're dead," the entity said as it sent another blast of magic against the shield. The totem inside of it glowed slightly less bright but stayed strong. "We need to get out and regroup."

"Fuck that," Vanessa snarled and hurled the broken remains of a metal chair at Ambrose's head. It went through his shield and hit him right in the middle of the shocked look on his face. He fell back, hands flying off the power sink, his forehead open and gushing blood. Akemi drove her feet into Jade again, and the woman convulsed.

The entity rose to its feet and sent a spell at Ambrose. For one second the man froze, realizing what was happening. The entity felt him gathering his magic for a counter spell, but it was already far too late.

Ambrose burst into flames.

The fire covered him head to foot, the roaring flames sending scorching heat through the room. An instant later, the sprinklers in the ceilings opened up, pouring gallons of water into the room. Ambrose tried to scramble to his feet, but Cassandra hit him with a blast of magic that made him convulse and fall to the floor. The entity crawled to its feet and stumbled toward the door, slipping on the soaked concrete.

Vanessa grabbed its shoulder, spinning the entity around and punching it straight in the nose.

Kana curled into a ball, trying to breathe through broken ribs. The heat from Ambrose's burning body had scorched her skin, but the sprinklers kept her from being seriously burned. She blinked, trying to focus through the driving water. She saw Akemi, rage and magic burning in her eyes, staring at Ambrose's smoldering body. Across the room, Vanessa was wrestling with Kana's body, throwing it to the ground and falling on it, fists pounding its face. Night raced toward them, slipping on the concrete and trying to grab Vanessa. Cassandra was approaching, her eyes on Akemi.

Akemi launched herself at the power sink.

Kana wrapped both arms around Akemi's legs. Sharp pain burst from her ribs, making her scream. Akemi lost her balance and fell, landing on Kana, making the pain worse. A moment later, Akemi's hands, still strong despite their age, wrapped tight around Kana's throat. Kana, already barely able to breathe, struggled against the lack of air. On the other side of the room, Vanessa screamed in pain.

"Jesus, Kana!" Cassandra shouted. "What did you do?"

Then, from Jade's memories, Kana found a spell.

Gritting her teeth and summoning all the physical and magical strength she could, Kana put her hand against Akemi's chest.

A burst of air, as powerful as the blast from an air cannon, hit Akemi dead center in the chest and sent her flying across the room. Even over the pounding of the water, Kana heard the crunch of Akemi's bones as her body smashed against the wall.

Then, a flash of white light filled the room and blinded her.

CHAPTER 22

K ANA BLINKED INTO THE BRIGHTNESS, her eyes aching and watering. For the longest time, the room stayed white, and Kana wondered if she'd gone blind. Then, white changed to blurry gray, the blurs became shapes and resolved into the burnt remains of Ambrose and Akemi's broken body lying against the wall. Kana groaned, tried to sit up, and cried out in pain.

"Night, look after her!" Cassandra ordered. "Vanessa. Can you hear me?"

Kana shifted her gaze from Akemi to Cassandra, who knelt, cradling Vanessa's head in her arms. Something was wrong with Vanessa's face, though Kana could not see what. Night appeared in front of her, reaching down.

"Jade? Are you all right?" Night asked. "I thought Akemi had killed you."

"I'm not Jade," Kana whispered, teeth gritting in pain. "Jade's dead. Akemi killed her. I'm Kana."

"What?" Night stared at her, mouth open. He closed it a second later to keep the water from pouring in. He looked half-drowned, and Kana suspected he still felt better than she did.

"Help me get to Akemi," Kana said, grabbing his arm. "Be careful, my ribs are broken."

Night did his best to help her to her feet without pain and didn't succeed at all. Kana stumbled to the wall where Akemi lay, gasping in pain.

"Try anything," Kana warned, "and I'll do to you what the entity did to Ambrose."

"You…" Akemi pulled in a shallow breath, "don't know… that spell."

"Jade knew it," Kana said. "And now I know everything Jade did."

"How?" Akemi's voice came out forlorn, confused. "How did you do it?"

"Get the fuck off me!" Vanessa's voice echoed through the room. "Where is that bitch?"

"Dammit, Vanessa," Cassandra snarled. "Calm the fuck down!"

Kana turned, and her ribs gave her a jab of agony. Vanessa looked awful. The skin on the left side of her face had become charred meat, her eyelid was sealed shut, and her hair was gone around the remains of her ear. Watching her limp across the floor, Kana could almost feel Vanessa's agony. Vanessa stopped in front of Akemi, wavered, and fell to her knees.

"My mother," Vanessa demanded. "Tell me what happened to her. What happened to me?"

Akemi didn't even look at her. "Kana… How?"

Vanessa pulled back a fist, but Cassandra caught her from behind, pinning her.

"Tell us what happened to Rachel Meadows," Kana said. "Then, I'll tell you."

The professor shook her head, the movement ponderous and slow. "I shouldn't have… underestimated Rachel… She helped with the shield research… She must have figured it out… but only could send her child. I detected the time travel portal opening and made Ambrose get her. I figured we might need her later."

"What happened to my mother?" Vanessa asked, her voice broken.

"Buried in Salem." Akemi breathed in slow. "Died April 1692. Probably the only real witch they killed."

"You fucking piece of shit," Vanessa whispered. "You bitch."

Akemi didn't look at her. "How? How did you succeed when I failed?"

"Because you're too much of a coward," Kana said. "You spent twenty years experimenting and forgot the most important thing you discovered."

Akemi squinted like she was having trouble focusing her eyes. "What?"

"A spirit attached to a body cannot stay in another body, whether that body is alive or dead," Kana said. "You learned that when you and Ambrose switched places. The reason you managed to take Professor White's body is that you were *both* dead, not just her. But with the other girls you killed, you were terrified to give up your life to switch bodies. That's why you always failed. In order to go into another's body, you have to have no other place to go."

Akemi stared at her, then, surprisingly, began laughing. The noise was weak and racked with pain. Kana tried to stand and nearly fell. Night caught her and picked her up, cradling her in his arms. Kana leaned into him, letting him take her to the control room. The sudden cessation of water pouring on her head made Kana gasp in relief. She waited until Cassandra came out, her arm around Vanessa's waist. Vanessa's head drooped.

"What about her?" Cassandra asked as they stepped through the door.

"Fuck her," Vanessa whispered. "Close the door and call your buddies. Let them deal with her."

"We have to get out of the house," Kana said. "The entity is still trapped here, and we can't fight it. It's too powerful for us."

"What?" Cassandra looked thoroughly confused. "Is it floating around?"

"It was in me," Vanessa said. "It took me over during the fight. Then it left and went into Kana."

"So… Kana's dead?"

"Jade's dead," Kana said. "I'm Kana."

Cassandra frowned. "I'm confused."

"Just get us outside," Kana said. "The entity can't follow us there."

"There's still a riot outside," Cassandra reminded her.

"Better than what's in here," Kana said. "We need to go."

"Ugh." Cassandra sighed. "All right, I'll deal with the riot."

Night kept carrying Kana. She leaned into him, in pain and exhausted. She wanted to get out of the building, to escape the city if she could, and find someplace to understand what happened. Behind her, she heard Vanessa whimpering in pain.

"You'll be all right," Cassandra said. "We'll get you an ambulance."

"You won't be," Vanessa muttered, though there was no malice in the words. "Some fucking cop. You didn't even notice I wasn't me."

"I was a little distracted, in case you forget," Cassandra said. "I'm sorry. It must have been hell."

"You have no idea."

"I want to know. But not yet. Can you make it up the stairs?"

"Yes."

Night carried Kana to the lounge and put her down on the couch. Cassandra let Vanessa gently down into one of the chairs. She pulled out her phone, pushed the button, and frowned. She pushed it again.

"Water damage?" Night asked.

"It's MLEA issue: waterproof, damage proof. You could run over it with a tank." Cassandra pushed the buttons again. "Fuck."

She went to the curtains, pulled it back an inch and stared. Night frowned at her. "What's going on out there?"

Cassandra didn't answer. Night went over, looked, and stayed staring. Neither moved. Vanessa groaned and stood up, and Kana followed her, hands clutched around her ribs.

"Night, what the fuck is going on?" Vanessa demanded. She hauled back the curtain just as Kana came up behind her.

Shipton University was gone. The trees were gone. The cars that had filled the road were gone, and the road itself was no longer curved. It ran in a long, straight line, and where Shipton's green grounds had once stood, now there were tall, square, gray apartment blocks, concrete and soulless with small slit windows dotting their walls. The sun had long since risen, and the sky above was yellow-gray with pollution. Lines of people wearing brown, sack-like tunics walked down the street, thick black collars around their necks.

"Oh, God." Kana turned from the window, clutching her ribs and gasping as she stumbled out of the room.

"Kana," Night called after her. "Where are you going?"

Kana didn't answer. She climbed the stairs at a slow, stumbling run, the fastest her body could manage, and cast her magic—Jade's magic—ahead of her, already knowing what she would find. She reached the second floor and went into the library. The big table stood empty, the notebooks and bag of disks gone.

"Kana?" Night's hands came down gently on her shoulders. "What's wrong?"

"The entity learned everything I learned when it took my body, including time travel." Kana stared at the empty table, then raised her eyes to the swirling haze of her magic above her. She read the patterns as easily as Jade had before and felt grief closing her throat. She leaned against Night, using him to stay upright as the last of her energy vanished.

"Kana?" Night's voice was quiet but urgent with concern. "What happened?"

"The entity went back in time," Kana whispered. "The shields must have protected the house, which means we're the only ones who know how things were, and we're the only ones who can stop it."

Thank you for reading Plague of Witches!

Dear Reader,

I hope you enjoyed *Plague of Witches*. It was my honor and pleasure to write for you.

Thanks for joining me on this fun and wild ride!

Get ready for many more adventures ion this series.

Also, if you're so inclined, I'd love a review of Plague of Witches. Without your support, and feedback my books would be lost under an avalanche of other books. While appreciated, there's only so much praise one can take seriously from family and friends. If you have the time, please visit my author page on both Amazon.com and goodreads.com.

https://twitter.com/JohnPatKennedy
https://www.facebook.com/AuthorJohnPatrickKennedy/
http://www.johnpatrickkennedy.net

CPSIA information can be obtained
at www.ICGtesting.com
Printed in the USA
LVHW031526060320
649226LV00002B/426